Baseline, John, and Eric were waiting for them.

The teenagers stared at them with wide eyes. One started to back off. The other pulled a blade from his back pocket.

"Gonna cut your ass, motherfuckers," the knife wielder snarled. He lunged forward.

At that moment, Baseline leaped. His hands grabbed the top of the clock far above his head. He swung backward for momentum, then kicked out with both huge feet.

He hit the charging teenager in the chest. The kid staggered as the air whooshed out of him. His knife hand sagged to his side. He stumbled to one knee as the twins seized him. Eric twisted the knife out of his hand.

"Where'd the other one go?" John asked.

Baseline dropped, his knees bending as his feet hit the platform. "Down the tunnel," he said. "We'll let the police chase him. Mrs. Jones' favorite son don't want any part of those tracks."

"Nice leap," Eric said.

Baseline smiled. "When it comes to soaring, I'm your man. 'Specially cause I don't like knives one bit."

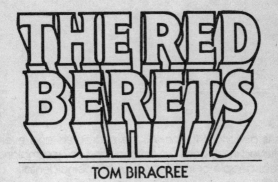

THE RED BERETS

TOM BIRACREE

PINNACLE BOOKS　　　　　**NEW YORK**

THE RED BERETS

An original Pinnacle Books edition, published for the first time anywhere.

First printing, February 1983

ISBN: 0-523-41704-7

Cover illustration by David Dorman

Printed in the United States of America

PINNACLE BOOKS, INC.
1430 Broadway
New York, New York 10018

THE
RED BERETS

prologue

**Headquarters, U.S. Military
Assistance Command
Saigon, Vietnam
November 8, 1972**

Major Joshua Hudson, staff psychiatrist, sat silent for a moment, pensively rubbing his index finger over his lips as he gazed at the soldier sitting opposite. Sergeant James Knight—five feet ten inches tall, powerfully built without being bulky, thick, closely cropped black hair framing a squarish face deeply tanned by months in the field—seemed to have stepped off a Special Forces recruiting poster. His voice, his manner, and, especially, the expression in his gray blue eyes conveyed the considerable intelligence and calmness under pressure that were reflected in his extraordinary combat record. From everything Hudson could determine, Knight was the last person he would have expected to be examining in a pre-court-martial interview.

Finally, Major Hudson sat forward and spoke. "Do you mind telling me about the incident two weeks ago that brought this whole thing about?"

"No, sir," Knight replied. "Although you should know my decision was based on a lot more than one operation."

"I understand. But I want to know what triggered your decision not to carry arms. It was this mission into Laos, wasn't it?"

"Yes, sir," Knight replied. "There were thirteen of us. The seven in my Special Forces team and six pilots we'd freed from the Pathet Lao. We were on our way back to the border when we came across this village that was held by some tribal mercenaries. They'd herded the villagers into the clearing and they ..." His voice faltered for a second. "They ..." He looked down, then back up at Hudson. "This gets pretty rough, sir."

"Go on, sergeant. There's not much I haven't heard."

"Yes, sir." Knight took a deep breath, then continued. "They had this girl. She couldn't have been more than eleven or twelve. They stripped her, bent her back over a jeep. One of them started to rape her. Another began sticking a rifle up her—her rear. A third beat her in the face with his belt buckle. They just tore her to shreds. Then they grabbed another girl."

Knight paused. Hudson could easily sense the deep emotion inside the sergeant. But he also remarked that he was totally in control of those emotions.

"What were you doing during this time?" Major Hudson asked.

"Most of the flyers were getting sick. We were all furious, but we couldn't do anything because the villagers were between us and them. We had to wait until they'd gone through four girls. When they moved the villagers, we hit them, with everything we had. I blew two of them apart myself, a little bit at a time to stretch it out. Then I threw my Armalite as far as I could into the bush."

Knight had been staring out the window to his right as he talked. Then he turned back and looked directly into Hudson's eyes. "I led the men back to the border. That was my job. But I knew it would be my last patrol."

"I understand how you'd feel that way," Hudson said. "You've been under a hell of a lot of strain for the last ten months."

Knight's jaw tightened. "No, sir. That's not it. I'm not suffering from combat fatigue. I'm not looking for a Section Eight discharge. I've come to the conclusion that the war is wrong."

Hudson raised his eyebrows. "What do you mean by wrong?"

"Sir, those tribal mercenaries were being paid by our side. To punish the villagers for giving supplies to the Pathet Lao."

"That's awful. But—"

"Even that didn't make up my mind," Knight

interrupted. He was leaning forward, his eyes glowing with intensity. "If that was an isolated incident, it could have been a mistake. But it's a pattern. The mistake is our being here. All the killing we do just produces more killing. I will not kill again."

Major Hudson had heard the words before, the antiwar rap of hundreds of soldiers looking for a way out. But something about this twenty-year-old staff sergeant was different. He didn't doubt for a minute that Knight deeply felt exactly what he was saying.

Hudson said, "Sergeant, you know you're leaving yourself open for a court-martial and a possible prison term. You know what that will mean when you get back to civilian life?"

"I know."

"You also know that a lot of people will call you a coward?"

"That doesn't matter," Knight said. "Besides, if my noncombatant status is approved, I've volunteered to extend for a year as a combat medic. I believe their casualty rate is higher than Special Forces."

"I believe you're right," Hudson said. "Well, that's all I have. You can go now."

Sergeant Knight stood, saluted, then pivoted. As Major Hudson watched the door close behind him, he suddenly knew what he was going to do. The chances of getting approval for a transfer to noncombatant status for any soldier in Vietnam were one in a thousand, and for a Green Beret NCO they were considerably worse. But Major Hudson was going to bat for this young man, with everything he could muster.

Hudson looked down once more at the papers in the thick personnel record file. Sergeant James T. Knight. Born, New York, New York, March 9, 1952. Home, 532 E. 6th Street, New York, New York. Well, if Hudson could pull off the miracle, he would see that Knight would go back to New York without a cloud hanging over his head. And that was important, because for one of the few times in his life Hudson felt he'd been sitting opposite a young man with the potential to be somebody. If he wasn't mistaken, he'd be reading about James Knight in the headlines some day.

New York City, 1982. Home of the Statue of Liberty, the Empire State Building, Central Park, Broadway, Coney Island. With its theaters, galleries, and museums, the capital of American culture. With its stock exchanges and banks, the capital of American commerce. A mecca for tourists foreign and domestic. By day a vibrant, exciting metropolis.

But when darkness descends, the mood abruptly changes. People scurry down increasingly empty sidewalks, casting fearful glances at ominous shadows. By midnight, hostilities have intensified. Most of the city's 6,400 miles of streets have become no-man's-land, where the vicious lay waiting in ambush, holding the city's 7 million decent, law-abiding people hostage in their fortified apartments and homes.

In the election of 1980, Americans gave the presidency to a man who promised billions of additional dollars in defense spending to stem the threat from international aggressors. But for the tens of millions of urban dwellers already living in a war zone, the new administration provided nothing except further cutbacks in already undermanned, overwhelmed police departments.

For a few courageous members of that population living in fear, it became apparent that the only path to follow was that taken years before by those enduring the yoke of Nazi occupation in Europe. With their backs against the wall, they began to rise up against the brutal minority that oppressed them. Their solution—fighting back.

one

The night was unusually warm for late November. The boisterous Thanksgiving Eve crowd at the social club had spilled out onto the sidewalk. Jim made his way through the knots of drinkers, a couple of whom interrupted their conversations to nod in his direction. When he got to the corner of Avenue C, he paused, debating for a moment whether he wanted to grab a sandwich or a couple of slices of pizza before heading back to work.

The thought of a few minutes' conversation with Granny Moore made him choose the sandwich. He turned left.

He'd only gone a few steps when he heard the scream. Up ahead of him, a woman had been shoved to the pavement. A teenager was pulling on a purse held by a shrieking little girl. As Jim started to run, he was horrified to see the teenager slash at the girl with a knife. The girl let go.

"Stop," Jim yelled, sprinting. The kid saw him, then darted between parked cars to cross the avenue. He never saw the Dodge that accelerated quickly to beat the light. Just before impact the driver stomped on the brakes. The tires screeched and the car skidded sideways, clipping the kid before crashing into a parked car.

Jim rushed up to where the little girl was lying on the sidewalk. He knelt to examine her. She'd been cut on the left forearm, and blood was streaming down over her hand. Quickly, he pressed his clean handkerchief to the wound. Then with his other hand he pulled off his tie and wrapped it around the girl's arm to secure the bandage.

By the time he finished, the girl's mother was next to him, loudly crying in Spanish that her poor baby was hurt. Jim put his hand on her arm and kept repeating that the girl would be okay until she started to calm. He told her to keep the girl still until an ambulance arrived.

Then he stood. In the street a crowd had formed around the purse snatcher who'd been hit by the car. Jim stepped off the curb and elbowed his way through the men.

The victim was writhing on the pavement. Jim saw immediately that his right leg was broken. He squatted to inspect for further injuries, calling out, "Step back. He needs some air until the ambulance gets here."

"Ambulance, shit," a harsh voice snarled.

"Punk motherfucker," growled another man.

The crowd was so closely packed he could

smell the whiskey on their breaths. He could also feel their anger.

"This kid needs air," he said in a calm tone. "Please step back."

A husky black man with a broad, crooked nose eyed him with hostility. "Who the fuck are you, asshole?"

"I'm a medic."

"Medic, shit," the man said. He stepped by Jim and kicked the kid viciously in the ribs. The youth screamed and writhed again.

"Stop," Jim shouted. He grabbed the big man's arm. The man shook him off, then threw a punch that hit Jim in the shoulder. Jim stumbled backwards.

"Teach you a lesson, boy," the man growled. He stepped toward Jim, cocking his arm to throw another punch. Jim, held by two men in the crowd, braced for the blow.

But the arm stopped in mid-stroke. The man grunted in pain, then grunted again as he doubled over. He stumbled for a couple of steps, then fell to his knees and vomited noisily into the street.

The crowd rumbled ominously. One of the men holding Jim released him and clenched his fists. Then he abruptly dropped his arms and melted into the crowd.

Jim turned. In the center of the circle was a massive bronze-skinned man with a totally shaved head. Huge arm and chest muscles bulged through his T-shirt and he wore sweat pants that contained thighs the size of tree trunks. Even the tough dudes from the avenue retreated as he glared.

Jim clamped him on the shouder. "Thanks, Renaldo."

Renaldo nodded toward the kid. "Take care of him."

Jim knelt and put his head to the kid's chest. His heart was beating rapidly but steadily, and his breathing sounded all right.

The whine of a siren grew louder. A half minute later, a police car screetched to a halt.

"Out of the way. Out of the way," the cops called as they pushed through the crowd. A graying older cop with a big beer belly reached the center. "What the hell's going on?"

Jim stood. "Kid snatched a purse. Ran into a car while I was chasing him."

The cop craned his head to look. "Lucky him," he said in a bored tone. "He gonna live?"

"Yea. But ne needs an ambulance."

"It's on the way," the cop said. He bent over to get a closer look. Noting the long, jagged scar on the kid's left cheek, he commented, "Savage Skull, huh? They're coming in all over the place."

A second cop emerged from the crowd, a younger officer Jim knew. "What's the story with the little girl?"

"Guess she tried to grab mommy's purse when it was snatched."

"We'll take her to the ambulance first, when it gets here."

"He needs it more," Jim said. "I'll take her to the clinic. It'll be faster."

"Okay," the cop said.

Jim turned to Renaldo. "I'm going. Thanks again."

"Stop by later?" Renaldo asked.

"Sure."

"Here, let me do that."

"Okay," Jim said, getting to his feet. He stepped back away from the treatment table and watched.

It was like magic. The doe-eyed eight-year-old Puerto Rican girl who had been squirming like an eel when he tried to clean out the dirt-caked cut became a lamb as soon as Sara touched her. Jim never failed to be amazed at the instant rapport Dr. Sara Cummings—out of Greenwich Country School, Vassar College, and Harvard Medical School—had with the Lower East Side street urchins who streamed into the Lower East side Health Clinic on East Eighth Street.

The girl's tears had dried, and as Sara swabbed the wound she stared at her with awe, as if a fairy princess had come into her life. With Sara's silken blonde hair, her flawless skin the color of pale china, her trim, lithe body, she seemed a princess to Jim too.

For a moment he continued to watch, permitting himself the enjoyment of the fantasy that it was her daughter, their daughter, the doctor was comforting. Then came the familiar ache.

Sara reached for the needle to begin stitching. Jim turned and left the treatment room, closing the door behind him. He stopped in the waiting room to tell the girl's mother it would only be a few more minutes. Then he went into his small cluttered office and plunked himself down in his battered desk chair.

When Sara came in later, he was leaning back, feet on the desk, rubbing his nose with his index fingers. Sara followed his eyes to a tray that contained an impressively high stack of unpaid bills.

"That bad, huh?" she asked.

"Worse," he replied. "Three days before the end of the month and I just paid the last of the rent. Now all I have to worry about is the disconnect notice from the electric company, two months' telephone bills—"

"Your salary," she interrupted.

Jim grimaced.

"How long has it been since you've paid yourself?"

"Well," he said with a slight smile, "Let me see. A couple of weeks last month . . ."

"You're crazy, Mr. Knight," she said. "Is it worth it to go through all this? You're such a talented man. You could be doing so many other things than beating your head against the wall trying to keep this clinic open."

Jim looked at her solemnly. "Ask little Maria in there. She'd be sitting in the emergency room at Bellevue half the night with the ODs, the winos, the drunks who've been shot or stabbed. That's no way for a kid to have to grow up. It just burns me that . . ." He let his voice trail off. Then he sighed and said, "I'm sorry. I didn't mean to go off on a toot. Not when you've been nice enough to come down here on the night before a holiday."

"That's okay. We're not going to the country until tomorrow morning. Bill had to work late."

At the mention of her husband's name, his lips tightened. Then it passed and he said, "Over the river and through the woods, huh? I guess that's the traditional way to spend Thanksgiving."

A thought struck Sara. "Would you like to come? My parents would love to meet you, after all the stories I've told them about this place."

"And what about Bill? I know how fond he is of your volunteering your time down here."

She looked away for a moment. Then she said firmly, "What I do with my own time is my own business. And it's daddy's house I'm inviting you to."

He got up and put his hand on her shoulder. "Thanks for the invite. But the country's not my scene. I get nervous without the familiar crunch of broken glass under my feet."

She looked into his eyes. "You sure?"

He had the overwhelming urge to kiss her. But that would be a horrible mistake. He dropped his hand to his side and said, "Come on, Doc. Time to close up. Baseline's probably been waiting for you out front."

It took Jim a few minutes to lock the safe with the drugs, douse the lights, and secure the windows. Then they went out the front door and into the three-quarter darkness of East Eighth Street.

Two winos lounged comfortably in the doorway of the tenement next door to the storefront. An elderly couple carrying shopping bags shuffled along the dingy, trash-lined sidewalk toward them. Beyond, in the street, a pack of kids were playing an exuberant game of tag under a streetlight.

Jim held Sara's elbow protectively while he scanned both directions. "I guess—"

Before he finished, a yellow taxi, a beat-up 1976 Chevy, rounded the corner and screeched to a halt in front of them. A very tall, very skinny black youth about nineteen years old unfolded himself from the driver's seat and ambled over toward the sidewalk. As he approached, his face widened into a broad smile. "Hi ya, Doc."

"Ball game went into overtime?" Jim asked with a smile.

The kid pointed his index finger at him. "Got it, man. Then the fantabulous Baseline Jones got himself serious. I was flying so high the referees done had to stop the game to call La Guardia Airport to get me clearance to land. With a minute left, I dropped my neutron bomb and the ball game was O-V-E-R, done."

"Neutron bomb? What's that?" Jim asked.

Baseline's smiled got even wider. "That's my new slam dunk. It leaves the gym standing, but blows away everybody inside."

Jim laughed. "Baseline, you're a trip."

"That I am," Jones said. He turned to Sara and added, "Speaking of trips, you ready for the ride of your life with that same Mr. Jones, the A-onest cab driver in the entire momma-feathering world?"

Sara was chuckling and shaking her head. "I hope so," she said. She took a step toward the curb, then stopped and turned back toward Jim.

"I almost forgot," she said. "Happy Thanksgiving." She leaned forward, kissing him lightly on the cheek. Then she followed Baseline around to the passenger side of the cab.

Jim stood, motionless, watching the taillights of the cab disappear around the corner. For an instant, the street seemed unnaturally, forbiddingly still, as if time had stopped. Then through the night air came the familiar, piercing wail of a siren. Jim turned, trudging down toward Avenue C to get himself something to eat.

As he walked, the feeling of emptiness clung to him. Of all the women in the world he could have fallen in love with, he had to choose a hopeless situation. A brilliant doctor married to an older, sophisticated, wealthy businessman. A woman from a social class and environment that couldn't be more different from his own.

As he moved past the row of run-down front-stoop tenements, he thought ruefully about Sara's invitation to her father's estate in Connecticut. That he could feel alien thinking about a place with sunshine and trees and clean air was a symptom of how screwed up his world was. He was so accustomed to the squalid environment of the Lower East Side that the abnormal seemed normal.

The Lower East Side had always been a melting pot, the first stopping-off point for generations of immigrants. But it had always been a place where people had a sense of community, where decent, hardworking people didn't feel ashamed to raise a family.

All that had changed. By the time Jim got back from the army ten years before, he noticed a profound difference. Friends of his mother now hid behind three locks in tiny, airless apartments, terrified to venture forth. Crowding the sidewalks of the avenues were the new street life—prostitutes, drug dealers, savage teenagers, drunks, bag ladies, and every other kind of lunatic the city had to offer. The crime rate had soared, the streets were far filthier, the number of abandoned, burned-out buildings began to climb, and, worst of all, the decent people who remained, instead of feeling they were working hard to insure that their kids would have a better life, began to be overcome with a profound sense of hopelessness.

The change in the neighborhood during his time in the service depressed Jim. After his mother died, a year after his discharge, he had nothing to keep him there.

Nothing, that is, except his crazy pie-in-the-sky idea of turning the neighborhood around, of making it a decent place to live once again. His pipe dream was that if people were given a reason to hang on, improvement would come.

That's why he started the health clinic. At first it was just him and another ex-medic. Then Father Reilly from St. Anselm's showed him how to apply for government grants, and he was able to get real medical equipment. He wrote hundreds of letters and the publicity gradually brought enough volunteer doctors to keep the place open from noon to nine at night and on weekends.

Those had been the good days. Then the city's fiscal crisis hit social services hard. Even worse was the Reagan administration, with the budget cutbacks and the who-in-the-hell-gives-a-damn-about-poor-people attitude. Jim managed to get a few foundation grants and he'd run every kind of fund raiser from bake sales to bingo. But it got harder and harder every month, and he got more and more discouraged. He couldn't even pay himself, and he was two months behind on his own apartment rent. After eight years of hard work, all he saw ahead of him was a dead end. Unlike the movies he'd been so fond of when he was a kid, the plot of real life had the bad guys winning.

He was so lost in his morose thoughts that he had to stop for a moment at the corner of Avenue C to remember where he was headed. That sandwich he set out for a couple of hours ago. He turned, walking north. As he reached the corner of Ninth Street, he smiled. The lights were on in the small soda fountain and candy store on the corner. That meant Granny was still working.

Jim had known Granny Moore all his life. Granny was special. No one knew her age, but she'd been a neighborhood institution as long as anyone could remember. The stout black woman with the broad smile and quick, rumbling laugh had seen the area go from predominantly Jewish to the present checkerboard of blacks, Hispanics, and whites. Despite the change, her store had remained a neighborhood hangout for kids for generations. To Granny, children had always been children, without color, who needed to be coddled and listened to and watched carefully—and, occasionally, scolded. The children were her life, really, and the store just a business. In a better world, Granny might have been a teacher or a psychologist. But New York, at least not in 1982, was not a better world.

As he crossed the street, he saw through the window that Granny was just finishing scraping the grill. When she heard the door open, she turned and flashed that huge smile.

"Too late to get a sandwich?" Jim asked.

Granny looked at him in mock disbelief. "Too late for sandwiches tonight, boy. Only reason I'm here is I been waiting for Goldstein to bring me by my turkey. That man get later and later every year. But you just trot over here and let Granny give you a big Thanksgiving hug."

Jim walked over and was enveloped. After a moment he pulled away and kissed her on the forehead. "If you were a little younger, I'd be tempted to take you out for a date right now."

"Oh, go on with you," Granny said, pushing him playfully away. "I got to get this place closed up and get on up to Harriet's with that big bird."

"You having a big dinner tomorrow?"

Her round face lit up even more. "Why child, are we having a dinner? You never lived till you seen the dinner we're gonna have. Ester's bringing her three in from Jersey and Harold and Johnny's bringing their broods in from Brooklyn. Why, I even think we'll tempt old grouchy George away from his football games to take a bite or two."

"That's great."

She stared at him a moment, a thoughtful expression on her face. "Why, Jimmy, what are you doing for Thanksgiving dinner?"

"I don't know. I thought I'd just catch up on—"

"You're coming to Harriet's, that's what you're doing. Why Ester'll be so glad to see you she'll probably eat you alive. And Harold mixes up that punch that sets me to giggling like a schoolgirl. We'll have ourselves one fine old time."

Her enthusiasm was infectious, as usual. But it didn't wash away all his gloom. "I don't know," he said. "I'd be a bother and—"

"Lord, you a bother? Jimmy, honey, you remember what you told me when your momma died? You said, 'Granny, you're the only family I got left.' And I felt so proud, 'cause I couldn't think of nothing better than to have a boy like you—excepting, of course, you had the bad luck to born white."

He laughed. "Granny, you could talk anybody into anything. I suppose if I don't come, I'll hear about it for weeks."

"Weeks? More like years," she said with a hearty laugh. "Now, you help old Granny by toting that big old bird down to the subway for me. I'll turn off these lights and we'll mosey right along."

"Boy, this bird is heavy," Jim commented as Granny fastened the padlock on the metal gates that covered her storefront.

"Twenty-six pounds. And wait till you taste what's inside. I'll make up the stuffing tonight so the flavor gets all mingled up. There's apples and chestnuts and all kind of good stuff in there."

"Sounds great," Jim responded. They chatted as they made their way west on Tenth Street, toward First Avenue. A cloud had passed over the moon, and with a couple of street lamps not functioning, the street was dark and lonely. Jim became conscious of the echoing sound of their footsteps on the sidewalk. Then the sound of a garbage can knocked over in an alley made him jump.

"What's that?" he barked.

Granny put her hand on his arm. "You jumpy tonight, boy."

Jim sighed for a second. Then he said, "Yea. Guess so. It's been one of those nights."

As they continued, he told her about the purse snatching and its aftermath.

Granny clucked, shaking her head. "Don't know about folks these days," she said."Things getting confusing, especially for an old lady like me."

"You're still a spring chicken," Jim said.

"More like early-winter chicken," she commented. "Here, you help old Granny down these steps and then you go on home."

They were at the subway entrance on First Avenue and Fourteenth Street. As Jim looked down the steps, the memory of the purse snatching came back to him again. He turned to Granny and said, "It's late, Granny. Why don't you treat yourself and take a cab home. That way you won't have to lug this turkey around."

"A taxicab? Child, who do you think I am, Mrs. John D. Rockefeller? Now, come on. Harriet's boy's waiting on me up in Harlem. He'll have got to thinking he'll starve to death tomorrow."

For a moment, Jim decided he'd tell her he'd take her in a cab. Then he realized he only had enough money on him for a sandwich. Thirty years old, and he didn't even have an extra five bucks.

"I'll ride up with you," he said.

"Wait one minute," Granny said. "You're gonna put me on that train and get yourself supper. You ain't too old to still mind your elders, are you?"

Jim sighed. "Okay, Granny," he said. Then he smiled as he picked up the shopping bag again. "I just hope this bird isn't as tough as you are."

two

The sign on the street-level door read Nude Models—$10 per session. Jim opened it, went up the stairs, continuing past the second-floor door bordered by blinking pink and white lights, up another more dimly lit flight to the third floor. As Jim walked into the large room, the smell hit him first, as it always did—a heady combination of sweat, rosin, and liniment, all aged for decades.

Only a couple of lights were on, and it took Jim's eyes a moment to adjust. Then he saw the gym was uncharacteristically empty. At almost any hour of the day or night, the place was a beehive of boxers sparring in the center ring, jumping rope, pounding away at the heavy bag, or playing their rhythmic tatoos on the speed bag.

Renaldo appeared in the door to the locker room. He was holding a mop.

"Hi," Jim said. "Huggins here?"

Renaldo said, "He's asleep in the back. Man getting old, Jimmy. Taking a nap every afternoon, and he's having trouble standing by the ring for more'n an hour at a time."

"He is in his eighties, after all."

"I know," Renaldo said. "Still, it hurts a lot to think of him passing on sometime. I shooed everybody out early tonight so he could get some rest. And so I could get some real cleaning done."

Jim smiled. "I noticed. Man's going to fight the number-one-ranked heavyweight contender in the world in three months, and he's playing janitor."

Renaldo's face remained serious. "I do what has to be done, Jimmy. No matter who he beats, a man can't be champion if he forgets who got him there. Like old Huggins. And you, Jimmy."

Jim felt a surge of warm emotion as Renaldo spoke. It was hard to see in the Samson-like twenty-two-year-old the thin, scared Puerto Rican kid that wandered, half dead, into the health clinic shortly after it opened eight years before. His first fourteen years of life had been the kind of nightmare that makes shocking tabloid headlines. His father disappeared before he was born, and his mother was a drug addict with a violent temper. Even as a baby, he was beaten regularly by his mother. He bounced from foster homes back to his mother, and dreaded both equally. The last time he'd been sent back home, he'd found his mother living with an older man who shared her temperament. After being locked in a room without food for three days, he'd broken a window, climbed down the fire escape, and fled.

Unable to face the idea of sending him back to his mother or subjecting him once more to the callous, revolving-door treatment of social services, Jim let Renaldo stay in his apartment. With proper rest and nutrition, the boy began to grow dramatically. When Renaldo was fifteen, he got an after-school job sweeping out Huggins's gym, and soon he found himself in the ring.

Xavier (Slapsy) Huggins was a legend in boxing. He'd once been a featherweight championship contender (as his equally aged crony Cube Crawford would say, "back in the days when Noah was building his ark"). His real fame, however, came as owner of the oldest gym in New York City and as trainer of nearly a dozen world champions. Huggins was a feisty bantom rooster of a man with a sometimes savage tongue, but he passionately loved boxing and boxers. Slapsy didn't give a hoot what nationality a man was, nor was superior boxing ability itself the way to win his esteem. Rather, what he most admired in a man was "heart," which in his definition meant loyalty, honesty, and self-sacrifice to achieve a goal.

Nobody had more heart than Renaldo. Slapsy said he'd never seen a boxer train as hard as the Puerto Rican boy. And outside the gym Renaldo was just as dedicated. He'd spent countless hours, for example, improving his diction so that he wouldn't embarrass himself or his people when he was interviewed on television and radio. And as he neared the championship, those interviews came more frequently.

It was still hard for Jim to believe the kid standing in front of him was the awesome puncher he watched on television. He was damned proud of him.

Jim clamped him on the arm. "Got a beer in that refrigerator. A couple of pieces of Luigi's pizza made me thirsty."

"Sure."

They walked past the door to the locker room to a tiny, hole-in-the-wall office. Renaldo pulled a can of Budweiser and a carton of orange juice out of the half-sized refrigerator under the desk.

Jim popped the top on the beer can and offered a toast. "To my rescue." He took a long swallow, then asked, "How in the hell did you get out there so fast?"

"I was washing the windows. I saw the commotion and decided to see what was going on."

"Good thing," Jim said. "The kind of days I've been having lately, getting beat up would be a highlight."

"I know," Renaldo said sympathetically. "Just hold on, Jimmy. When I get that title fight, all your troubles are going to be over. I promise you."

Jim smiled. "You've got a deal." Then he sighed and added, "But it's not just the money. I'm so tired of all of it. The constant hassles. The filth on the streets. That kid out there—it seems like there are more of them every day."

"There are more of them. The Savage Skulls. They're moving in like an army." He paused for a moment to take a swallow of orange juice, then added, "I'm not used to seeing you down like this, Jim. I think you need to get away for a few days."

"Sara asked me to come out to Connecticut. But I couldn't see myself—"

"Ah, Sara," Renaldo interrupted. "She was working tonight. Now I understand why you're more depressed."

Jim slowly shook his head. "I must be an idiot. All the women in the world, and I fall in love with one ten social classes above my head. Who also happens to be married."

"How does she feel?"

"I don't know. I mean, we're friends. And from what she's told me, I think her husband is a jerk, the way he treats her. But that's wishful thinking. She's married, and I have to get her out of my head."

"I don't know, Jim," Renaldo said. "When I was a kid, I used to think there was nobody lower than me. Now, I can't believe what's happening. You have to have faith."

Jim raised his beer can. "To faith."

Renaldo touched the can with his orange-juice carton. "To faith."

Jim drank. Then he said, "You know, you're sounding more and more like my father these days. You keep forgetting you're my kid brother."

Renaldo grinned. "It's all that beer you drink. Rots your brain."

"Then how come Huggins hasn't rotted clear away."

"He just shriveled," Renaldo said. "All his cells are made of leather now. He couldn't weigh more than a hundred pounds. But I'm going to try to fatten him up tomorrow."

"Where you going?"

"Maria's family. In Washington Heights."

"Fine lady, that Maria," Jim commented. Renaldo's girl friend was a beautiful Dominican girl who was in a ballet company.

"Where are you going?" Renaldo asked.

"Granny's sister's place."

"Granny's a fine lady too."

"It's just like Huggins," Jim said. "Granny's getting old too. I worry about her."

"All we can do is enjoy them while we can, Jimmy. And that will be for a while yet."

"I hope so," Jim replied. He drained the last of his beer, then said, "On that note, I'll hit Huggins for another Bud."

Granny left the LL train at the Union Square station, one of the busiest in the New York subway system. Like the other big interline transfer points, the station was a sprawling underground catacomb of arcades and passageways and platforms. And through the maze prowled predators that made the station one of the most dangerous in the city.

Granny Moore had a lot of other things on her mind besides crime as she struggled to tote two heavy shopping bags down the long corridor that lead to the IRT platform. Nearly twelve o'clock and she still had a powerful lot of work to do when she got to Harriet's. Still, it was worth it. Jimmy coming up was the capper that would make it the best kind of day.

She finally reached the end of the corridor, then walked down the steps to the uptown tracks. The platform was more empty than it usually was when she closed up around nine. A dozen people, maybe, were waiting for the train. Couple of other old folks, three men who looked like they'd had way too much to drink. Down at the end, a couple of kids, pacing restlessly.

Granny was restless too. She kept leaning over, staring down the black mouth of the tunnel. Tonight of all nights she wanted that express train to come quick. Finally, she heard the approaching train give off its first distant vibrations. Then, gradually, the level of sound increased. Looking southward, Granny Moore saw the front car that in the darkness of the tunnel looked like a four-eyed monster, with its amber and white marker lights over the white sealed-beam headlights. As the "monster" emerged into the light, it became six, battered, graffiti-soiled subway cars.

The brakes sighed, the train settled, then the doors rattled open. Granny picked up the shopping bag with the twenty-six pound turkey, hauled it inside, then collapsed into the seat by the door.

Lord, she was exhausted. Since her seventi-

eth birthday two years ago, she'd been short-
ening her hours, opening up at 7:30 A.M. instead
of 6:00 A.M. and closing at 9:00 P.M. instead of
11:00 P.M. Today, thought, she'd been on her
feet an extra three hours. Walking over, talking
to Jimmy, with Thanksgiving on her mind, she'd
forgot how tired she was. But when she'd been
hauling herself to this platform, the weariness
came flooding back. If Harriet's boy weren't
there to meet her, she didn't know what she'd
do. Maybe she should have taken a cab, like
Jimmy said.

The train started with a jolt. She looked
around. She saw a half a dozen people staring
at the floor or reading the paper. In the far
corner, a filthy old drunk sprawled over two
seats. Whenever she got to feeling low, the
Lord reminded her of the greater burdens he'd
bestowed elsewhere. Hard as her life had been,
she'd had more than her share of blessings.

Her family was the biggest of those blessings.
And she hadn't wanted to tell Jimmy about the
best news of all until tomorrow. Harold's youngest daughter, Cynthia, had been accepted
by Harvard Law School.

Granny couldn't get over it. Her own flesh
and blood sitting right there in those classrooms
with the Kennedys and all those rich folks. That
was the reason she'd started saving every single cent she could. Cynthia was going to have
real nice clothes, not hand-me-downs or twenty-
dollar dresses off the rack at Alexander's. She
was going to be just like the rest of the students.
And when she got to graduation three and a

half years from now, Granny was going to sit in the audience watching her. Granny was already so filled with pride at the thought that she was like to burst.

The train rattled to a stop at Forty-second Street. The doors opened, a handful of people got on, the doors slammed shut. Then the train moved on. Three stops to go. Granny leaned back, her fleshy arms folded on her ample lap, her eyes closed.

She heard the door between cars open and shut. But she didn't open her eyes until the train jerked to a stop at Eighty-sixth Street.

The two of them were standing directly in front of her, holding on to the straps hanging from the horizontal bar above her head. They were both young, no more than fourteen or fifteen. Their dress was standard ghetto—Converse sneakers, pegged jeans, shirt opened to the waist with the sleeves of their denim jackets cut off.

Though she wasn't the worrying type, Granny started to get concerned. It was the expression on their faces that bothered her. They both had this fixed, brittle smile and they stared at her with hard eyes that made them seem far older than they were.

The train started in motion. The taller one spoke. "Give us the purse," he ordered.

Lord, she thought. That voice. They were just children, except maybe gone a little wrong. What right did they have to the $54.87 she was taking home to add to Cynthia's clothing fund?

"Give it to us," the boy said again.

She looked around for help. Everyone on the car was looking away.

The boy on the left grabbed her bag. She held on, and he pulled her off the seat. She fell hard onto the subway car floor, still holding on for dear life. It was hers, the money so hard earned.

Then the knife plunged into her back. Once, then again. Her eyes quickly dimmed and her grip on the strap of the bag immediately loosened. She felt dizzy, like with too much wine in the park on a Sunday afternoon. She was nauseous and thought she'd throw up. She heard their feet pound down the car, the doors open. Then she heard her own terrible drawn-out groan. Then nothing.

three

The moment the door opened, the moment he saw Ester's face, so red and puffy from weeping, he knew. She clung to him, and he felt her body shake. A numbing sense of despair engulfed him. His spirit seemed paralyzed. He sat in that small, tidy Harlem apartment, with family and the scores of friends who stopped by, until he felt so smothered by grief he couldn't breath.

So, finally, he escaped. When he hit the street, the crisp, cold November air seemed to break open a new bitter well of feeling within him. He could barely contain his swelling rage. Unable to bear the thought of sitting in a subway car, he started walking.

He moved south on Lenox Avenue, then west on 110th Street. Past the corpses of buildings, their windows tinned over, their interiors gutted by fire. Past garbage-strewn alleys and stripped cars perched on old milk crates. Past the tawdry line of bars and pizza parlors and candy stores.

He drew long looks from the human jackals perched on stoops and leaning against doorways along the route. He was an incongruous sight, a white man dressed in his one good sport coat and tie, the outfit he'd donned to please Granny. On a normal day, he'd have been mugged before he'd gone five blocks. But today the aura of violence must have been upon him. No one said a word or took a step toward him.

If anyone had, he would have been a dead man. Jim hadn't felt this kind of anger, this outrage, since a long time ago. Since he'd stood in the jungle outside a tiny hamlet in the mountains of Laos.

As he walked up the steep hill toward Morningside Heights, his face set in such a rigid, grim mask his jaw began to ache, he thought: this city is more dangerous than the front line in Vietnam. At least in Nam they'd had weapons to defend themselves. The big cities of this country today seemed to have written off decent working people as if they were worthless lottery tickets. To call the city a jungle was an insult to jungles.

The cops were supposed to provide protection. If the President of the United States came into town, or some foreign leader, about a thousand cops would be lined up elbow to elbow to make sure nothing happened. But in the rest of the city their numbers were so few that collectively they had the effect of one man pissing on a forest fire. And with the courts and jails the way they were, getting caught for anything less than murder was like getting a traffic ticket. For every criminal the cops caught, fifty more got away.

When Jim reached the top of the hill, he paused to catch his breath. Ahead of him, across the Hudson River, the sun was hanging, blood red in the haze, on the horizon. As he stared at that sun, the determination came to him. Granny Moore's death was not going to be just a statistic. Her senseless murder was not going to be filed away with the other two thousand slayings in the violence-ridden city. He didn't know how or in what way. But Granny's death was going to mean something. No matter what he had to do.

Detective Vinnie Civitello cradled the phone between his shoulder and ear as he opened the bottom drawer of the battered, paper-strewn desk. Behind him, the peeling green wall was covered with wanted posters and police memorandums. As Jim waited, his eye wandered from grim, unsmiling face to grim, unsmiling face, and he thought, How many lives has each of them shattered?

"Yeah, yea, I'll hold," Vinnie muttered into the mouthpiece. He pulled out of the drawer a nearly full bottle of Jack Daniels bourbon and a couple of small paper cups. He motioned with the bottle to Jim.

Jim shook his head.

Civitello gestured with the bottle again. "You

look like you need a belt," the detective said.

Jim took the bottle. He unscrewed the cap and poured a couple of shots.

"Yea. I'm here. Shoot," Vinnie said into the phone.

Jim watched the detective's pen poised over a pad. Vinnie kept saying, "Uh huh. Uh huh." But the pen hardly moved.

Then Vinnie hung up the phone, downed the bourbon in one gulp, and leaned back in the swivel chair.

"Well," Jim asked, "what are they doing?"

Vinnie scowled, his heavy jowls creasing like a bloodhound's. "Same fucking story all the time from those shitheads. Transit police. About as useful as tits on a bull."

"What are you trying to tell me?"

Vinnie rubbed his left ear. "They don't have nothing. When the punks split at 125th Street, so did the rest of the people on the car. The only guy who didn't was a drunk who wouldn't have woke up if the Russian army moved in. No one else on the train that they could find saw anything."

"Goddamn it," Jim exclaimed in frustration. "Somebody must have seen something. If they couldn't have helped Granny, the least they could do is come forward."

Vinnie leaned forward, grabbed the Jack Daniels, and poured himself another slug. He downed it, grimaced as it burned its way to his gut, then said, "Look it, kid. You ain't no cherry, the operation you run. Half the people on the subway that time of night are drunks or perverts or muggers or homicidal maniacs themselves. The other half are too scared to say boo."

"That's ridiculous."

"Ridiculous, huh. Lemme tell you about this guy who lives down on Rivington Street. Got back from the army a few months ago with some country chick he married who didn't know from nothing about life in our fair city. She was looking out the window one day, saw some kids boosting batteries from cars. She called the cops and they got nabbed. Two nights later, the kids and a half dozen of their buddies bust into their apartment. They tied the guy up, raped his wife a few times apiece, shoved a shotgun between her legs and pulled the trigger. Then they blew him to pieces. End of citizen cooperation."

A surge of anger hit Jim. The muscles of his face squeezed in around his eyes and he could feel the vein in his temple pulsate. "So what are you telling me? We should just give up? What in the hell is this world coming to when the cops give up before they start?"

Vinnie gestured out the window. "This is what it's coming to," he said. "Jim, you're a bright, decent guy with a big future. Take my advice. Go back to your clinic, pull down the shades, lock the door, then drop the key down the nearest sewer. Get on a bus or a train or a plane until you get to a place were the houses are a mile apart and the stores don't have gates over the windows and kids leave their bikes in the driveway overnight and where they think angel dust is something that falls off of halos. That's where you'll be able to live like a human being again."

Jim stared for a couple of minutes at the door to the office. Then he faced Vinnie again and asked in a calmer voice, "So you think I should run away? That's the answer?"

Vinnie shrugged.

"Why do you stay here, Vin? Tell me that. Why in the hell do you stay?"

"In the words of our mayor, I'm a fucking wacko."

"No, Vin. I'm serious."

Vinnie picked up the stub of a fat cigar from an overflowing ash tray, lit it, then watched the first thick cloud of smoke drift upward toward the cracked ceiling. Finally, he said, "Here's the way I see it, kid. Despite the fact I look like a dumb, greasy guinea, I'm not like most of the guys here. They think we ought to put a twenty-foot-high fence around the Lower East Side. They think everybody's an animal. But I know different."

He paused to take another drag at the cigar. "I'm gonna throw some numbers at you. Last year, we logged about six hundred thousand felonies in this city. With the ones that didn't get reported, maybe the real total was twice, even three times that, I'll allow. That's a lot of crime. But when we nail a guy, we find the guy's done not one crime, but twenty or thirty or fifty crimes. Even if the average is only ten crimes apiece, which is very conservative, that means 97 percent or 98 percent of the people in New York are decent, hardworking, law-abiding people.

That means the ones who do all the shit, the ones that make the cities hellholes, are less than 3 percent."

"I believe that," Jim said. "But what are you trying to tell me?"

"I'm trying to say that I believe someday we good guys are going to find a way. A way to get rid of that 2 percent or 3 percent scum and take back the city again."

"You mean, someday the giant is going to wake up and find out how strong he is?"

"That's it. You see a little of it. When I was at the 46th Precinct in the Bronx, I saw the Italians on Arthur Avenue, right in the middle of all the decay of the South Bronx, keep the neighborhood the way it was ten, twenty years ago. Somebody strange walks down the street at 2:00 A.M., the precinct gets calls. Girls walk home from baby-sitting at midnight and nobody thinks twice. That's what I mean."

"That's interesting," Jim said. He sat back, forefinger on his lips.

"What are you thinking?" Vinnie asked.

"What are the chances of the transit cops finding Granny's killer?"

"What are the chances of my going home and finding Bo Derek nude on my bed?"

"Seriously, Vin. I mean it."

"The chances of the punk getting nailed sometime for something are pretty good. Probably for snatching a purse, which means he'll be back on the street in about two minutes. But the chances of connecting the guy to Granny and getting a conviction ..." He shook his head. "Probably fifty to one."

"I thought so," Jim said. "If the transit police can't find Granny's killer, maybe I can."

Vinnie looked concerned. "Look it, Jimmy. I didn't mean that. All you'll do is get yourself stabbed too."

"Maybe. But I'm not going to take it anymore, Vin. I can't do that to Granny. I don't know how. But whoever attacked her is going to pay."

Vinnie studied Jim for a while. Then he smiled. "Maybe you can do something. You want some advice?"

"That's why I'm here."

"Now, this is off the record. If somebody asks, your good buddy Detective Civitello didn't say nothing. Right?"

"Of course."

"Good. Here's what you do. Get a buddy or two. Dress good enough so you don't look like punks, but not so good you stick out. Then ride that train a few nights, about the time Granny got killed. A lot of people get off work at the same time every night, ride the same train home every night."

"So?"

"So you can strike up a conversation. People are always scared. But they respond when someone's friendly, somebody who makes them feel safe. Get them talking, you might just find out something."

Jim felt a strange excitement begin to build in him. "Great idea. I can see it working."

"One thing, though," Vinnie cautioned. "Anybody gives you a lead, anything gets pointed out, you go to the cops. You learn anything, hand it over. I got some buddies on the transit police, I'll make sure they follow through. Promise?"

Jim rose and extended his hand. "Promise. And thanks, Vin. Thanks a hell of a lot."

four

"Jim."

"What is it?"

"Come. Look at this."

"Damn it, I'm busy," he snapped. He proof-read a few more lines. Then he put down the pencil and rubbed his eyes.

Shouldn't take it out on Juanita, he told himself. The clinic's receptionist was perpetually cheerful and effervescent. Today, after the emotional shock of Granny's death and a sleepless night, he felt strung out and exhausted. He was only in the office because he had to proofread the final draft of a vital proposal for emergency funding for the clinic.

He leaned back in the chair, clasped his hands behind his head, and closed his eyes.

A couple of minutes later, he heard Juanita at the door. "Jim?"

He opened his eyes. "Sorry, Juanita. I didn't mean to snap."

"That's okay," she said. "There's this man. He's here to see you."

"I'm really busy. Can you take his name and—"

"He came in a limousine," Juanita interjected.

"A limo?"

"That's what I called you to see. A big gray one, with a chauffeur and everything."

"Who is he?"

Juanita handed him an expensive, embossed business card that read Manhattan Community Development Associations, Inc. Anthony Brown, Director.

Jim stared at it, puzzled. He'd never heard of the group before. But he couldn't afford not to see people who drove up in limousines. He told Juanita to show him in.

The man who walked in the door and extended his hand had the build of an ex-pro football linebacker. He was tall, about six three, with broad shoulders, a barrel chest, a thick neck, and a square, rugged-looking face. He was dressed immaculately and expensively, however—three-piece black pinstripe suit, silk shirt, diamond tie pin, Gucci loafers.

Jim shook the huge proffered hand and asked, "What can I do for you, Mr. Brown?"

He smiled. "Call me Andy, Jim. And the reason I'm here is to do something for you."

"Me?"

"That's right. Let me explain. The group I represent are investors who are concerned with turning things around in marginal areas of the city. You'd agree that the Lower East Side is marginal?'

Jim smiled wryly. "If your margins are wide."

"Exactly. We enlist the cooperation of forward-looking businessmen in the area to improve property values, services, that kind of thing."

"I'm not sure I understand."

Brown reached into his jacket and pulled out an envelope. He handed it to Jim and said, "Perhaps this will make it clearer."

Jim opened the flap and saw green. He counted twenty crisp new $100 bills. He held the bills in his hand for a moment, not believing what he was seeing.

"What is this?" he finally asked.

"A contribution," Brown replied. "our investors are family men, and they believe the strength of an area rests with families. Health care for children is an important family service. We've heard of the fine work you've done, and we don't want to see your clinic close its doors."

"I don't know what to say. Except thank you. We're really up against it, to tell you the truth. This will buy us some time."

Brown looked at Jim with a hint of amusement. Then he said, "You've got a lot of time. You see, you'll get an envelope like this every month. If that's not enough, you let me know."

Jim was flabbergasted. "God, will this be enough? It's the whole difference. And if one of these grants comes through," he added, picking up the proposal on his desk, "we won't even need that much."

Brown reached out and gestured toward the

proposal. Jim gave it to him. Brown leafed
through the pages for a moment, then ripped
the proposal in half.

"Hey," Jim said with a flash of anger.

Brown got to his feet. "You don't need these
people. I told you, the neighborhood will take
care of its own."

Jim stared at the huge man. The whole situation didn't make sense to him, and that worried
him. "What do I have to do for this? You want
monthly reports?"

Brown smiled again. "You keep on doing
what you've been doing. And that's a real fine
job." He started for the door, then turned. "Oh,
yea. You have my card. You need anything,
call."

Jim watched him go. Then he picked up the
stack of $100 bills and thought, I should be
jumping up and down for joy right now. This
money was manna from heaven, the kind of
miracle that happened on television shows.

Maybe that's why he didn't trust it. It was all
so vague, this neighborhood development as-
sociation. How could they give him money in
cash, without even asking for a receipt? Why
had they chosen him to receive the largess?

Jim continued to stare at the money. Then he
thought, I'm being ridiculous. He would certainly
have to do some investigation. But in the the
meantime, he had bills to pay, including his
own long-overdue rent.

The doors of the LL train opened at Union
Square station. They got out and walked up

the stairs, then wound their way to the IRT platform.

"Which train, Jim?"

Jim didn't respond. He was lost in thought. It was weird, the first time on the subway since Granny's murder. They were taking the same route, the same one she took every night of her life.

"Jim, you been popping some of those pills you hand out?"

This time Jim responded. He looked at Eric and John and said, "I wish I had. Why?"

"We want to know which train to take."

"The express. We're getting off at 125th Street."

"Thank you, sir," the twins said in unison.

Jim smiled. Eric and John Siebert lived above a hardware store that their great-grandfather, a German immigrant, had started eighty four years before. With their blond hair, their blue eyes, and their husky builds, they looked more like Minnesota farm boys than the street-wise city kids they were.

All the years he'd known them, Jim still had trouble telling them apart. They were identical, except for one thing—John, for some inexplicable medical reason, had been born totally deaf. That defect, however, had made less difference in his life than in any other handicapped person Jim knew. Because he didn't want to be separated from his brother, John early in life became a skilled lip-reader. He learned to speak, and he went all the way through public school in regular classes. This fall, the twins had started studying engineering at Hunter College. Their proud father, Heinrich, was planning to retire from the hardware business in sixteen years, on the hundredth anniversary of the store. And he'd decided that was long enough for his family to be merchants. It was time for his sons to become professional men.

The express squealed to a halt in front of them and they climbed aboard. The half-filled car was graffiti covered and filthy. The thought struck Jim: what an awful place for Granny to die. What an awful place for anyone to die.

Jim and the twins rode in silence. At Forty-second Street, the Grand Central Station stop, there was an influx of riders. They included three teenagers swaying to the beat of deafening loud music blaring from their "box," the huge portable radiotape players carried by so many city kids. Playing radios on the subway cars was illegal. But there was no transit cop on the car, and most of the passengers gritted their teeth.

Then an older, heavyset man wearing a dirty green coveralls and a baseball cap looked up from his newspaper. "Hey," he shouted. "Turn that off."

The kids stared. The biggest, a lean black kid about sixteen, said, "You talking to us?"

"I said turn that thing off. It's not allowed."

The kid nudged his friend with his elbow. "We got ourselves a real music lover here."

The three kids moved over to stand in front of

the sitting man. The leader said, "Who the hell you think you are, motherfucker?"

The man, intimidated, stared away. The tall kid grabbed the box and shoved it up against the man's ear, knocking off his baseball cap. The man tried to lean away, but another kid pushed his head against the speaker. "You like that, motherfucker?"

"That's enough."

The tall kid turned. Jim was standing behind him.

The kid's eyes flashed angrily. "We got another asshole wants to . . ."

His voice trailed off when he saw the husky bodies of Eric and John move up behind Jim. He looked from one to the other, taking in the grim expressions on their faces. Then, in a show of bravado, he started to smile. He turned and started to say, "These motherfuckers want . . ."

His mouth dropped open when he saw his friends had fled to the next car. He glanced back at Jim, then started to back away.

"Turn it off," Jim commanded.

The kid stopped for a second, then grabbed the handle of the door between cars.

Jim moved forward. "I said, turn it off," he shouted.

The kid turned the radio off. Then he quickly went through the door.

Jim sighed in relief. He patted Eric on the shoulder. "Thanks for backing me up, guys."

They started back toward their seats. Then they stopped, stunned.

The passengers were applauding. Two elderly ladies in the corner started it. Then a mother and her small daughter, a couple of men in business suits, a priest. Then the whole car joined in.

Jim sat, smiling and nodding. His face felt warm, and he knew he was blushing a little bit. But he felt a tremendous rush of satisfaction too.

"I feel like Superman," Eric commented.

Jim turned to him. "I never did anything like that before. I guess I was thinking about Granny, and I found myself moving."

"It was great," John said. "People ought to do that more often."

"They should," Jim said thoughtfully, "they really should."

The inside of the Harlem funeral parlor was packed and hot. After forty-five minutes, Jim excused himself and stepped outside for some fresh air.

The night was clear and cold. the buildings on either side of the Hillside Funeral Home had been demolished, and a cold wind whipped through the opening, swirling papers on the sidewalk. Chilled in his sport coat, Jim found the scene desolate. He was ready to go back inside when the yellow cab pulled up in the No Parking zone in front of the canopy.

Baseline Jones unfurled himself from the driver's seat and Renoldo came around from the passenger side.

Baseline put his huge hand on Jim's shoulder. "Bummer, man. A real bummer."

"Yea," Jim said. After a pause, he turned to Renaldo. "Slapsy coming?"

"Tomorrow. To the funeral. He's really broken up."

"Did you talk to him about helping me out for a few nights?"

"He's all for it. Anything to find out who did this to Granny."

"And I'm in too," Baseline added.

Jim was surprised. "You drive the cab at night. You know I've got the twins to help?"

"I need a vacation from that rolling junk heap. Besides, all you guys is ugly. Real ugly. You know what I say, 'If the ladies are riding and their looks are fine/You'll need the charming body of the fantabulous Baseline.'"

Jim chuckled. "What an ego. How do you live with yourself?"

"He's deaf," Renaldo said. He ducked a playful swipe from Baseline, then asked Jim, "When do we start?"

"Tomorrow night. Meet me at the clinic at nine. That'll give us time to talk first."

"Good."

Jim clasped his hands around his elbows, then said, "Burr, it's cold. Let's go inside."

Renaldo walked up the stairs. Jim was about to follow when Baseline grabbed his arm.

"Just a second, man."

"What is it?"

"The word is out that a man laid a pile of bread on you today."

"How did you hear about that?"

Baseline grinned. "Like every other warm female body on the planet, your lovely Juanita dreams of running her hands over the magnificent frame of Baseline Jones. Unlike all but a few of those females, the lucky chick occasionally gets her chance."

"I should have figured as much."

"Well," Baseline said, "I figure anything that bails you out has to be A-OK with the Baseline. Only thing is, that dude that laid the bread on you has pissed off some people I mean *pissed*, pissed."

"Who's that?"

"I picked up old man Goldstein the other day. He was going on and on about this guy coming in and offering to buy his building."

"He said he represents a group of investors," Jim said.

"Could be. But Goldstein said the dude had a lot of trouble taking no for an answer."

"So what are you trying to tell me?"

Baseline shrugged. "I don't know. I'm always suspicious of the man. I don't want to see my good honky friend Jimmy get into trouble."

Jim smiled. "Thanks. I was planning to check out the guy anyway. I'll talk to Goldstein."

"Don't mention my name," Baseline cautioned. "I don't want any big dudes out looking for my body."

Jim looked at his friend for a moment. Then he said, "Seriously, Baseline. You don't have to ride the subway with us. We're not looking for trouble, but there could be violence."

Baseline stepped back, a broad, incredulous expression on his face. "Brother, this man's been doing violence for years to grown men in short pants who foolishly steps on a basketball court. And, of course, to the bodies of select young ladies. I'm ready for anything."

A warm feeling passed through Jim. "Thanks," he said.

"Come on," Baseline said, an uncharacteristically somber expression on his face, "now we go inside. Time to do some mourning for a fine lady."

five

The older one, a lanky sixteen-year-old, moved casually and confidently down the street, his body swaying slightly, as if he had a record playing in his head. The boy with him was much slighter, and as he walked he cast anxious glances at the eerie shadows cast by the darkened buildings.

They crossed the street, their feet crunching the broken glass from a trashed Oldsmobile. The taller kid stopped on the sidewalk and looked around.

"Maybe he's not coming, Cisco," the younger boy said nervously.

His brother glared at him. In the faint light of the streetlamp, the discolored scar on his left cheek glowed like a bad burn.

"You're too old to be a pussy no more, Ton," he said harshly. "You gonna be a Skull, you're in this. Understand?"

Tony nodded.

His brother looked at him searchingly for a moment. Then he said, "Come on."

They ducked through the gaping hole in the chain link fence into the park, which was more like a scar than an urban oasis. The asphalt was strewn with the litter, and the playground equipment yawned at awkward angles. In the shadow of the neighboring building, vague shapes were sprawled on park benches like discarded empties in a gutter.

Cisco lead his brother to the far side of a squat, square building in the middle of the park. He scouted around, then pulled a joint out of his jacket pocket. He lit it, took a deep drag, then offered it to his brother.

Tony shook his head.

Cisco grabbed his right hand and stuck the joint between his fingers. "I told you, shithead. Dude offers you some blow, you take the blow. Dude offers you some wine, you take a hit. You piss anybody off you ain't gonna be a Skull. Then you ain't my brother. You ain't shit."

Tony's hand was trembling as he put the joint to his lips. He sucked, noisily, but not taking in much smoke. Holding his breath, he handed the marijuana cigarette back to his brother.

"Better," Cisco said. "Better."

Tony leaned against the wall and closed his eyes. He breathed deeply, trying to control the wild pounding of his heart. He was scared to death. But there was no place to go.

His whole thirteen years, it seemed like things were being stacked on top of him one by one. He was half Italian and half Hispanic—"greasy as a guinea, dumb as a spic" went the taunts. Soon after he was born, his father split for good. His Italian mother, disowned by her family after her marriage to George Melendez, lay around in bed all day eating, drinking, and cavorting with the endless stream of "uncles" who moved in and out of the small, dark, filthy tenement apartment.

So Tony grew up on the streets. He'd always been small for his age, and quiet and more timid than his peers. He would have tasted a lot more harassment than he had if it hadn't been for Cisco, who reveled in being one of the baddest dudes around. When Cisco joined the Savage Skulls, everybody left his kid brother alone.

That was terrific for Tony. But now the time had come that he'd always dreaded. The time when he got old enough to prove himself. To join the Savage Skulls.

Gang life terrified him, the fighting, the stealing, the drug dealing. The alternative was worse. He'd have to walk down these same streets every day as, in Cisco's words, "a punk," "a pussy." He might was well go up on the roof and throw himself off, rather than have the crap beaten out of him a little bit every day.

He'd been thinking about that more and more. He'd gone up on the roof a couple of times, testing himself, getting close to the edge. But he didn't think he'd have the courage to jump either.

"Where in the hell is that landlord?" Cisco grumbled. "Gotta be past twelve. I—"

A powerful flashlight beam hit his face.

"Drop the joint," said a man in a deep, commanding voice.

"But—"

"But, shit. You got a job to do, and I don't want you stoned out of your skull."

"Okay. Okay," Cisco said. His brother was amazed at the unaccustomed deference in his voice.

"Listen," the man said, "here's the job. You know how to make Molotovs?"

"Sure."

"Make two. Got that in your thick spic head. Just two."

Tony saw his brother nod. As the man issued his orders, Tony stared. His eyes gradually adjusted, and he could make out the faint shape of a man in an overcoat holding the flashlight.

"Got that?" the man concluded.

"Sure," Cisco said. He paused, then added, "What about the bread?"

The man reached into a pocket. Several bills fluttered into the circle of light, then fell to the pavement.

"A bill now. A bill after the job is done."

"Hey. The going rate's three hundred. I can't do . . ."

The flashlight shut off. They heard footsteps moving away around the side of the building.

An hour later, Cisco and Tony were moving slowly down Avenue B. When they moved past the blaring music coming from the open windows of a second-floor social club, Cisco asked, "You got the gas off your hands?"

"Yea."

"You sure?"

"Yea," Tony repeated. His voice was a squeak.

"The building's halfway down the next block. We go up to the second floor. The empty apartment is the one with the smashed door. We pop in the Molotovs and split."

"The empty apartment? You mean people live there?"

"Relax," Cisco said. "We ain't out to kill nobody. Two cocktails won't get the building. This is a warning. When everybody splits, we'll take the whole building. That's the way it works. Got it?"

"Yea." Tony's mouth was so dry he felt his tongue stick to the roof of his mouth. He was trying desperately hard not to gag.

The turned the corner. In the middle of the block, they walked up the steps of the building. Empty wine bottles and beer cans littered the landing. When they plunged into the blackness of the front hall, the stench of fried fish and urine hit their noses.

"Put your hand on my back," Cisco whispered.

Tony did as he was told. He crept behind his brother up to the second floor.

"Now," Cisco said. He flicked the lighter. The flame startled Tony, and he almost dropped the mayonnaise bottle full of gasoline. Cisco lit the cloth crammed into the top of the bottle full of gasoline, then lit the wick of Tony's bottle. Cisco hurled his cocktail into the doorless apartment to their left. The bottle shattered, then with a roar a stream of fire jumped up the wall.

For an instant, Tony froze. A door opened upstairs and somebody shouted. In total panic, he heaved the bottle and fled down the stairs.

He could hear Cisco ahead of him, but he was blind in the darkness. Then he heard a body crash to the floor of the landing.

"Shit!" Cisco cried.

Tony nearly stumbled over his fallen brother. "What's the matter?"

"Fucking bottle. My ankle," Cisco panted. "Help me."

He looped his arm around the neck of his slender, shorter brother. The weight nearly toppled Tony, and he staggered as they moved outside. When they reached the sidewalk, Cisco lurched and Tony felt himself falling. He reached out with his right hand to brace the fall. When the hand hit the ground, he felt a stabbing pain. The sidewalk was littered with broken glass. A shard had sliced a deep cut in his palm, and a stream of blood poured out.

"Come on," Cisco shouted. Above, they could hear the crackle of fire in the second-floor apartment.

Tony somehow got to his feet. His brother hoisted himself up and draped his right arm around Tony's shoulders again.

They were three buildings down when they heard the sirens.

"Faster," Cisco hissed. "Faster."

Tony tried to speed up, but he lost his balance and they fell again.

On his knees, catching his breath, Tony saw the flashing lights of the police car turn the corner behind them. He leaped to his feet.

"What are you doing, asshole?" Cisco yelled.

The police car pulled to a halt in front of the building in which they'd started the fire. Tony took a deep breath, ran back toward the building, then darted across the street through the beams of the police car's headlights.

"Hey," Cisco heard the cops yell. They got out of their car and started to chase Tony.

Ignoring the intense pain, Cisco got to his feet and lurched down the street. By the time the cops nabbed Tony, he'd hailed a cab on the next avenue.

Jim lay on his back, staring at the ceiling. With the streetlamp right outside his third-floor apartment, the room was never dark. Although he was totally exhausted, he couldn't sleep.

As he'd done so many times, he traced with his eyes the network of cracks in the ceiling of the almost closet-sized bedroom. The patterns were endless. There had been nights, mostly in his youth, when the cracks seemed to be a road map to a future of limitless prosperity and happiness. Now, they seemed to represent an inescapable maze.

He'd been all right at the funeral home. He'd taken an odd kind of comfort in the rituals of mourning; in the presence of his friends; in the existence of his plan to do something to make Granny's death meaningful. But when he'd returned home, to the untidy apartment in the shabby tenement in which he'd lived most of his life, the bottom seemed to fall out of his mood.

The heart of his depression, he'd decided in the two hours of tossing and turning, was being alone. It was not that he was lonely in the conventional sense, for he had a lot of good friends. Rather, it was the lack of somebody lying beside him. Someone whom he loved and who loved him. Someone with whom he could share the deepest feelings, his doubts and fears. Someone with whom he could weep.

He wondered if the core of his problem was the need to be strong. He'd always been the one to be responsible, to take charge, to stay levelheaded. He'd begun to suspect the reason he hadn't married was that subconsciously he feared opening himself up.

Maybe that was why he'd fallen in love with Sara. Since she was unattainable, she was "safe." And his ability to function despite the pain of unrequited love made him feel like a martyr to his work—his commitment to the betterment of his community.

Tonight he felt closer than ever to abandoning that commitment. Maybe Vinnie Civitello was right. He was too bright, too talented to bang his head against the wall, scratching every month to pay the rent on a tenement apartment in the middle of a slum. Maybe he should—

He sat up in bed as he heard the whine of the siren passing beneath his window. Another siren came by a moment later, then a third. He tossed off the blanket and padded across the floor to the window.

Minutes later, he was dressed and on the street. Two blocks away, fire engines blocked the street. As Jim approached, he could see, in the pulsating red lights, figures jerkily racing back and forth, like actors in an old silent movie. A chattering crowd watching the firemen put a ladder up to a third-floor window from which thick, black smoke was bellowing. Firemen smashed the remaining glass, which showered down into the street. Then a powerful stream of water blasted through the window, hitting the flames with a roar.

Jim's first thought was to look for the injured. He moved through the crowd, asking questions. Then he spotted a cop he knew, a young Irish guy who played basketball sometimes over at the Catholic school gym. The cop told him that everyone seemed to have fled the building safely.

"We got the perp," he added. "A kid. I think Timmy's getting ready to take him off to Bellevue."

"Why?"

"Punk cut himself trying to get away."

"Where is he?"

"I'll show you," the cop said.

The kid huddled in the back of the police car looked about eight years old. Jim opened the door.

"Let me see it," he said. The kid extended a hand wrapped in a blood-soaked handkerchief. He unwound the cloth and took a look.

"This needs cleaning and stitching right away."

"I said we're taking him to Bellevue."

"That'll take most of the night. Why don't we run by the clinic. I'll take care of him."

"Fine by me," the cop said. "The quicker, the better."

"This is going to hurt," Jim said as he looked into the dark eyes of the wounded boy. Jim could see he was scared to death. Somehow, he didn't look like the type to be throwing Molotov cocktails.

Jim started stitching the wound. He was proud of the skill he'd perfected under the worst of combat conditions in Vietnam. The boy didn't flinch, and Jim finished quickly.

As Jim bandaged the cut, he asked, "What's your name?"

The boy looked away.

"Come on," Jim said. "I saved you a trip to Bellevue. Least you could do is tell me your name."

There was no response for a moment. Then the boy turned "Tony."

"Tony what?"

"Tony Melendez."

"Tony Melendez. Nice name. Too nice a name for a kid who starts fires."

Jim saw the boy stiffen. He looked away again.

"Why'd you do it, Tony?"

No response.

"You're too young to get into that kind of crap," Jim said. "Take it from me. I grew up in this neighborhood. I've seen what happens.

You're gonna spend the rest of your life with those punks who think they're so cool, huh?"

Tony turned. His eyes narrowed as he looked at Jim with curiosity. "You grew up here? You—you in a gang?"

"No. Gangs are for punks. I made up my mind I didn't want to be a punk."

Tony stared at him.

"How about you?" Jim asked. "You going to be a punk?"

Jim could see the boy fighting back tears. The boy pulled away.

"Okay," Jim said. "If you ever want to talk about it, you stop here. This time, you're lucky. You're too young, so they'll take you home to momma. Next time could be worse. You think about that."

six

The cold drizzle intensified into a steady rain as they trudged up First Avenue. They hurried down the steps to the subway.

Baseline took off his Windbreaker and squeezed it like a wet rag. "Damn, what a night," he said.

"You should have worn something heavier," Eric said.

"Heck, I ain't used to this," Baseline complained. "It's always seventy-five degrees and dry in that cab of mine."

"Well, you're not in the cab," Jim said. "But if you're going to start bitching, maybe you should be."

He turned and shoved a $5 bill into the token booth slot. "Five," he said.

As he waited for change, Renaldo came up next to him. "Hey, Jimmy," he said in a low voice. "Cool it, huh? We're all a little uptight."

Jim swept up the tokens and the change. He

looked up at the tall, rugged boxer, meeting his eyes. Then he nodded, acknowledging the criticism.

Jim moved over next to Baseline. "Sorry about that," he said.

"That's cool," Baseline said. "But I hope these cars got some heat."

Jim smiled. "Not too much heat, I hope." He handed out the tokens. "Let's go."

Jim walked to the edge of the tracks, peering impatiently down the black tunnel. As they'd sat in the clinic tonight, sharing pizza and talking about the plans for riding the subway, Jim had felt increasingly foolish. It was like a bunch of grown men playing cowboys and Indians.

The only thing that kept him from calling it off was that Vinnie Civitello, a detective he respected, had recommended the attempt. That, and the lingering emotions he retained from that morning, standing next to the grave site in the drizzle watching Granny being lowered to her last resting place.

He pivoted and started pacing. Eric came up next to him.

"I got a question, Jim."

"Shoot."

"You remember what happened last night? With those guys with the radio?"

"Yea."

"Are we going to do it again?"

"What do you mean?"

"If there's some trouble. Are we going to help?"

Jim pursed his lips. At length, he said, "I don't

know. That's not why we're riding the subway. I don't want anybody getting hurt."

"We got Renaldo with us."

"We won't start any violence," Jim said firmly. "We're not trying to do the cops' job."

Eric shot him a dubious look. "We're not? Then what are we doing?"

Jim grimaced. He really didn't have an answer.

Minutes later, the LL train screeched to a halt. They boarded and rode in silence the two stops to the Fourteenth Street Station. As they headed for the IRT, Jim said, "Granny's train left here at 11:48. A number 5 train. I want to wait for that one."

"Jim, I just thought of something," Renaldo said. "Granny was attacked on a weekday. Tonight's Saturday."

"I know. But a lot of people work shifts through the weekend. I want to get a feel for what we're doing."

"What are we doing, exactly?" Baseline asked. "My brain ain't working too well in this cold."

"Granny was riding in the next to the last car. People get into habits. Probably other people take the same cars going home every night. Renaldo and I will take that car, you get the one ahead, Eric and John the one behind."

"Why do I get to work alone?" Baseline asked. "Why don't I get the big guy?"

"We're here to talk," Jim said. "Talk to people who look like they're getting off work. And you talk twice as fast and twice as much as anyone else."

"Ouch," yelped Baseline.

Two trains, an express and a local, came through. The train they were waiting for was three minutes late. To their surprise, the next to the last car was empty. When the doors opened, they found out why.

"Yuch," Baseline said, holding his nose. Somebody had vomited in the corner of the car.

"We'll do the cars on each side," Jim said. "Renaldo and I will go with you."

Jim hopped on the next car just before the doors closed. The seventy-two-foot-long IRT cars contained forty-four seats. A little more than a third of them were occupied on this train. Most of the people sat staring forward blankly, their faces fixed in the expression of absolute neutrality that is the mark of the subway rider.

Jim nodded toward the front of the car. Renaldo and Baseline started in that direction. Jim decided to try a squat, balding man wearing a green work shirt. On the pocket was stitched Jessie. Asst. Mgr.

Jim sat down next to him. "Excuse me, sir."

The man ignored him.

"Excuse me."

The man scowled. "Yea?"

"Were you riding this train Wednesday night?"

"What if I was?"

"Were you?"

The man looked at him sourly. "Buzz off, buddy." With a snap, he opened a folded copy of the *Daily News*.

The heavyset black woman on the other side of Jim had sidled away. When Jim questioned her, she stared at him for a moment with wide, anxious eyes. Then she nodded her head no.

Jim got another quick no before the train rattled into Forty-second Street. More people got on than got off. Jim thought, this is going to take a long time. He was about to move across the car when he heard a loud voice say, "Ladies and Gentlemen. May I have your attention."

Baseline was standing in the center of the car.

"Mr. Jones is my name," he went on, "and information is my game. May I ask if anyone was riding this train Wednesday night."

Silence.

"Too bad for you. My friend Mr. Knight has $500 he's looking to give away to somebody that was."

"Five hundred bucks!" exclaimed the man Jim had started with. "For what?"

"My friend Mr. Knight lost something on that train. And he'll pay $500 to the lady or gentleman that helps him get it back."

"What'd he lose?"

"The person who found it will know. Now, was any of you fine people on that train?"

Two people, a kid about fifteen and a seedy-looking gray-haired man raised their hands. Both of them were dead ends, however.

Jim conferred with his friends, when the train stopped at Fifty-ninth Street. "Good idea, Baseline. That's a hell of a lot quicker than talking to people individually."

"No luck, though," Renaldo said.

"Do it again," Jim said. "I'm going forward to talk to the conductor. We'll get off at 125th Street and head back south."

Jim went through the doors into the next car, the middle car on the train. The conductor was standing by the door to his booth.

Jim approached him. "Can I talk to you a minute?"

The conductor looked at Jim. He was young, maybe late twenties. His hair was cut short, his uniform was immaculate, and the gold Transit Authority emblem on his hat shone brightly.

"Sure," he said.

"Were you working on this train Wednesday night?"

"Why?"

"A lady was murdered. A friend of mine."

"What happened?"

"Purse snatching," Jim said. "I guess she tried to resist."

The conductor shook his head sadly. "That's a mistake. These punks are killers."

A pang of excitement rippled through Jim. "What punks?"

The train started to slow. "Just a second," the conductor said. He opened the door to his booth. Then he inserted his key into the panel and turned it right. When the train rolled to a halt, he inserted the door key and pressed the button to open the doors.

The conductor depressed the foot pedal that operated the public address system. "This is Eighty-sixth Street. Change for the local upstairs.

This is the number 5 train to Dyer Avenue. Next station stop will be 125th Street. Watch the closing doors."

The doors shut and the train started to move. The conductor kept his head out the window the required five car lengths to insure that no one was caught in the doors. Then he locked the cubicle and asked Jim, "What were we talking about?"

"The purse snatchers."

"Yea. Last couple months, there's been a crime wave on this line. And the number 4 line too. They think it's the same group. Where did this lady get it?"

"Between Fifty-ninth and Eighty-sixth."

"Humm," the conductor murmured thoughtfully. "Mostly they hit in the Bronx. Stations are closer together. They wait their chance, hit it, then they're out the door and into the street. They don't waste time, these guys. They've also cut a few people."

"What are you doing about it?"

"Me? I gotta stay here and do my job. They won't work a car with the conductor or motorman, because we got radios."

"What about the cops?"

The guy shrugged. "We're lucky if we got one on for a few stops all run. They probably got some kind of lookout system, these muggers. We need a guy with a gun in every car, if you ask me."

Jim stood, swaying with the train, as he pondered the information.

"Anything else?" the conductor asked.

"No," Jim said. "But thanks a lot."

"Where are we, man?" Baseline asked.
"Dyer Avenue."
"Where in the heck is Dyer Avenue? And what are we doing here anyway?" the lanky basketball player asked.
"Waiting for the train. We'll be headed back soon."

Jim, too, was freezing, standing in the brisk wind that had arisen after the end of the rain. They were on an elevated platform, thirty feet above the street below. Although automobile traffic was fairly heavy, the spot felt remote and desolate.

The feeling of desolation was enhanced by the long subway trip through the South Bronx, the worst of New York's wastelands. The cars had become increasingly empty as the train moved north out of Manhattan. The passengers who did shuffle on and off seemed sullen, defensive, and, above all, fearful. Jim had picked up that sense of fear like a tuning fork. He found himself tensing at every stop, and when the doors opened between cars.

A few groups of teenagers had passed through. One had lingered to stare at them for a while. At Renaldo's suggestion, they'd agreed to deal with problems by staring right back, presenting a stern united front. In that case, it had worked.

Still, Jim felt exhausted and depressed. By the time the train pulled in, the bright lights inside the car, the shelter from the wind, made the prospect of the ride almost appealing.

They were the only passengers in the car until the third stop. A kid and his girl friend got on and started necking. At Pelham Parkway, a toothless old woman in a filthy tattered overcoat staggered in and went to sleep.

Eric looked at Jim. "Sad, huh?"

Jim just shook his head.

Twenty minutes later, a half dozen other people were in the car hurtling through the tunnel in Manhattan. Even though there were plenty of seats, a lone teenager stood, holding the pole, at the rear of the car.

"Man's got the right idea," Baseline grumbled.

"What's that?" Renaldo asked.

"All bundled up. Must be warm."

Renaldo glanced at the kid. He was wearing a knit cap pulled down to his eyebrows, and a scarf covered most of the lower half of his face. He wore thin, black leather gloves.

The train stopped at 149th Street. The teenager moved to the door, straddling it as he looked forward. Then he stepped back inside as the doors closed. He did the same thing at the next stop.

Jim noticed the behavior. The kid was almost military in the way he moved and the rigid alertness with which he stood.

The kid straddled the doors again at 125th Street.

"Catch that?" Jim asked Renaldo.

"Yea."

As the train rumbled on, Jim's mind turned away from the kid. He yawned. Then he thought, a holiday Saturday night. Not that he'd had any plans. But the others—"

He bolted to his feet when he heard the scream. They were at the Eighty-sixth Street station. Jim sprinted outside the car. Way up ahead near the front of the train, a black woman was yelling for help.

The conductor was with her when Jim and the others pulled up.

"My purse," the woman was crying, "my purse."

Without a word, Jim raced up the steps, out the gate, and up the steps again to Eighty-sixth Street. He stopped, his head turning.

The street was crowded with pedestrians. Eighty-sixth Street was one of the main thoroughfares on the fasionable Upper East Side, and the restaurants and night clubs catered to a late-night clientele. The purse snatchers had only needed an instant to disappear.

"Damn it," Baseline exclaimed as he came up next to Jim.

"I know," Jim said. "We must have missed them by a minute."

"That's not what I mean. We gotta pay to get back on the train."

"I'll pay," Jim said. "But first, what about a beer?"

They were on their second tall Weiss beer at the Hoffbrau House when Jim interrupted a discussion about the Knicks basketball team. "I've got it." he said in an excited tone.

"Got what?"

"That kid on our car. He must have been a lookout."

"You're probably right," Renaldo said. "So what?"

Jim smiled. For the first time that night, it came back to him a little bit. That feeling of power he used to feel leading patrols in Nam. Of knowing what the enemy was going to do and outthinking them.

"Next time we'll be ready," he said. "Next time we'll get them."

seven

The doorbell roused Jim from a sound sleep. He blinked his eyes, trying to focus. His mouth tasted like sandpaper, and he felt a dull, unpleasant throbbing in his temple. He knew then he'd had a few too many beers last night.

He slumped back down on the pillow. But the doorbell rang again, then a third time. He grunted, hoisting himself to his feet, and shuffled through the small living room to the front door.

"Who is it?"

"Jim? It's Sara."

The sound of her voice jolted him. His head cleared, and he was conscious that he must look like a wreck. He ran a hand through his unkempt hair. Then he turned the bolts of the two locks and pulled open the door.

"Oh, Jim," she said, throwing her arms around him. She held him tight, so he could feel her breathing.

74

Then she pulled back. "I'm terribly sorry about your friend. You must feel terrible."

"How did you find out? The paper?"

She shook her head. "The old Jewish gentleman on the first floor. I asked what apartment was yours."

"Mr. Weinstock. He's a nice man." He looked at her for a moment. He noticed her face looked drawn and tired, and there were dark circles under her eyes. "If you didn't hear about Granny, why are you here? I thought you were spending the weekend in Connecticut."

"I am. I was, rather." She lowered her eyes, biting her lower lip. Then she said, "Actually, I came in to take you for a ride. I have mother's BMW. It's such a nice sunny day. I thought—I thought you'd like to get out of the city for a few hours."

He appraised her for a second. Then he decided not to ask any more questions now. He said, "Sure. Great idea. Give me a couple of minutes to put this body in shape."

"Heavy date last night?" she asked.

"Night out with the boys. I'll tell you about it later."

While Jim showered, Sara inspected the living room, which had the appearance of a parlor in her great-aunt's house. Against the far wall was a mahogany loveseat with gold and green flowered upholstery, padded arms with lace antimacassars, and cabriole legs with padded feet. Flanking the loveseat were end tables covered with damask tablecloths on which sat identical lamps. On the left was a six-foot-high glass-fronted cabinet, which contained a set of fine china, a set of glassware, salt and pepper shakers, candle holders, glass figures, and other odds and ends. On the right stood two wooden-legged armchairs on either side of a table covered with framed photographs.

The first photo that caught her eye was of a chubby little tyke in an old-fashioned sailor's suit. She picked it up, smiling when she recognized from the eyes that it must be Jim. There were a dozen other photographs of him, some with his parents or other relatives. She was particularly amused by one in which his hair was no more than a half inch long—an army photo, she assumed.

Above the table, in an oval convex frame, was a very old photograph of a beautiful young woman. She wore an old-fashioned, high-necked white blouse, and a ribbon tied to her full, light-colored hair. Her cheeks had the full flush of youth, and her lips were formed into a pleasant smile. The most striking feature, however, were the eyes—sharp, sparkling, intelligent.

"My grandmother," Jim said, coming up behind Sara.

"She's beautiful."

"Yes, she was. She was still beautiful when I knew her, and she was in her eighties. She died at ninety-four, without losing a bit of her wit. For a Polish immigrant who came to this country without the most rudimentary education, she was a remarkable woman."

"Great," Jim said, draining one container of coffee and opening another.

"I'd like to hear about Granny, Jim. If you feel like talking about it."

"Sure."

As they sped up the Harlem River Drive, then across the George Washington Bridge to New Jersey, Jim talked about the murder and his reaction. He concluded by describing the subway ride the night before.

Sara looked at him with concern. "That sounds awfully dangerous, Jim."

"It might be. But I don't care. You know, I couldn't get over the expressions on the faces of the people on the train last night. It wasn't only that they were afraid. It was a sense of resignation they gave off. They looked passive, defeated."

"That's pretty profound," Sara said.

"No, not profound. And not original. That's the way people looked in Vietnam. One day we'd walk through their villages, barging into their huts. The next day the VC would come through, kidnapping a few young boys, raping the women. The third day the South Vietnamese army would do the same thing. The only way they could survive was to become numb."

"That's awful."

"Well, it's happening here, in the cities. And we don't have millions of soldiers and planes and tanks and artillery. We're letting ourselves be defeated by a handful of arrogant, immoral punks."

Sara didn't respond for a moment. Then she

said, "I see what you mean. But we have the police to deal with them."

Jim snorted. "There's not nearly enough police. Other people have to do something."

She glanced at him with concern in her blue eyes. "Why you?"

"It's something I have to do. I don't know why. But I have to."

He could see she was upset. He waited a moment, then said in a light tone, "Enough of this. I'm starved. Let's stop somewhere."

"I'm way ahead of you," she said. "I have a fabulous lunch in the trunk. Sandwiches, smoked salmon, bagels, all kinds of cheese, two bottles of wine. Think you can wait until we get to the park?"

"Sure."

They drove along in silence along the north-bound side of the twin ribbons of road that wound through the forests, which were still lovely despite the fallen leaves. Just short of the state line, Sara parked in a scenic overlook. They walked out onto an outcropping of rock hundreds of feet above the magnificent mile-wide Hudson River.

As Jim stood, staring out over the expanse of blue water as the crisp wind whipped around him, he thought: what a magnificent sight this must have been when Henry Hudson sailed upriver in 1609. How in the hell have we managed to screw things up so badly since then?

They walked back to the car. Twenty minutes later, they reached a picnic table in a scenic glen in Bear Mountain State Park. Sara spread a tablecloth while Jim opened the white wine. When he poured two glasses he offered a toast. "To happiness."

Sara touched his glass. As he took a sip, Jim noticed her face becoming solemn.

"Disappointed in the wine?" he asked.

She took a deep breath. Her head was bowed, her lips compressed. Then she met his eyes. "Jim, Bill and I are splitting. For good."

He was surprised. He looked at her cautiously. "I'm sorry to hear that," he said.

"You shouldn't be sorry," she said. "It was wrong. Right from the start."

"How?"

She walked a couple of steps away, toward the leaf-covered path. She spoke without turning. "I've always been the baby of the family. My next youngest brother is eleven years older than I am. I was used to the company of older people, used to being spoiled. I don't think I ever dated anyone my own age. It would have been a surprise if I hadn't married a much older man."

"Did you love him?"

She turned back toward Jim. "I thought so. I certainly felt a great deal of affection. The problem was, I never got anywhere near the center of his life. He treated me well. We had some good times. He was even proud of my academic achievements, that I was a good doctor. But only so far as it didn't interfere with what he wanted to do. When he wanted a wife, I had to play the role he expected of a wife.

And that isn't what I want out of life. Not anymore."

He looked at her intently. When he spoke, he found his voice was tight. "What did Bill say when you told him?"

"He thought I was being silly," she said. She walked back over to the table and picked up her wineglass. "Bill's the typical surgeon, used to playing god. He treats this "crazy" notion of mine as if it were a diseased appendix. A swipe or two of his scalpel, and the problem disappears. But he's wrong. This is the first healthy thing I've done in years."

"I don't know what to say."

"Don't say anything," she said. She stepped toward him, put her hands on his head, and pulled it toward her.

Their lips met. He felt her mouth open, his tongue reached out to hers. An intense emotion flooded through him. He pulled her impossibly tight. His body pressed against hers until he thought he could feel the wild beating of her heart.

Finally, they parted. Their eyes remained locked as they struggled for breath. Then her lips curled into a smile. "That was my confession," she said.

"I guess I like confessions," he said.

"What about some lunch?"

He almost didn't let her go. But then he dropped his arms and said, "Sounds good."

It was dark when Sara halted the BMW in front of Jim's apartment building.

"Here we are," she said.

"I guess so," he said. He put his hand on her shoulder and added, "Thanks for the terrific day."

She smiled, then moved toward him. They kissed again, this time longer and more gently. His hand moved, she arched her breast toward it. As he cupped it, he could feel her tremble.

When they broke, she said in a thin voice, "Shall—shall we go upstairs?"

He closed his eyes. He could feel the sexual hunger raging within him, bringing a kind of madness to his head. But there was something he couldn't exactly name fighting against it.

"What is it?" she asked. "I'm sorry if I—"

He kissed her gently. "You don't have to be sorry. The only thing is, it's too soon for you. You just made the decision this weekend. I—"

"You want to be sure I'm sure. Well, I am."

"I believe you are," he said. "I hope and pray you are. This is so important to me. To us. I think we should wait."

She smiled. "You're right. You're an incredible man."

He kissed her a last time, then opened the car door. "I'll call you tomorrow."

"Okay. And Jim, promise me. Keep yourself safe. I couldn't bear it if anything happened to you now."

eight

The building was a typical Lower East Side tenement. The lock on the front door was busted, the glass missing. The hallway was littered with beer cans and cigarette butts and blackened bottle caps.

When the door to the fourth-floor apartment opened Tony Melendez gasped in surprise. He was escorted into a living room that looked like one of those displays in Macy's. The floor was covered with thick gold shag carpeting. He saw a twenty-five-inch console color television, stereo speakers that must have been four feet high, chrome-and-glass coffee and end tables, and a huge brown sectional sofa.

He was still gaping when Torres, a cocky kid about his brother's age, nudged him and said, "Come on."

Tony followed him through the living room toward the rear of the apartment. Torres knocked on what looked like a bedroom door. The door was opened. Tony found himself facing a tall, stern Irish-looking guy holding a .45 caliber pistol.

The guard inspected them for a moment, then called out over his shouder, "It's Torres with the kid."

"Bring the kid in," came the reply.

The guard motioned to Tony with the pistol. "Wait outside," he said to Torres.

When Tony walked into the room, he saw that it had been turned into an office. The same gold shag carpeting was on the floor. The left wall was covered by floor-to-ceiling shelves that held a portable television set, a stereo system, a bar, a half-sized refrigerator, and a safe. To the right, a small sofa and two armchairs were grouped around a coffee table. At the far end was a four-drawer file cabinet and a big desk.

As Tony moved forward, the chair in front of the desk swiveled. Sitting there was a lean man in his late twenties. He had closely cropped curly hair, light skin, and an angular face disfigured by a long, ugly scar on his left cheek. The scar ran to the corner of one of his deep-set black eyes that were almost hypnotic in their intensity.

Tony stood still, trembling in the presence of the powerful ghetto figure he'd seen only at a distance—Salvadore Santos, head of the Savage Skulls.

Santos looked Tony over, his eyes lingering briefly on his bandaged left hand. Then he said, "Sit down, kid."

Tony sat on the sofa, nervously looking down. Everything had happened so quickly since Fri-

day night when he and Cisco had crept into
that building with the firebombs. After the endless hóurs in the police station, the cops had
driven him home to his mother, who was so
drunk she didn't understand what the hell they
were saying. The next morning she'd cuffed
him around a little bit when she found out she'd
have to get her ass out of the house to go
down to family court with him. Then she'd sent
Tony out for a couple of six-packs and soon
she was watching television as if nothing had
happened.

When he went out on the street, Tony was
amazed to find that he was some sort of hero.
Older guys, his brother's friends, went out of
their way to clap him on the back. His brother
was holed up at a girl friend's place for a few
days, in case the cops came after him. But he
sent word he was proud of his little brother.
That was another first.

Now was the biggest surprise of all. The summons from the head of the biggest gang on
the Lower East Side, maybe in the whole city. In
the last year or so, guys had come from all
over to join the Skulls. Santos even lorded it
over other gangs by riding around in a big
black Cadillac. The word was out that the Skulls
were into some heavy shit.

Santos got up out of the desk chair and
ambled over to one of the armchairs. He was
wearing a silk shirt open nearly to the waist,
brand-new jeans, gleaming boots, and a thick
gold chain around his neck.

"What's your name again, kid?" he asked.

"Tony."

"Tony, sir," snapped the Irish guy.

Santos waved. "That's okay, Cide. Kid don't know yet. Kid's got some balls and brains, though."

A flush of pride went through Tony.

"Want a beer, kid?" Santos asked.

Tony was about to say no. Then he remembered what Cisco had told him. "Yes," he said. "Yes, sir."

Santos smiled. "See. Kid's a quick learner. Get us a couple a beers, Cide."

When they had Heinekins, Santos asked, "How's the hand?"

"It's okay."

"They take you to Bellevue?"

Tony shook his head. "That guy did it. At the clinic."

"Fucking Knight," Santos remarked. "He's a candy-ass turkey, that guy. Second time he helped out one of the boys, though. Cide, make a note we do something for the guy. Send him a case of booze."

The Irishman walked over to the desk.

Santos turned back to Tony. "Good thing you did the other night. Kept your cool, didn't rat. Saved Cisco from a fall, and he's one of my main men."

"He's my brother," Tony said.

"We're all going to be your brothers," Santos said. "You want to be a Skull, right?"

Tony shifted a bit. But with those eyes on him, all he could say was, "Right."

"Well, you're a lucky man. Every dude with half a brain wants to be a Skull. For what you did, I'm going to waive the initiation. You're going straight into basic training. How'd you like that?"

"I'd like that. Sir."

"Good. You see, kid, the Skulls ain't no gang like those jive-ass punks hanging around all day zonked out of their brains, cutting each other up over a piece of pussy or a bottle of booze. The Skulls are an army. We've got connections with the big guys, and we're gonna own this whole town real soon. Real soon."

Santos paused to take a sip of beer. Then he continued, "Now, you gotta understand, when I say the Skulls are an army, I mean it. You'll be assigned to a squad led by a lieutenant. First you'll do some training missions. You'll make a little bread. That's gonna have to be enough, because I don't want no free-lance stuff. No mugging, no shoplifting, none of that shit. You got that?"

Tony nodded.

"A punk about your age, thought he was a smart ass the other night, got hit by a car pulling a mugging. He was lucky, because I would have broken both his legs. That's what happens to Skulls who don't follow orders. Understand?"

"I understand, sir."

Santos smiled. "See, bright kid." His expression grew more serious, and he leaned forward again. "One more thing, kid. We got a way to deal with traitors. Guys who talk to another gang, guys who talk to the cops, guys who run off their mouths to anybody."

He pointed to the Irishman. "That man's name is Homicide Healy. Way he got his name is, he's the best at any kind of killing you can name. He can kill you fast, or he can do it real slow. You rat on us to the cops and you'll be found in the trunk of a car with your balls in your mouth. Now, is that clear?"

The menace in Santos's voice was so strong that Tony's throat tightened, nearly pinching off his voice. "I—I got it," he managed to stammer.

Santos leaned back and drained the beer. "Terrific. One last thing. You get your scar. Cide?"

Healy opened a drawer in the wall unit and took out a gleaming straight razor, a small plastic vial, and a folded paper bib. At Santos's command, Tony got up and followed the gang leader and the Irishman into the bathroom. Santos motioned him to sit on the john.

Healy tied the bib around Tony's neck. When Santos opened the razor, Tony's eyes bugged out in fright. He had the urge to jump up and run. But he fought against his fear, knowing that the consequences of that would be worse than what he was going to face.

Grinning, Santos pushed Tony's head to the right. The cutting was less painful than Tony had thought, more a pricking than a sharp pain. Worse was the feeling of the blood flowing down his cheek.

Santos dabbed at his cheek with a towel. Then he opened the vial and poured some fine reddish powder into his hand. When Santos applied the powder to the cut, Tony grunted with pain. He bit his lower lip, and he could taste the salty blood.

"That's sawdust," Santos said. "It stopped the bleeding. And it makes sure you have a real nice scar. So everybody in the world will know you're one of us. Forever."

The booming voice could easily be heard over the noise in the gym. But the body it came from was withered and gaunt, as if it had been left in the sun to dry too long. The thinness of the old man was further emphasized by the five-sizes-too-large sweat shirt he wore. He also sported a red beret on his head and a big fat cigar was stuck in his teeth.

"Goddamn it, the body. The body," he shouted apoplectically. His face was red as a beet, and his eyes threatened to burst from their sockets. "Damn it," he snarled, reaching beside him to ring the bell.

"Come here," he comanded. Renaldo, breathing noisily through his mouthpiece and sweating profusely under his protective headgear, obeyed.

"Listen," Slapsy Huggins said, "You ain't fighting no fat truck driver from Queens this time. You go head-hunting like that, Thunder Wilkins is gonna turn you into Puerto Rican porridge. You gotta go to the body. Cut the heart out of him. A man can't punch if his gut feels like he swallowed a medicine ball. You got that through your thick head?"

"I'm trying," Renaldo panted.

"Then try harder. Go on."

Slapsy rang the bell, and the fighters moved toward each other.

"Stick and move," Slapsy yelled. "Stick and move."

Renaldo's jab, short, sharp, lightening fast, flicked out once, then a second time. His sparring partner, a blocky white guy, danced back, shaking his head slightly. Renaldo jabbed again, then unleased a wicked left hook to the side of the rib cage. His opponent grunted.

"Double up on that," Slapsy shouted.

The sparring partner retreated. Renaldo was after him like a cat. Two series of jabs, a right feint, then Renaldo nailed him with two hooks to the body. The sparring partner doubled over. Renaldo unleased a frightening right uppercut to the jaw. His opponent straightened, staggered two steps back to the ropes, then collapsed in a heap to the floor.

Renaldo checked to see that he was okay. When the guy was able to get to his feet, Renaldo walked over to his trainer. "How's that, Slapsy?" he asked with a smile.

"The guy's a stiff. I could take him, for chrissake. Let's get another goon in there."

"That's twelve rounds today, Slapsy. I'm beat."

Huggins shook his head in disgust. He turned to the short, bald-headed man next to him. "No guts today, Cohen. These guys all want it handed to them on a platter." He shook his head again, then said to Renaldo, "All right. Have it your way. A half hour on the speed bag."

Huggins watched Renaldo duck between the ropes on the other side of the ring, jump to the floor, then head for the speed bag in the corner. Huggins nudged Cohen. "That's the next world champion. Power, speed, guts. You mark my word."

Cohen, a nervous-looking, pot-bellied man in his late fifties, just nodded. "Can we talk now, Huggins?" he asked.

"Come on," Slapsy said. He shuffled stiffly across the gym to his office.

"Beer, Cohen?" he asked.

Cohen shook his head.

Slapsy got one for himself, eased himself into the chair behind the desk, and took off his beret. "So what's the problem?" he asked.

"Those guys. They came to see me again. At home. They made another offer for the building."

"They offer you more?"

Cohen grimaced. "Five thousand less. Huggins, I'm frightened. I don't like this."

"So sell."

"And lose a lifetime's work? My business, my son's business. And your gymnasium. Do you want to move?"

"My gym?" Slapsy roared. "They told you that?"

"Why do they want the building?" Cohen asked. "To run a dry goods store, maybe? Bah. I know how they work. They spend nothing, they kick everybody out. Then there's a fire. And they build an apartment building. They want no gym."

Huggins picked up his cigar, which was nearly

as fat as his wrist. He puffed on it, thinking. Finally, he asked, "Have these bums threatened you?"

"In words, no. But the voice, the eyes—you know such men, in your line of work."

Slapsy's eyes narrowed. "No hoodlums ever took over any of my boys. I've stared down more than a few in my time. And kicked an ass or two."

Cohen looked at him imploringly. "So what do I do? You know my boy, he's delicate. I'm no fighter either."

Slapsy chewed on his cigar. Then he said, "Tell you what you do, Saul. If you think it's as bad as you say. You sell."

Cohen's eyes widened and he popped out of his chair. "Sell? But—"

"Slapsy waved him down. "Relax. You sell the building to me. For $1."

Cohen stared at him in puzzlement. "One dollar? What is this?"

"If Slapsy Huggins owns the building, these bums will have to deal with me. They gonna come in here with muscle with all my boys our there? No, not when there are hundreds of buildings that are easy pickings. When the heat's off, I'll sell it back to you."

Cohen sat, chin resting in his hand. "I don't know."

"Don't you trust me? Christ, I'm too old to lie."

Cohen smiled. "Please. Of course, I trust you. Thirty-one years, never one day late with the rent. I trust you like family." He got to his feet.

"But I have to think. I want to talk to my wife, my boy. You'll be here tomorrow?"

"Where the hell else would I be?"

"Then we talk. And thank you, Huggins."

nine

Transit Police Captain Bill Devlin, a hefty, crew-cut man in his fifties, pried a Lifesaver from a roll on his desk, popped it in his mouth, then offered the roll to Jim.

"No thanks."

Devil put down the roll and leaned back. "Let me explain something, young man," he said. "In 1975, we had over 3,600 transit cops. Today we have 2,600. The system has 476 stations, and operates as many as eight to nine hundred trains an hour in rush hour. That's just too much ground and too many trains to cover."

"I realize that," Jim said. "That's why I'm here. To tell you how you can stop a crime wave on the IRT. A six- or eight-man team of plain-clothesmen can nab this gang. Even with bad luck it wouldn't take more than a week."

"I'm afraid I can't do that," Devlin said. "The public wants a uniformed presence on the subways, and that's what they're getting. What would the riders of all the other lines in the city say if they found out I assigned eight officers to one train?"

They'd probably applaud. At least you'd be doing something positive."

Devlin's round face turned red. "I don't appreciate wisecracks when I've given up my own good time to meet with someone. I said I'd inform the officers on that line of what you suspect."

"They haven't been able to make a single arrest in six months," Jim snapped.

Devlin glared at him. "I think this meeting has ended."

Jim stood. "I know it has. The next time we meet, it will be at the trial of those hoodlums."

"I'm warning you," Devlin said. "I'll have no vigilantes riding my trains."

"Your trains?" Jim scoffed. "If they belong to anybody, they belong to the hoodlums. They should be my trains, and the trains of the millions of decent people in this city. We aim to take them back."

Jim turned and opened the door.

"One step out of line," Devlin shouted at his back. "One of you so much as spits, you're in trouble. You hear me?"

"Jim, this is Chang," Renaldo said. "He's made chop suey out of every Golden Gloves lightweight in the city."

Jim shook hands with the trim Chinese youth, who looked older than his seventeen years.

"And this is Rafael. He may be skinny, but he's tough."

"I know your sister," Jim said. "She's been treated here."

Rafael, who went five nine, maybe 125 pounds soaking wet, scowled. "She was here when that husband of hers beat her. I find him, he's gonna wish he was fighting Renaldo here."

"We set to go?" Eric asked, coming back from the bathroom.

"We're waiting for Baseline," Jim said.

"As usual," Renaldo commented. He turned to Jim, "I can't believe what that transit cop told you."

"I couldn't either. It was as if I was the criminal. He sounded as if he didn't care if full-scale war broke out on the IRT, as long as it didn't disrupt his schedule or bring any political heat."

"That's what my father always complains about," Eric said. "The other day, he called our councilman to—"

"That's all right, don't stand up," Baseline announced as he walked in the front door. "Your hero is here. With his brand new A-1 all-star recruit." He turned and put his arm around the person who entered with him. "Jimmy, this is the sensational Marguerite Washington."

"How do you do?" she asked, flashing a dazzling smile. The black girl was tall, taller than either Chang or Rafael, and she had a lithe, athletic-looking body.

Jim shook her hand. "This is a surprise."

"Now don't you go worrying 'cause Marguerite is a female," Baseline said. "You are in the presence of a lady that plays the meanest game of basketball in the entire New York City high school system. I mean, she has moves that would turn Magic Johnson into a bunny rabbit."

Jim looked at her. "I don't know. You understand what we're doing? It could get dangerous."

Her dark eyes flashed with determination. "I can handle myself," she said firmly. "I've been in some pretty tight spots—without seven men on the same train. Besides, I have to be a part of this. Granny was my great-aunt."

Jim reacted with surprise. "I didn't see you at the funeral."

"I was at a basketball tournament in Philadelphia. My daddy didn't want to call me with the bad news. I'll have a tough time forgiving him for that."

If Jim had been asked earlier about bringing a girl along, he would have categorically said no. But the girl in front of him was street savvy, tough, and determined.

"Okay," he said. "Thanks for coming. Now, I'll explain what we're going to do."

He picked up a cardboard box and opened it. "I want each one of you to take a whistle."

"Wow!" Baseline exclaimed. He blew a whistle, then shouted, "Fouell. Number 22, for mugging. Gets one shot in the slammer."

Jim smiled. "Okay, clown. But that's the last whistle I want to hear unless there's trouble."

"I don't understand," Rafael said. "Aren't we going to be together?"

"No," Jim said. "This group that's been working the trains has a lookout in every car, or, at least, in more than one car. So one of us is going to be in each of the eight cars. If something happens, when the doors are open the whistle gets blown and the rest of us come running."

"What about between stations?" Chang asked. "What if we're involved with something and can't whistle?"

"Try not to get involved. I don't want anybody taking on a guy with a knife, or a group of guys. Is that clear?"

"We might not be able to help it, Jim," Renaldo said. "I think we ought to have a backup system."

"That dude on the train the other night popped out at every station," Baseline said. "Suppose we do that."

"Good idea," Renaldo agreed. "Stick our heads out the door. If a head's missing, we investigate."

"All right. That's fine," Jim said. "Remember, though, we're not riding the train to get involved with rough stuff. No thief's going anywhere until the train stops. Unless it's a matter of life or death, you sit tight until those doors open."

The number 4 train pulled into Fifty-ninth Street. Doris Bunker squeezed through the single door that opened, then collapsed into a seat. She put her two shopping bags between her legs and caught her breath. For once she was glad the subway ride to the North Bronx would take forty-five minutes—she'd need the time to get her strength to walk home.

Despite her exhaustion, she had a sense of satisfaction. The Thanksgiving sales had been even better than she'd hoped. She was well on her way to making the upcoming season the kind of Christmas she'd planned.

Six months ago, the idea of any Christmas at all seemed impossible. That's when her father, Harry, who was only forty-four years old, had the massive heart attack. Doris had sat with her mother in that dingy waiting room at Montefiore Hospital for nearly forty-eight hours, before the doctors told them that Harry was probably going to live.

The propects of his ever going back to the loading docks were slim, however. Thank God they owned the small brick house, which they'd purchased when interest rates were still reasonable. But buying food for the family—which included Doris's thirteen-year-old sister, ten-year-old brother, and the eight-year-old twin boys— took every cent they could scrape together, including all of Doris's earnings from her waitress job at the Crystal Coffee Shop.

After the heart attack, Doris had immediately abandoned her plans to go to school part time in the fall. She was only nineteen, she could go to school anytime. What really hurt her was the gloom that had settled over her family. That's when she came up with her plan for Christmas.

Her parents had always insisted she take the express bus to and from work. But that cost $5.00 per day, compared to $1.50 round trip on the subway. Doris calculated that if she took the subway for six months, she'd have $300 to spend on Christmas presents.

Taking the subway was awful. There were delays, and it was dirty and smelly and scary. Every time it got to her, though, she could see in her mind's eye the delight and surprise on the faces of her family, especially her father, when they woke up on Christmas morning to find piles of presents under the tree. The image never failed to bring tears to her eyes.

Tonight, she'd fought the crowds in Alexander's for nearly three hours, searching out the very best bargains. Tomorrow night she'd do the same, then she'd be nearly done with the shopping, before the prices went up. Then, when she had the time, she'd go over to Mrs. Coffey's house to wrap the gifts.

She was thinking about buying Mrs. Coffey a nice gift for storing the presents. Then she noticed the man staring at her, a man who must have gotten on at the last stop.

Suddenly, she was nervous. She wasn't used to being stared at. All through high school, she'd been so scrawny that hardly any boys noticed her. Lately, she'd started to fill out and, looking at herself in the mirror, she had to admit she was getting a little bit pretty. Her mother had told her many times that the women in her family were late bloomers.

"Hey, Roy."

She heard the voice and involuntarily glanced over. The man had nudged a dozing friend. They were both a lot older than she was. They were both dressed in filthy clothes, their hair was unkempt and greasy, and on their faces was at least a week's stubble. As she looked downward, she noticed her hands shaking.

"Piece of pussy over there, Roy. Hey, sweetheart. Sweetheart."

Doris's hands tightened around the handle of a shopping bag. She shot a look toward the front of the car. Darn it, she thought. She was always so careful to sit in the car with the conductor. Tonight, she was so tired she forgot.

"You want to fuck, baby? How about it? Or how about I take a nibble on that pussy of yours?"

The panic was rising in Doris. Her mind raced. Could she get up and try to make it into the next car? No. The best thing was to ignore them. When they got to the next stop, she'd change cars.

She smelled him before she saw him. He stood in front of her, swaying with the movement of the car. "How about a blow job, honey?"

Her heart was racing so fast she thought it would burst. Please let the next stop come, she thought.

He grabbed her face and twisted it toward him. His eyes were funny, like he was crazy or on something. "What's wrong, bitch? You don't like me?"

"Go away," she sobbed. "Go away."

To her horror, the man picked up one of her shopping bags. "No," she cried.

He flung it against the far wall. She could hear glass breaking.

"Suck me," the man roared. "Me and Roy."
He reached out for her. She ducked.

"Why you—" the man started, cocking his
arm.

The next thing Doris knew, the man had doubled over. He fell to his knees, coughing.

A blond teenage boy stood there, glaring at
him.

"Son of a bitch," the man grunted. He dove
for the legs of the teenager, John Siebert. John
stepped back and kicked him in the ribs. Then
the other man grabbed John from behind, hook-
ing a forearm around his throat. John struggled,
kicking at his legs, but the man held firm.

The first man, saliva drooling from his mouth,
slowly got to his feet. He reached inside his
pocket and pulled out a knife. "Bastard," he
snarled. "I'm gonna cut your balls off."

Then train pulled into a top. The man with the
knife staggered backward a step, hit the vertical pole, then regained his balance. The rest
of the passengers in the car were frozen, like
spectators at a sporting match.

Doris huddled there, terrified. She tried to
scream, but panic had closed her throat. The
man with the knife started toward her rescuer.

Then she heard the whistles, one, then a chorus. Through the door sprang a tall black girl.
The man with the knife saw her out of the corner of his eye. He spun and started to lunge.

She kicked him hard between the legs.
He doubled over. She stepped forward and
chopped with both hands on the back of his
neck.

Through the door other figures came flying. Two grabbed at the man holding her rescuer, while two more secured the man on the floor.

An immense bubble of relief broke inside Doris. Someone put a hand on her shoulder. "You all right?"

The tears of relief made Doris unable to answer. The rest of the passengers on the car rose to their feet and cheered.

An hour and a half later, Doris reached the steps of her small house.

"I don't know how to thank you," she said to her companion.

He took her elbow and pulled her forward a bit.

"The streetlight," John said. "I need it to read your lips. That's why I didn't know the jerks were harassing you."

"You were there on time. You and your friends. I'll never forget this as long as I live."

"I've got to go back to meet my friends. You okay?"

She nodded. Then she leaned forward and kissed him on the cheek.

He reddened and smiled. Then he headed back toward the subway stop.

Explaining to her distraught parents took an hour. But she was still too keyed up to sleep. In the small room she shared with her younger sister, she rose, turned on the small Tensor light on the desk, took out a sheet of paper, and began to write a letter. Every morning on the way to work she read about all the bad things happening in New York. She was going to write a letter to the *Daily News*. Somebody had to tell the world there were still heroes left.

ten

"I ought to be Spiderman, the places I have to go," Vinnie Civitello groused. "Ruined another pair of suit pants, on top of everything."

"What happened?" Jim asked as he poured the detective a cup of coffee from the pot in his office at the clinic.

"They've been using an old tenement on Avenue D as a shooting gallery. The other day a patrol car sees a couple junkies wander in, then leave in a big hurry a couple minutes later. They check it out, then radio us. I wish to hell they'd radioed in about that rotten stair. I went through nearly up to my ass, and a nail cut the hell out of my leg."

"Did Ben give you a tetanus shot?"

"If you pricked my finger, I'd bleed tetanus vaccine. The privilege of working in this fair city."

"You didn't tell me what you found in the building," Jim said.

104

"What else? A stiff. Six slugs in the gut. Terminal indigestion." He took a big pull on his coffee, then added, "Something's going on, Jimmy. I can feel it."

"Who was the dead guy?"

"A nobody. Small-time street dealer. Those guys get it all the time."

"So?"

"So it's usually a desperate junkie. Or they've been cheating their connection, maybe. The thing is, we must have had a dozen killings like this in the last few months. And a lot more of the old familiar faces have vanished. I think somebody muscled them out of the neighborhood."

"Who?" Jim asked.

"My guess is the Savage Skulls. Santos has big plans. He sees himself as a real Godfather type."

"Santos is a bully," Jim said with feeling. "I've known him all my life. We went to school together, until he dropped out. I don't think he has the brains to be anything more than a thug."

Vinnie shrugged. "Maybe not. But he's keeping his gang in line. We haven't picked up many of them for mugging, shoplifting, the usual crap. That's what puzzles me about the drug thing too. If the Skulls were taking over, they'd be out there selling the stuff. We haven't seen much of that. The junkies are desperate."

"Santos will make mistakes," Jim said. "Especially with that temper of his. He becomes a wild man."

Vinnie looked at Jim appraisingly through a

cloud of cigar smoke. "I hear you're not bad at losing your temper yourself. You pissed the hell out of Bill Devlin."

Jim scowled. "I don't want to tell you where he's got his head firmly wedged."

"Don't bother. Just tell me what kind of trouble you've been getting into."

When Jim finished, Vinnie said, "Well, kid, you've crossed the line. You really thought out what you're getting into? Or why?"

"I'm taking it day to day. All I know is, riding the subway last night felt right. Stopping those jerks from molesting that poor girl felt right."

"And you're going back out tonight?"

"Yes," Jim answered. Then he asked, "What do you think about it?"

"Well, let me tell you a story," the detective said. "Up in the Bronx, in this small park, they got these two statues. One of them's a guy, one a girl, and they're both naked. Greek-style statues. Anyway, they sit in this park a few feet apart for a hundred years, through rain, snow, all kinds of stuff."

"Is this a serious story?" Jim asked with a grin.

"Shut up and listen. One day, this low cloud appears in the sky. From the cloud comes this voice that says, 'Statues, you've been very good these last hundred years. As a reward, you'll become alive for one hour.'"

"Well, then there's this thunderbolt. The boy and girl look at each other, then go running off hand in hand into the bushes. They thrash and moan and pant, until the voice in the sky says, 'Statues, you've got five minutes left.'"

"So the boy statue says to the girl, 'You want to do it again?'"

"The girl thinks for a second, then says, 'Okay. But this time you hold the pigeon and I'll shit on it.'"

Jim roared with laughter. When he collected himself, he said, "That's terrific. But what's it supposed to mean?"

Vinnie drained the last of his coffee and hoisted himself to his feet. "It means," he said, "that we've put up with enough. It's time we start shitting on the pigeons who've been shitting on us. Good luck, kid."

Tony was the last one to arrive.

"You're late," Torres snapped.

"I'm—I'm sorry," Tony stammered. "The number. It's not on the building."

"That's your problem. Give me twenty."

"What?"

"Twenty pushups, scumbag," Torres demanded. "The Skulls is an army, man. You may be a hot shit, getting in with no initiation. You still follow the rules, or you out. Now, drop."

Tony followed instructions. As he grunted through the pushups, he wished he was anywhere else.

The flush of pleasure at being a hero had passed. If anything, he felt more scared than before. The scar on his face seemed to glow, a neon sign that seemed to announce, "I'm on the other side." He no longer had the choice, to be a Skull or walk the hard path of respectability.

He hadn't been late because he couldn't find the building. He'd walked by the playground at his old elementary school. The older kids were out, the sixth-graders. He stopped, watching them playing stick ball, laughing, taunting each other and the girls that happened by.

Just two years ago he'd been one of them. Now he felt a hundred years older. He wasn't a boy, but a man. Even school was behind him—he'd been warned by his brother that the Skulls were a full-time job.

As he finished the pushups, his left hand began to throb. He checked the bandage, but there was no bleeding. The cut had healed well. He had to go back to get the stitches out.

"All right, Melendez," Torres said. "Meet the squad. That's Rascal. And Gomez. Ice is the big guy ..."

Tony went around the room, slapping five. The rest were about his age, maybe a little older. They all looked tough, especially a Chinese kid whose arms were covered with tattoos and who had a crazy look in his eyes.

"All right," Torres announced. "We're gonna go over some guns. Show you how they work and all that shit."

"Fuck, who don't know that," scoffed a surly-looking black kid with bad skin.

"You, asshole," Torres said. "I ain't talking about no Saturday-night specials. I mean real guns. That other stuff couldn't stop no old lady. When you have to stop something, you have to stop it."

Torres turned to Tony, "Right, Melendez?"

Tony met his gaze. "Right."

"Good. But before we get to that shit, I want to make an announcement. We're going out tonight."

"Where?"

"None of your business," Torres snapped at the sallow-faced Puerto Rican kid. "Be here by eleven. Remember, have something to cover your face. Understand?"

There was a chorus of "yeh's."

"And you," he said to Tony, "you were something with big pockets. You're carrying."

"Carrying what?"

"The weapons, man. We get nailed, one guy takes the fall. You're the new boy, and you're it."

"What year was that, Slapsy?" Cube Crawford asked.

"It was back in 1919. A month after Dempsey took the heavyweight title from Jess Willard. Hottest August in a hundred years, and I couldn't get a fight nowhere but New Orleans. I thought I'd sweat so much I'd come out a featherweight."

Crawford, a very heavy seventy-one-year-old black man, cackled as he bit at his cigar. He was one of the best men in the fight game, and he'd worked with Slapsy on and off for forty years. A lot of their time, especially in the last few years, had been spent swapping stories for the benefit of the young fighters in the gym.

Crawford turned to Chang, the Golden Gloves lightweight. "This old coot was managing Slapsy, he loved his whiskey like a pig loved slop. Feed him a bottle, and he'd sign anything."

"He damned near got me killed that fight," Huggins said. "I was number four contender. Number two was the Cajun kid named LeBraun. Benny Leonard was lightweight champ at the time, and we got a handshake that the winner of our fight would get a title shot. Problem for me was, since LeBraun was number two, he was in the driver's seat."

"Things haven't changed much," Cube offered. "Game's still rotten as a dead coon in a hollow log."

"It was worse back then," Slapsy countered. "That drunken manager signed a contract for me to fight this guy somewhere in the backwoods of Louisiana. I'd have had to kill him to win, then it would have taken General Pershing and the whole American Expeditionary Force to get me out of there. So I put my foot down."

"You fought in New Orleans?" Chang asked.

"That was almost as bad. Crowd was 80 percent Cajun, and the referee was a guy named Perez who turned out to be LeBraun's second cousin. I don't remember who the judges were, but they were probably his uncles or something."

Slapsy took a big sip from his beer, wiped his mouth, then continued, "Anyway, the fight gets going. LeBraun was a boxer. No power, but his jab was always in your puss. I was more of a slugger, and in the first few rounds I got in some good shots. Opened up a nice cut under the right eye, and I had him puffy in a few other places."

"Remember that, kid," Cube said. "You're in the Gloves now, where they stop the fight for a hangnail. You turn pro and you cut a guy, you work the blazes out of it."

"That's what I was going to do," Slapsy said. "Came out for the fifth round loaded for bear. Then he stuck me with a couple jabs and I saw red. I mean literally. The son of a bitch had something on his gloves that stung the hell out of my eyes."

"You complain to the ref?" Chang asked.

Slapsy grimaced. "Perez? He could have pulled out a gun and shot me, and Perez would have started to count me out. I got back to my corner after the round, I was in big, big trouble."

"What did you do?"

Slapsy grinned. "I was stumped. But I had an old corner man, name of Horsehead Jones. Ugliest guy you ever saw—he had this hair, you turn him upside down, you could have sanded the floor with his head. Horsehead carried this box with every kind of patent medicine, liniment, and lotion known to mankind.

"Now, Horsehead worked at the track when he wasn't doing a fight, and he had this clear stuff that they used to blister a horse's leg, to bring the soreness out. Drop it on the floor, this stuff, and it would eat a hole in the carpet. Anyway, Horsehead's all pissed off 'cause he had a big bet on the match. So he tells me to really go at LeBraun in his corner in the beginning of the round, even if I had to get myself hit. Then I was supposed to get on my horse and run the rest of the round. Which I did."

"I don't understand," Chang said. "How'd that do any good?"

"Just before the round, Horsehead slips this kid $5. The bell rings, the Cajun and I go at it, his corner's yelling and screaming. The kid sneaks over and pours this clear stuff in his water bucket."

Slapsy leaned back, hooked his hands around the back of his head, and smiled. "Why, I'll tell you. After the round, LeBraun sits down and gets a whole spongeful of the stuff in his face. In his eyes and in that cut. A second later he howled like a banshee, leaped clear over the ropes, and started running around that arena like a chicken with his head cut off. I nearly split a gut."

"So what happened? You win?"

"The fight was called no contest. Two months later I tore up my shoulder sparring, and my career went down the drain. At least that cheating bastard didn't get the best of me, though." Slapsy shook his head in satisfaction at the thought. Then he added, "Now, that's enough loafing for you, young man. You got some working out to do."

"Yes, sir," Chang said with a grin.

When Chang opened the door, a man in a business suit was waiting outside. He asked to talk with Huggins alone. Slapsy nodded at Cube, who left.

The man introduced himself as Anthony Brown. Slapsy listened to him, his head cocked suspiciously. When Brown finished, Slapsy said, "That's a lot of fancy words. I'm still not sure who these people are you represent or what in the hell they want with this building."

"Who they are is not important," Brown said. "What they're doing is making a commitment here. Mr. Cohen reacted hysterically. We're not trying to force out businesses. On the contrary, rehabilitating the commercial buildings will help us attract people to the residential housing we're purchasing. Mr. Cohen's dry goods store and your gym can continue to operate, at reasonable rents."

Slapsy stared at the immaculately dressed Brown, who sat calmly under his gaze. Finally, he said, "Let me tell you what I think. I've been in the fight game for sixty-five years, and I've seen every kind of smooth-talking sharpie and con man on the face of this planet. There's nothing wrong with the words you're saying. But behind them there's one hell of a scam going on. I don't know what it is. I don't care what it is. Maybe you don't know. Despite the way you're all dressed up, I think you're the muscle, not the brains."

Brown's face darkened. "Wait a second, pops."

"Don't call me pops," Slapsy said angrily. "Just get the hell out of here."

Brown got to his feet and looked at Slapsy menacingly. "You don't know what you're doing."

"I know exactly what you're doing. I don't give a damn who you represent."

Brown pounded his fist on the desk. "You're gonna care, pops. Let me tell you."

"And let me tell you something," Slapsy replied. "I've never been able to put up with your type. I see you on this block again, I'll talk to everybody in the city to find out what the hell you're up to. I know a lot of people. A lot of people."

Brown glared for a moment. Then he left, slamming the door behind him.

eleven

The woman who plunked herself down in the seat next to where Marguerite Washington stood carried a copy of the *New York Post*. Marguerite looked over her shoulder at the front-page headline: "Laughing Teens Held in Brutal Slaying of Two Retarded Brothers."

The woman turned the page. Marguerite's eyes were drawn to other headlines: "Pregnant Mom Murdered"; "Bandits Beat Up Aged Widow for $15"; "Cops Subdue Drug-crazed Gunman in Shooting Spree."

Marguerite turned away before the woman turned the page again. These stories always disgusted and infuriated her. That's why she felt so proud when she'd taken the knife from the man the night before.

Pride was the motivating factor in her life. From the time she was a little girl, her momma and her dad had instilled that feeling in her. Being female, being poor, being black, people would say a lot of things to her, she was told. If she had pride, she should ignore them and sail on through.

So that's what she had done. No matter how bad the teachers were, she did her homework every night and asked for more. No matter how much grief she took from the boys, she got out on the playground with them, honing her basketball skills until she could beat half the boys one on one. Her determination not to walk the neighborhood in fear was her motivation for the karate classes that stood her in such good stead last night. In another year, she'd have her black belt.

With all her accomplishments, she should be satisfied. She wasn't, however. She had a restless nature that led her to want to do more and more.

The train pulled to a halt. Marguerite stepped out the door, looking first forward, then back. Everybody was in place.

She stepped back inside, checking the passengers in the car, alert. Although they didn't know it, they were going to get home safe tonight. That made her feel proud.

"Off," Torres ordered. Tony stepped out onto the platform, keeping his hands in his pockets so the knives didn't rattle. The overcoat, borrowed from Cisco, seemed to weigh a hundred pounds. Tony had never felt more conspicuous in his life.

The nine Skulls clustered around. "Rascal," Torres said. "You take the next express on Fifty-ninth. Get on the local and go to Fifty-first. If there's a cop there, your job is to get him the hell away."

Rascal, a blocky white kid, nodded.

"The rest of you know what to do. We'll wait two trains, then go to Eighty-sixth and get a local. I'll move through the train with the kid here to pick a target. If I give the sign at Fifty-ninth, we hit."

"Why we hitting in midtown, man," a voice complained. "Tons of cops."

"This is training, shithead," Torres said. "If it's right, we won't have no problems. Got that?"

There were no objections.

Tony leaned against a post. Gomez offered him a cigarette. Tony took it, then leaned forward for a light.

The smoke made him slightly dizzy, but he didn't cough. He said to Gomez, "You done this before?"

"Sure, man. No sweat. Just like the dude says. We check it all out. We grab the loot and split."

"What if somebody puts up a fight?"

Gomez grinned. "That's what those blades is for, man."

As the train rattled past the darkened Yankee Stadium on the elevated Bronx tracks, Jim was lost in thought. He was wondering if the whole magic day with Sara on Sunday had been nothing more than a dream.

He must have called her ten times in the last two days. He got her receptionist, then her answering service. Evidently, she'd had a number of emergency cases. Maybe, he told himself, she'd tried to call him at home when he was out on patrol last night.

Or had she? Maybe she'd had second thoughts? Maybe she'd gone back to Bill? Maybe she'd decided that a starving pie-in-the-sky do-gooder wasn't worth the gamble?

The urge to stay home to wait for a call had been strong. But he'd made a commitment to patrol.

Funny, he thought, the word *patrol*. So much of what he was doing now was like a flashback to the war—even to his half-formed reasons for getting involved.

During those months in Saigon, when he didn't know whether he was going to be court-martialed, discharged, or sent back out in the bush as a medic, he'd tried to think back to his exact reasons for making the decision to join the army. It wasn't the desire to fight or to pursue a military career. It wasn't the fear of the draft—he never thought about waiting until they came to get him. In fact, it wasn't a well-formed, cohesive reason at all. The best he could come up with was that he felt it was his responsibility to help when an emergency confronted his country.

Now he was back on the front lines in a different kind of action. Again, he felt driven by responsibility—to Granny, to the city he loved despite its problems. That was why he'd fallen back on his military training. To the concept of patrol.

He didn't know, however, what was in the future. If they found Granny's killers, they could quit. But what if they didn't? Every night they spent out here represented a sacrifice for everyone. He knew that he should formulate some plan, some schedule. He'd have to talk to Renaldo and the others. Maybe they'd give it until the end of the week. Or two weeks from last Thursday, the night of the murder.

Still, those kinds of plans wouldn't help if Sara called tonight. The thought of what he might be missing gave him a cold feeling inside.

The train slowed as it approached the Eighty-sixth Street station. When the car stopped, he moved across the car to the open door. Eric came running up. "Jim," he said. "I saw a pack of teenagers running up the stairs to the local tracks."

"Let's go," Jim said. He took the stairs two at a time, followed by the rest of the patrol. But at the top, he saw the doors of the local slam shut, and the train pull away.

"Damn," he muttered.

"What will we do?" Eric asked.

Jim pondered a moment. Then he said, "Eric, you, John, Rafael, and Chang wait for the next local. Renaldo, Baseline, Marguerite, and I will take the next express to Fifty-ninth and transfer."

"What are we looking for?" Rafael asked.

"Trouble," Jim said.

The train lurched to the right as Tony was between cars. He stumbled, then caught himself on the safety wires. Three feet below him hissed the sparks from the friction of the contact shoes of the car rubbing against the third rail, which carried 600 volts of direct current.

A hand grabbed Tony's overcoat and pulled him back up. Tony followed Torres into the next car.

Torres walked down the aisle, slowly surveying what he called "the meat." At the end of the car, he approached Trynoski, a wiry Polish kid who seemed to have a permanent sneer on his face.

"Nothing," Torres said in a low voice.

"What about them?" Trynoski asked.

In the middle of the car, a young guy about twenty-five, dressed in an expensive-looking dark suit, necked with a girl.

"Nah. Rents they pay, these young dudes don't have no bread except on payday. Today's Tuesday."

As they moved on to the next to last car, Tony breathed a little sigh of relief. Maybe they wouldn't find a target that suited Torres. They could just go home.

The farther they moved toward the rear of the train, the emptier the cars. On the left was a group of giggling high school girls. A couple of heavyset women who looked like cleaning ladies going home swayed with the moving train. A Hispanic couple concentrated on a fussing baby. At the far end was a middle-aged, grey-haired man with a white apron sticking out below his car coat.

Gomez was stationed in this car, the hood of his parka pulled up over his face. Torres nudged him, and they all moved into the last car.

Torres turned to Tony. "Blades. For me and Gomez."

"Who?" Gomez asked.

"Guy in the brown coat. Looks like he just closed up his deli or something. He's got a bagful of food. People like him don't shop in delis in that part of town unless they own them."

Tony stood there, braced with fear.

"I said *blades*," Torres snapped.

His hands were shaking as he grabbed the handles. He barely managed to avoid dropping them as he passed them to Torres and Gomez.

"What do I do?" he asked.

"If it's cool, the train will move. Stay on. If there's some shit, hit the tunnel."

The express pulled into Fifty-ninth Street. Jim led the way up the long flight of stairs. The local was still waiting. Jim sprinted, throwing himself between the doors of the head car just as they were closing. The doors reopened, and Renaldo, Baseline, and Marguerite joined him.

"Man, this is worse than a double-overtime game," Baseline panted.

"Typical male," Marguerite teased. "Do more talking than training."

"I'll run circles around you any day, momma."

"Hold it," Jim interjected.

"What?" Renaldo asked.

"The other end of the car."

"Gotcha."

They surrounded the teenager wearing the

black gloves, army jacket, and a wool scarf wrapped around his face.

"What's going on?" Jim demanded.

"Huh?"

"What's going down, man?"

The teenager tried to bolt. Renaldo grabbed him by the shoulders and turned him around as if he was an inflatable dummy.

Jim pulled the scarf down. He saw the scar on his left cheek. "Savage Skull."

"Let me go," the kid shouted.

"We're going to find a cop," Jim said. The train was stopping at Fifty-first Street. "Bring him along, Renaldo."

Jim reached the open door when he heard the angry shout. At the opposite end of the train, he saw an older man struggling with an attacker. Another came up behind and Jim saw the glint of steel. Then the man tumbled to his knees.

Baseline and Renaldo were already on the move. A black kid came out of a car and threw a rolling block at Renaldo. He hurdled the kid like a sprinter, but another kid hit him with a shoulder. The muscular boxer veered into Baseline and they both went down.

Jim, right behind, avoided the pile up. He saw the backs of the thieves as they sprinted up the stairs to the street. He was about to give chase when he heard the victim gagging.

In an instant, he made his decision. He knelt. The man had been stabbed in the lower back. Quickly Jim stripped off the man's coat, then full-length butcher's apron underneath, then the shirt and undershirt. He ripped a long strip from the apron and began binding the wound to stop the flow of blood.

Renaldo knelt beside him. "Call an ambulance," Jim said. "And the cops."

Tony watched in horror. When he saw the conductor join the crowd surrounding the man who'd been stabbed, he knew the train wasn't going to move.

He had three options. One was to stay where he was. But even if he ditched the two remaining knives and the gun, the scar on his cheek would identify him.

He could try to get to the exit. But they would be watching that. He couldn't let himself get caught. He'd be an accessory to murder.

That left the tracks. He felt smothered by despair. He breathed deeply, trying to dissolve the huge knot of panic inside him.

The car was fortunately empty. He moved to the back, took a last deep breath, then opened the door.

He dropped to the tracks and looked around. If he hugged the wall, he'd stay away from the third rail. He moved slowly into the darkness, his hands on the rock, which was slimy with mold. When he got twenty feet or so from the cone of light from the platform, he stopped to let his eyes adjust. The red light from the signals provided a murky kind of vision.

He started forward again. He went fifty, sixty steps. Then a clatter sent a spasm through him. He stopped, absolutely frozen.

It was several seconds before his mind identified the scurrying sound. Rats.

He hated rats. But he couldn't let that stop him. Once again, he moved.

The first vibrations came from the walls. Then he heard the first sound, like the faraway rumble of a thunderstorm. The rumble got louder and he felt the ground beneath him shake. He couldn't decide whether to cling to the wall or throw himself to the ground.

When the train passed beneath him, an express on the level below, it was moments before he could bring himself to move. He felt totally drained, and light-headed, as if the oxygen had been cut off from his brain.

He scarcely remembered negotiating the distance to the Forty-second Street subway station, slipping up onto the platform, then making his way to the street for the long, chilling walk home.

twelve

Jim hadn't gotten to bed until after three in the morning. When the alarm went off four hours later, he felt like he had a hangover. Three cups of coffee and an ice-cold shower failed to banish all the fog. For the first time in months, he was a few minutes late for work.

The waiting room was jammed. The cold, damp November weather produced a near epidemic of flu cases, especially among the many elderly people living in drafty, inadequately heated apartments. They'd come in three or four days a week—as much to get fussed over and to be warm as to get treatment.

Juanita came out from behind the desk to greet him.

"One of those days," Jim said.

"Dr. Carter is going crazy."

"I'll take the other examination room. I'll look at the repeats."

125

"You can't," Juanita said. "There's a reporter here to see you. From the *Daily News.*"

Jim hurried into his office. From behind, the person inspecting the photographs on the wall looked like a slender boy dressed in a corduroy sport coat, jeans, and boots. But when she turned, Jim saw a woman with the youthful face of a high school cheerleader—full, rosy cheeks, sparkling eyes, button nose. Her light brown hair was pulled back and fastened into a ponytail that swung when she moved.

"I'm Jim Knight," he said, extending his hand.

"Jill Prentice," she said.

Jim was surprised. He'd read Jill Prentice's thrice-weekly column for years.

She smiled with amusement at his reaction. "I know," she said. "I don't look like my picture."

"You do look much younger."

"I'm really an ancient twenty-nine."

Jim smiled. "To me, you're still a kid. Anyway, I'm delighted to meet you. I'm a big fan of yours."

"Thanks," she said. "Now that we have that out of the way, do you have a few minutes?"

"Of course. I always have time to talk about our work here."

"It isn't the clinic I came to talk about. It's a letter from a very grateful young lady named Doris Bunker."

For the second time, Jim was surprised. "Oh, I see." He paused for a moment, then added, "There really wasn't much too it. Some friends of mine saw her being harassed, and we stepped in to help."

Jill looked at him knowingly. "If that was all there was to it, I wouldn't be here. But I talked to Doris, and she said you've been riding the subway every night. Do you want to tell me about it?"

Jim pursed his lips. Then he said, "It sort of sounds silly. Like we're playing cops and robbers or something."

"Why don't you let me be the judge of that?"

Jim looked at her. He instinctively felt she was a person he could trust. "Okay," he said. "I will."

He talked for nearly forty-five minutes. When he finished, she commented, "That's remarkable."

"What's remarkable?"

"What you're doing. And why. And what you've seen. Doris was right. There's a story here."

"I don't know," Jim said.

"I do," she said. "I want to go with you tonight."

He frowned. "It's dangerous."

Jill smiled. "You didn't read my columns on the Women's Detention Center on Riker's Island? I was locked up for a week with some decidedly dangerous females. I've become a pretty good free-lance claw-and-scratcher. Besides, the *News* has a great insurance plan."

Jim thought, Why not? The guys deserved some reward for riding with him. And maybe the publicity would produce a lead that would help nail Granny's killers.

Jim rose and extended his hand again. "Welcome aboard."

It had started to snow after midnight. The air

had been absolutely still, so the big, fat snow-flakes drifted downward gently. They softened the light from the streetlights and blanketed the sidewalks and cars and garbage cans. The effect was out of a Christmas movie, like *Holiday Inn* or *White Christmas*.

Tony Melendez, however, didn't notice the fairy-tale scene around him. He hadn't gone home. Instead, he'd walked the streets in the snow, becoming increasingly cold, wet, and hungry. He was also confused, scared, and terribly alone.

As the snow tapered off in midmorning, he walked eastward, toward the East River, under the thick, gloomy, leaden-gray sky. He remembered taking the same walk last summer, on a perfect, warm July day. Maria, a shy, pretty girl next door who was in his class at school, had made thick sandwiches, which she carried in a bag with fruit and corn chips. He'd stopped at the bodega for Twinkies and a quart of Dr. Pepper.

Playfully, they'd skipped along, laughing, chattering about the year gone by. They'd crossed the ball fields, then sat and spread their picnic out in a remote corner where they could see the blue waters roll by. Though the roar of traffic was in the background, the city—with its ugly tenements, the filthy streets, the gangs—seemed miles away. They watched the sea gulls soar and dive overhead; they held hands; then, shyly, they kissed. At that moment, the world had seemed like a wonderful place to Tony.

Now that world was gone. He was no longer a boy. If he rejected the Skulls, he was an outcast, a traitor. If he stayed in the gang, he was a criminal.

He walked slowly up the ramp to the elevated walkway over the FDR Drive. At the top, he halted, staring out into the river. It seemed hostile, dangerous, as it rushed by—just like life. A plunge into the water, a few brief moments of suffering, and it would be over.

He shook as he stood, the desperation building in him. He started forward. Then he slipped on the snow and fell. He got his hands out barely in time to avoid hitting chin first.

It took him a moment to catch his breath. When he did, he noticed his hand ached.

Then it came to him. The image of the man who stitched his cut. He remembered the concern on the man's face, the feeling that he cared.

Tony took a last look at the water. Then he turned and headed back down the ramp.

"A cigarette, Santos?" Anthony Brown asked, offering an open gold case.

"Thanks," the Savage Skull leader said. He was the slightest bit uncomfortable out of his turf, in the plush office on lower Park Avenue.

Brown continued pacing as he talked. "You did a good job cleaning out those pushers. You do the same job protecting our people when we start up, you'll make a lot of money. No slipups, understand?"

"Sure," Santos said. "My guys are trained. They follow orders."

"They'd better. I ..." Brown's voice trailed off at the sound of a knock. A tall, muscular man in a gray suit opened the door. "His car is outside."

"Thanks," Brown said. He looked back at Santos. "You also clear on the other assignments. I want those torch jobs done right. Okay?"

"Sure."

Brown smiled. "Good boy. You can go."

The other man held the door open for the gang leader. Then he asked Brown, "The kid doing all right?"

"Yeh. You did a good job picking him, Mike. The kid's smarter than average. And he wants to be a big shot."

Brown lit a cigarette, then sat down behind the desk. "He'll be a big shot for a couple, three years. Then we won't need him anymore."

"That quick?"

"Things are going crazy in this city, in real estate. Look at Chelsea, whole blocks being renovated. Same thing's got to happen on the Lower East Side. That's why we're buying more and more stuff now. By the time we burn the buildings out and collect the insurance bucks, it'll be time to replace them with fancy co-ops and townhouses. And you know what will happen to commercial property. Rents will go up five, ten times."

"Sounds easy."

"It is easy, when the punks do all the work.

No sense in using people from the Family. If the punks get caught, who gives a shit?"

"What about the drugs?"

Brown smiled. "That's mine. That's my deal. The old man went along with the idea of getting the pushers off the streets. Crime rate goes down, makes the area seem a little better when the boom hits. Then I came up with the perfect way to sell our stuff."

"How's it going to work, exactly?"

Brown told him.

Mike shook his head in admiration. "Got to hand it to you. Sounds perfect."

"It is perfect. Long as our friend Santos does his job, we're going to make a fortune."

Jim saw the scar on his cheek first. When he spoke, his voice was cold. "You want to see me about the hand?"

Tony stood, trembling. Then he turned and started to run out of the office. When Jim caught him at the door, he saw the boy was crying.

An hour later, he'd heard the whole achingly familiar story. What was different in this case was that Tony had a conscience. Jim's heart went out to him.

Jim called out for some sandwiches and soft drinks. While Tony ate, Jim sat back and pondered. On the one hand, he had the boy's welfare to consider. On the other hand, Tony's membership in the Skulls presented an exciting opportunity. For one, it was a chance to find out what Santos's plans were and what his connection to Andrew Brown was. And, more importantly, it was a chance to find the killers of Granny Moore. From hearing Tony's story, Jim was convinced that one of the Skull's "training" patrols committed the crime that cost Granny her life.

By the time Tony had finished his meal, Jim had made up his mind.

"We have a problem, Tony," he said. "One of them is your age. I can arrange for a place for you to stay. But if your mother raises a stink, there's nothing I can do."

"She won't," the boy said. "She doesn't care."

"Is she on welfare?"

"Yes."

"Then she'll care. Her check would be cut. But that isn't the only issue. The other one is the Skulls. Right?"

Tony's lips tightened.

"From what I know about Santos, and from what you've told me, I think resigning from the Skulls isn't going to be easy. It could be dangerous."

Tony shifted uncomfortably in his chair. "I know. What can I do? I don't want to go out with them again."

Jim met his anxious eyes. "Tony, I'm going to level with you. What I have in mind involves risk. But it just might mean the end of the Skulls. And an end to your problems."

"How's that going to happen?" Tony asked. "They got so many guys?"

"There's more of us. More good guys. If everybody helps, if everybody stands up to them, they'll disappear."

"I don't know what you mean."

"What I mean is, I'd like you to stay with the Skulls for a while. Go to the meetings, go on patrol. Then let me know what happens."

"You mean spy?" Tony asked in a voice tight with concern. "They'll kill me."

"They won't find out. You'll do this only for a little while. I'll rebandage your hand; you say it got reinfected. Every couple days you come in to have the bandage changed."

Tony's face was pale. Jim could see his hands clench and unclench. "What if I get caught. On the subway. The cops, they'll . . ."

"I can't make a firm promise," Jim said. "But I have friends on the police. I promise I'd testify on your behalf."

"I don't know," Tony said. "I don't know." His mind was spinning. He had come to this man seeking a way out. Instead, he seemed to be getting deeper and deeper.

"Tony," Jim said. "I know you want to do the right thing. Saving your brother from being arrested, that was brave, even though he deserved to be caught. Now you have the chance to be a real hero. You don't have to do anything but go along. You don't have to call attention to yourself. Just listen." He paused for a second. "It might make this neighborhood a nice place to live. For the decent people."

"A real hero," Tony said to himself. For the second time today, the image of Maria, the girl from his class, came to his mind. The guys in the gang were already starting to notice her. He knew what happened if a girl didn't let them do what they wanted to do. And what would happen, he thought, to the kids in the playground, the ones he saw yesterday? They'd have to make the same choice he was faced with.

When he tried to speak the first time, his voice was so choked with emotion that no words came out. He swallowed, then tried again. "I'll do it."

Later, Jim saw again in his mind's eye the adult resolve on Tony's child's face. He struggled with the feeling of guilt at talking the boy into a dangerous action. Tony's decision was as brave as any he'd seen in the war in Vietnam.

Despite the risks involved, though, Jim still felt he'd made the right choice. Vinnie had summed it up properly. Jim had crossed the line. In his own mind, he'd declared war on the Savage Skulls.

thirteen

"Slapsy."

The old man grunted. But his eyes remained shut.

Renaldo stood in the doorway, smiling. Slapsy swore he never napped; yet half the time when Renaldo came into the office he was in the same position—arms crossed, head on his chest, eyes closed. The way he snorted when he was awakened always reminded Renaldo of Grumpy the dwarf in Walt Disney's *Sleeping Beauty*.

Renaldo decided not to wake Huggins. Harvey and Eduardo were watching the place. Besides, he got the impression that Slapsy wasn't too thrilled with having him gone every night. He'd been preoccupied and out of sorts lately.

If the truth be known, Renaldo missed the gym too. That was the sacrifice he was making. Around ten o'clock, when the crowd thinned out and he got things in order, they'd sit around. Renaldo, Slapsy, Cube, maybe a couple of others. Slapsy'd pass around the beer and tell stories.

Some people thought the stories about the fight game years ago were boring. But to Renaldo, they meant that he was part of a sport that had tradition, a real history. The fight world was his family now. The former champions were his ancestors, and Slapsy was his surrogate father. When he became champion, he would follow in the footsteps of the best of them.

He glanced at the clock. Time to leave. He took a last look at Slapsy, then quietly closed the door.

"Man, that dude was done in! He even had a stiff neck looking up to watch me fly. Mr. Big Shot from Brooklyn, my ass. He was so low after the game, he didn't open the gym door, he just crawled his way out through the crack. Now, that's a story, lady."

Jill laughed.

"Enough, Baseline," Jim said. "You want to give the twins a call to see what's holding them up?"

Baseline saluted, executed a sloppy about-face, and went out the door.

Jill asked, "Is he really that good?"

"All-city high school player last year."

"How come he's not in college?"

"First of all, until about this time last year, he couldn't read at all."

"You're kidding?"

"I wish I was. He's in a special program now. He's worked his butt off, and he's made real good progress. Hell, even without reading he could have gone to a bunch of junior colleges. But his mother has six younger kids at home. Baseline drives a cab six nights a week to help her out."

"That's great."

Jim smiled. "To quote you this morning, 'There's a lot of good stories in the Big Apple.'"

"Jim. I—I—"

Jim turned to see Sara in the doorway. He had been sitting on the edge of his desk, and he stood.

"Sara," he said. "I've been trying to reach you. I ..." His voice trailed off as he remembered that Jill was standing next to him. He made the introductions.

Jill shook hands, then excused herself.

They stood, looking at each other. Jim broke the silence. "I've been trying to—"

Sarah stepped forward and kissed him. He put his arms around her and pulled her tight to him. The kiss unlocked a store of feeling that swept over him like a blast of hot air.

Then she rested her head on his shoulders and said, "I've missed you."

"I must have called a dozen times."

"I was hiding," she admitted. "I had a lot of thinking to do. The freedom is so new to me."

"I understand," Jim said.

"Good. We've got a lot of talking to do. I thought we could have dinner. At some nice little place in Soho."

Jim sighed. "I can't, Sara. Not tonight."

Her expression darkened. "Why not?"

"I've got to go out. To ride the subway. That's why Jill is here, to do a story for the *News*."

"Can't the rest of them go? You've been out every night, haven't you. Can't you give it up for me?"

"The rest of them have given things up too. Until this thing is through, I've got to be out there."

Her eyes flashed anger. "You sound just like Bill. Everything is wonderful until it conflicts with your schedule. All men are alike."

He stiffened, then turned away. There was a war going on inside him. There was nothing he wanted more than to spend every moment with the woman he'd been in love with for months. Yet, on the other hand, there was the duty that weighed so heavily on him.

Sara put her hands on his shoulders. When she spoke, her voice was soft, "I'm sorry, Jim. It's not fair."

He turned. "No. It's my obsession that's—"

She put her finger on his lips. "It's not fair of me. I've been hiding the last two nights, doing what I had to do. I've got to recognize you've got obligations to clear away, too. As much as I want you, I have to understand."

He leaned forward and gently kissed her on the lips. "Thank you. I promise. It will be over soon."

She smiled. "When can I see you?"

"Early dinner tomorrow? Six o'clock?"

She kissed him. "I love you," she said. "Even if you are crazy."

*   *   *

"No fuck ups," Santos said. "Anybody fucks up, they get a call from my friend Homicide Healy."

He turned to Garcia. "You got the jack?"

Garcia nodded.

"Once you pry the cellar doors open," Santos continued, "everybody drops into the basement. And everybody goes out that way. If we leave the metal gates over the windows, it'll be tougher for the firemen."

"What if the cops come by?"

"They won't," Santos replied. "Torres is taking care of that. All you need to worry about is what you do inside the building. Soak that stuff good—the bolts of cloth, ribbons, all that stuff will burn like hell."

He looked at a hulk of a white kid. "Walsh, your job is the stairs. And Brownie, you get this," Santos added as he removed two sicks of dynamite from a bag. "All you have to do is put this on the ceiling. Right in the middle of the store. Make a nice chimney for that fire to get upstairs fast."

"How do I light it?"

"The fire will take care of that," Santos said. "Any questions?"

There were none.

He smiled, stretching the vivid scar on his cheek. "We're gonna see this one on the news tomorrow. You do your job, we'll be stars."

The scream came just as the doors were closing. Jim dashed forward and pounded on the conductor's cubicle. "Open the doors," he shouted. "Open the doors."

The train started to move.

"The emergency cord," he shouted back to Renaldo. Renaldo pulled the cord and the train stopped abruptly.

The conductor's door opened. The burly man in the blue suit was red faced with anger. "What in the hell—?"

"Open the doors."

"Is there someone caught?"

"Open them, damn it," Jim hissed.

The conductor disappeared. A moment later, the doors opened.

Jim ran out onto the platform and whistled. Then he heard another scream.

Jim sprinted toward the stairs of the elevated station, the 161st Street–Yankee Stadium stop. He could hear the feet of his friends pounding behind him. He halted at the bottom of the stairs, at a sign that said To IND.

Baseline was next to him. "Down there."

The underground IND station was nearly deserted. Jim heard moans off to the left, down a darkened corridor. He turned the corner, then stopped.

Two teenagers were on either side of a young girl whose pants had been pulled to her ankles and whose blouse was torn in front. A third boy was on his knees, zipping up his pants.

"Stop," Jim yelled.

The two on their feet took off. The boy on his knees started to get up. Renaldo landed on him, pinning him with his massive body.

Jim led the pursuit. The rapists darted down the stairs to the southbound platform. "Get the other side," Jim told Baseline. Then Jim hurried down the stairs. The platform was empty. The two teenagers had jumped down to track level, vaulted the guard in the middle, and raced toward the platform on the other side.

Baseline, John, and Eric were waiting for them.

The teenagers stared at them with wide eyes. One started to back off. The other pulled a blade from his back pocket.

"Gonna cut your ass, motherfuckers," the knife wielder snarled. He lunged forward.

At that moment, Baseline leaped. His hands grabbed the top of the clock far above his head. He swung backward for momentum, then kicked out with both huge feet.

He hit the charging teenager in the chest. The kid staggered as the air whooshed out of him. His knife hand sagged to his side. He stumbled to one knee as the twins seized him. Eric twisted the knife out of his hand.

"Where'd the other one go?" John asked.

Baseline dropped, his knees bending as his feet hit the platform. "Down the tunnel," he said. "We'll let the police chase him. Mrs. Jones' favorite son don't want any part of those tracks."

"Nice leap," Eric said.

Baseline smiled. "When it comes to soaring, I'm your man. 'Specially cause I don't like knives one bit."

It was three hours later, nearly 2:00 A.M., when

they were through. Jill said, "Let's get a cab. The *News* will pay."

"That's a good idea," Jim said. "And it's a good thing you were along tonight."

"I can't believe it," Renaldo said. His voice still showed the anger from his recent experience. "Those goddamn transit police were going to book me for assault. On the word of that scrawny punk who'd raped a thirteen-year-old girl."

"I think the cop put him up to it," Jim said. "It's that attitude again. Like we were the criminals."

"The cop assigned to that station was sleeping or something," Jill said. "If you hadn't come along, he wouldn't have had to stir. The girl probably wouldn't have filed a complaint."

"I felt so sorry for her," Jim said. "On the other hand, she shouldn't have been in that subway station at that time of night either."

"That's another story," Jill said. "But I've got a terrific one to write about what you did tonight. What happened afterwards makes it even better."

"Are you sure you should include that?" Jim asked. "We have enough trouble with the transit police as it is?"

Jill smiled. "You asking a reporter to cover up?"

"No. But—"

"Jim," Jill said. "The only way to change that attitude is to bring it to light. You're doing the right thing. I'm convinced of that. And I'm sure the public will be too."

Just then they spotted a cab. They hailed it, and it pulled to the curb.

"I'm still furious," Renaldo said as got inside. "Even if we did work it out."

Jim smiled. "Take it out on the punching bags tomorrow," he said.

Renaldo smiled too. "You're right. Slapsy's going to see a real tiger in the ring tomorrow."

fourteen

The digital clock read 2:34 when Slapsy stirred. Funny, although he found himself napping more during the day as he got older, he also found himself unable to sleep for more than two or three hours at a time at night. He got up, stretched, and started out the door to check to see that the gym had been locked up properly.

Actually, he didn't mind not sleeping eight hours. He really loved this time of night. As he slowly shuffled across the floor of the gymnasium in the faint red light of the Exit signs, he was struck by the rich smell of the sweat-soaked canvas, the leather, the liniment. Invariably, the odor touched off a succession of scenes from his storehouse of memories.

Even though Slapsy knew in his heart he wasn't the man that he was physically, he had seldom been happier. Age had finally blunted the driving passions, the ambition that had buffeted him since he was a young boy. The gym was his world now. He had all the money he would ever need, all the fighters he could train and regale with stories, and he had Renaldo to look after the place so he didn't really have to worry about details. Finally, he had one more crowning pleasure to look forward to—fastening the championship belt around Renaldo's waist.

Slapsy fussed around for a few minutes, tossing discarded towels into the bin, emptying some half-filled cups of water that had been lying around. Then he picked up a pair of gloves someone had left near the heavy bag. He started back to put them in the storeroom.

Then he heard a roar, like a subway train was passing beneath him. The windows of Cohen's store below shattered, and a faint odor of smoke reached his nostrils.

"Darn," he said aloud. He turned toward the office to call the fire department.

The blast knocked him off his feet. He hit a mat by the wall, then slid to the floor. Flames were dancing through the hole, the thick smoke billowed like a cloud toward him. For a moment, he watched, his heart beating so rapidly he thought it would burst. Then he collected himself.

When he tried to stand, he started choking. He dropped down to take in the fresher air near the floor.

The flames blocked the path to the windows. Like a swimmer, he pulled himself toward the door to the stairs. His eyes fastened on the faint glow from the still shining Exit sign. He could feel the temperature building in the wood beneath him.

"Come on, Slapsy," he growled. "Remember the Boxcar Reilly fight. Remember, you tough son of a bitch."

The smoke was thicker now. He was still moving, but he couldn't see the sign. Maybe the light had gone out.

Every movement of his body was agony now. His chest ached from breathing the foul air. "Come on, Slapsy. Come on. Come ..."

"Christ almighty!" the chief exclaimed as his car turned the corner onto Avenue B. He reached for the radio to call for a second alarm. Then he jumped out, put on his white hat, and began to direct the fire-fighting operation.

Within seconds after the pumper pulled up, a 2½-inch line had been stretched to a hydrant and water started to pour into the first floor. Ladders were stretched to the roof.

A fireman touched the chief's arm. "A woman says there's a guy who lives on the second floor."

"Get somebody in there, quick."

Three fireman donned Scott air-pacs and scampered up a ladder. The smoke was so thick it was impossible to see. The heat to the right, toward the fire, was too intense to go that way. One fireman dropped to the floor, then headed toward the left-hand wall, sweeping the area in front of him with his arms moving in a breaststroke pattern.

Over the radio, the chief announced that the

building was in danger of collapse. The fireman inside only had a few minutes before he had to pull out.

He was just about to turn back when he felt something soft. He pulled himself forward and felt the shape of a leg. He pulled the leg toward him, laboring so hard he was using air in big gulps. Finally, he hooked his arms around the shoulders, got to his feet, and pulled. He couldn't see a thing. It would have to be blind luck that would get him to the window.

The fire buffs were jammed six deep behind the police barricades. Jim elbowed and shoved his way behind Renaldo until they reached the sawhorses. A cop stopped them, but Jim hurriedly explained. The cop pulled back the barrier to let them through.

What Jim saw in front of him made him abruptly halt. From that distance, the fire scene had the same haunting beauty of a night battle viewed from a helicopter or a distant hill. In the middle of the block, amidst the dark buildings, was an angry box of fire. The flames danced and hissed like a tormented monster as two pumpers poured water through blown-out windows. Whirling blue and red bubble lights reflected kaleidoscopically off the fire equipment that glutted the street. Firemen moved through the path of headlights like jerky figures in a nickelodeon.

"Come on," Renaldo yelled anxiously. "We've got to find Slapsy."

Jim followed him forward, and the closer they

got, the more the true ferocity of the fire became apparent. The air was so gray and thick with ash that breathing was like chewing putty. Exhausted firemen slumped against a stoop, their faces blackened like minstrels, mucus dripping from their noses and mouths.

Stepping over stretched hoses, Jim moved around a rescue vehicle, then froze. In front of him, two rescue men labored over a fire fighter felled by smoke. One clamped the mouthpiece of a resuscitator tightly over the mouth, the other pumped rhythmically on the man's chest.

As he stood, motionless, watching, he flashed to those vignettes that ran like a film loop in his mind: the sharp crackle of semiautomatic rifle fire, the thunderous boom of mortar shells, the unholy screams of the wounded men, then himself, the medic, dashing forward frantically to stop the blood spilling into the filthy rice-paddy slime.

He could feel it now, as if it were yesterday. The shock of being at war, of being under enemy fire. And here he was in another war. Only this one was being fought in his territory, and the victims were his friends.

"Jim," Renaldo said, shaking him. "The guy said they got him out."

"Who?"

"Slapsy. They took him to Bellevue. Let's get a cab."

They paced in the dingy waiting room of the Bellevue Hospital Burn Center. At first, when they'd heard Slapsy was alive, they'd experienced a sudden, absurd leap of hope. During the long ensuing hours, however, darkness once again firmly entrenched itself in their souls.

For what seemed like an eternity, they had no word on his condition. When a doctor had finally come out, he was somber and brief. Huggins had suffered severe smoke inhalation and 80 percent of his body was covered with burns. His condition: "Extremely critical."

Renaldo slumped into a chair, rubbing his hands into eyes reddened from exhaustion and tears. "I should have been there, man. I should have been there."

"The fire spread like crazy, the firemen said," Jim commented. "What could you have done?"

"Something. I could have done something," Renaldo said, an edge creeping into his voice.

"You probably would have ended up there next to Slapsy," Jim said.

"I would have done something. Instead I was chasing around like an idiot."

Jim took a sharp breath. "I'm sorry, Renaldo. It's my fault you weren't there. I had you away helping me. Maybe you could have done something."

Renaldo breathed slowly and deeply, his huge chest rising and falling. Then he looked up at Jim. "No. You're right. What was I going to do, fight the fire with my fists?"

"Maybe you would have reacted more quickly. Maybe—"

"Forget it, man," Renaldo said. "Anyway, we're both too tired to try to figure out anything."

"You're right," Jim said.

"Gentlemen," a nurse said, standing in the doorway. "You can see him now, for a few minutes."

After the dimly lit waiting room, entering the intensive-care unit was like walking into a sunspot. The bank of overhead lights blinded them at first. As they waited for their eyes to adjust, they became aware of the slow, mechanical hiss of the respirator. The sound was mournful, desperate, infinitely sad.

Jim took a deep breath to compose himself. Then he watched Renaldo pull back the green curtain around the bed.

What he saw pierced his heart like an arrow. Jim involuntarily gasped, then stepped back.

Like the victim of a medieval torturer, Slapsy was spread-eagled on a steel-arched Stryker frame. His body was covered with a cooling blanket in a desperate attempt to lower his body temperature. Jim averted his eyes, and they came to rest on a bank of instruments monitoring his condition. One had a digital display that read 104.2.

Jim forced himself to look at Slapsy again. Before he looked at the old trainer's face, he noticed that even the tips of his fingers and toes that emerged from the blanket were charred and oozing.

Suddenly, the fingers of one hand uncurled, reaching out. Renaldo stepped forward to touch those fingers, and they closed around his.

Jim looked at Slapsy's face. He shuddered. The hair and eyebrows were gone. Every inch of Slapsy's skin was covered with a thick white cream. All he recognized were the dark eyes.

Renaldo spoke. "Slapsy. It's the fourteenth round, man, and you're behind on points. You got to pull it out. You've got to—" Emotion choked off his voice. Tears were running down his face.

Jim moved closer. As he did, he breathed in a sweet-sour smell, like that of a dying orchard.

Slapsy couldn't speak. But Jim could see in his eyes that he knew they were there. Huggins looked at Renaldo, then at Jim, then back to Renaldo. Then his eyes closed.

The nurse came up to them. "He needs his rest. You have to go now."

"How is he?" Renaldo asked. "Does he have a chance?"

The nurse sighed. "I don't know."

"You've got to know. Is there anything else you can do?"

Jim took him by the arm. "We've got to go. They're doing all they can."

Renaldo took one look over his shoulder. Then he walked with Jim out of the room.

They walked home from Bellevue, down the cold, empty streets in the half-light of early morning. They walked in silence, the only sound the slap of concrete beneath their feet. Renaldo went to his girl friend Maria's apartment. Jim headed farther south, toward home.

When he turned down his block, the first red streaks of dawn stained the gray black sky. He could hear the deep growl of a Department of

Sanitation truck compressing garbage on the avenue behind him. A few people on their way to work trudged toward bus stops or the subway.

In two hours, Jim had to be at the clinic. He debated stopping for breakfast. But he decided he needed a shower and a change of clothes first.

He was so tired that when he opened the door to the foyer of his building, he didn't notice the small figure huddled in the corner.

"Jim."

"Tony. What are you doing here?"

The boy scrambled to his feet. His hair was matted.

"I have to tell you. The fire. The Skulls, they did it."

Jim's exhaustion suddenly slipped to the back of his mind. He grabbed the boy's arm. "How do you know?"

"I'll tell you."

Jim suddenly realized it was freezing in the foyer. "Come on upstairs. We'll have something warm to drink while we talk."

"We didn't go on the subway tonight," Tony said. "Torres took us to this building, on Seventh Street. Then we waited. For a long time, way after midnight. Then Torres got up, and we spread out around the block as lookouts. Torres stuck a rag in the gas tank of a station wagon. Then he lit it. A minute later, the car blew up. God, it was something."

Jim grimaced in disappointment. "Is that all? A crummy car fire?"

"No, no," Tony said. "Later, when we ran, Torres was bragging. He said we got an important job. The fire department was supposed to come to put out the car. When another building was set on fire, they'd be too late to stop it."

A lightning bolt of rage zipped through Jim. "Damn!" he said through clenched teeth. He couldn't believe it. A thought burned through his brain—if the firemen had gotten there earlier, they might have saved Slapsy before he was so badly burned. The determination came to him—he'd revenge this if it was the last thing he ever did.

He looked at Tony. "Why did the Skulls start that fire in the building?"

"I don't know."

"We're going to find out," Jim swore. "We're going to find out."

fifteen

"Paging Dr. Cummings, Dr. Cummings, call on 1207."

Sara stopped, went to the nearest nurse's station, and dialed 1207.

"Dr. Cummings, hold for Dr. Cummings, please."

It was three or four minutes before her husband's voice came on the line.

"You could at least call yourself, Bill," Sara said.

"You're very difficult to track down. Besides, I was on the phone to Oman. The sheik is a patient of mine."

"I know," Sara said. "But I'm sure you didn't call me just to discuss your prestigious patient list."

There was no response for a moment. Then a distinctly cooler voice said, "I've heard from your lawyer."

"Well?"

"I think you need a new lawyer. He doesn't

ask for a thing. His goal seems to be to get this over with as quickly as possible."

"Those were my instructions," Sara said. "I don't want your money. I told you that."

"Very laissez-faire of you. I see spending time with that Robin Hood of yours has had a more egalitarian effect than I would have thought."

"Robin Hood?"

"Prowling around the subways protecting the poor from their oppressors. Very noble."

"How did you know about that?"

"You didn't see the *News* this morning?" he asked. "Makes your chap a candidate for sainthood, at the very least. That will be very comforting when you're living in some cold-water flat surrounded by all the street urchins he brings in."

"Bill, that's enough," she snapped. "I don't have to listen to this."

"What you have to do," he said angrily, "is come to your senses. One week, you're a happily married wife. Less than ten days later, you've filed for divorce to moon over some social worker. You're like a spoiled child who—"

She slammed the receiver down. She stood, trying to control her trembling. How could he talk to her like that? He was the one who was like the child, throwing a tantrum every time he didn't get his way.

Well, he wasn't getting his way this time. She'd made up her mind. Whatever happened with Jim, she and Bill were irrevocably through.

The thought of Jim reminded her about Bill's reference to today's *Daily News*. She searched the nurse's station to no avail. She found one in the visitors' lounge.

She found it on the page opposite the editorials. She recognized the picture of Jill Prentice in the center of the page.

The headline read, "A Candle in the Night."

It began: "When darkness comes, much of New York City huddles under a blanket of fear. The night belongs to the hunters, the vicious thugs who stalk their prey in the streets and alleys and subways. Each night, in a city in which over half a million felonies occur each year, the screams of victims echo every night, unheard or, far too often, unheeded if heard.

"Last night, in a deserted subway station in the Bronx, such a scream rent the chill air. But this one did not go unheeded. A terrified girl was rescued. Three rapists were handed over to the police. The reason was a very special man named Jim Knight and a group of his friends who, in the words of Eleanor Roosevelt, would 'rather light a candle than curse the darkness.' "

Sara felt an odd mixture of emotions stir within her as she finished the column. She did feel a sense of pride at Jim's actions and ideals being described in such glowing terms. On the other side, though, she was jealous and a bit angry. She was tired of the city, of its pace, its demands, it problems. She wanted to build a new life with the man she loved.

But the article made it seem like Jim had chosen a new life, one that didn't include her. There was even a woman connected with it, the columnist. She must have an ulterior motive for writing a piece like that, she and Jim must have—

Stop that, she suddenly told herself. It's not fair to Jim, to speculate.

What was fair to both of them, though, was a long, frank conversation. Upset at the fire, Jim had canceled the dinner last night. She picked up the phone to dial him. They'd have to talk soon.

Jim looked at the two lighted buttons on the phone. They hadn't been dark for more than a few seconds all morning. He shook his head and said, "Vinnie, I didn't want all this."

The detective puffed on his cigar. "You got it, kid."

"There must have been thirty, forty kids in here today, wanting to sign up. Sign up for what?"

"Like it or not, you've started something, Jim. Something important."

"Vinnie, I run a health clinic. I do a pretty good job, but it's all I can do to handle the work that entails."

Vinnie leaned forward. "You've got a chance to do more than that. Not that your work here isn't important. But you can have an effect on the whole Big Apple. Maybe on the whole country. They all think of New York as a place where nobody cares. Where somebody like Kitty Genovese is getting knifed on the sidewalk and thirty people close their windows to keep out the noise, then go back to bed."

"I know," Jim said, "But—"

"Let me finish, will you? Now, all of a sudden, you've got thirty, forty kids, maybe a lot more, who want to help you take this city back from the hoodlums. Remember when we were talking about how it's 2 percent of the people in this city who make it miserable for the rest?"

"I remember," Jim said. "But it sounds like you're saying I should lead some sort of army."

"That's it, Jimmy. An army. An army of good, decent people, out on the streets, riding in the subway, looking after each other. That's the way it should be."

"I abhor violence."

"Who said anything about violence? These punks, they're all cowards. They see ten, twenty people on a subway train who aren't afraid of them, they'll run and hide. Go back to the sewers where they belong."

"Why don't you lead them?" Jim asked.

The detective shook his head. "Not me. Not a cop. Besides, it takes somebody who can communicate with the kids. It's the teenagers who are going to get involved in this, Jim. At least for the most part it will be kids, because they've got the time. And you've got a way with kids. You're a natural leader."

Jim winced. "That's what they told me in Special Forces. And look what I ended up doing. Killing civilians, setting villages on fire—Christ, I was a war criminal."

Vinnie looked at him hard. "Do you really believe this is the same thing?"

Jim held his breath for a moment. Then he

exhaled and said, "No. It's not the same thing at all. I guess it just seems like such a huge new commitment. I guess I just need a little time to figure out what it means."

"I understand. You take that time. Don't let an old grouchy cop lean on you."

Jim smiled. "An old grouchy cop you're not. I appreciate everything you've done."

Vinnie raised his eyebrows. "What have I done? Oh, there is one thing. I checked with the fire marshals. That fire was absolutely, definitely arson. That the Skulls did it surprises me like if you told me Christmas was on December 25. The problem is nailing them."

"Somebody must have seen something. The street's always full of people."

"So somebody's going to testify, then maybe fly to Tahiti for the next hundred years or so? No, the answer is in finding out why they burned it. The arson guys tell me there's been a big jump in burning buildings for insurance. They think it's an organized ring, and I'll bet the Skulls are doing the torching for it."

"What about that guy Brown who came to see me?"

"Good bet. He's probably tied in to the Mob. It would help if I saw the guy."

"Would a picture help?"

"Is the Pope Catholic?" Vinnie replied. "Also, anything that would tie the guy into Huggins would help."

"I'll do what I can," Jim said. "I've got to go over to meet Renaldo soon. We're going to the hospital."

"How's Slapsy doing?"

Jim pursed his lips. "Not well. But there's always hope."

The windows of the first floor had been boarded up. But through the open space where the second-floor windows had been, Jim spotted the flash of a lantern.

He yelled, "Renaldo, is that you?"

Minutes later, the fighter's head appeared. "Come up. The stairs are okay, except for a couple weak spots. Watch your step."

The walls were totally blackened, and the stairs were covered with ash. Jim carefully picked his way upward.

In what had been the gymnasium, nothing recognizable remained. The floor was covered by a foot of sodden, splinter-laden ashes, except in the center, where there was a gaping hole where the ring once stood. The walls had been burned through to the brick. As Jim's eyes adjusted to the semidarkness, he could see that the Coke machine in the far corner had melted to about a third its normal size, and was now an absurd *S* shape.

The heat must have been intense, Jim thought. He was amazed that the firemen got Slapsy out alive.

"Over here," Renaldo called out. "Go around by the back wall. That's the safest."

Jim moved carefully across the floor. The dampness was thoroughly chilling him, and the thick stench of the burned rubble clung to him like a blanket. He coughed when he tried to take a deep breath.

When he joined Renaldo, Jim said, "Unbelievable, huh?"

Renaldo grimaced. "Yea. Let's go back this way."

They went through the storeroom to Slapsy's small office. The room had sustained heavy smoke damage, but the furniture was intact.

Renaldo picked up something and tossed it to Jim.

Jim caught the soft, damp object. He brushed off some ash, then recognized it. "Slapsy's red beret," he said.

"Slapsy said he won the thing off Frenchy LaRouche in a card game. I think that was a story. I think Slapsy bought it because it made him look jaunty."

"It fit. Slapsy was a real bantam," Jim said. Then he added, "Is a real bantam, I mean."

"Those sons of bitches," Renaldo said. "It would almost have been better if he'd been killed in the fire. He's just going to have to suffer incredible pain before the end."

"Maybe he'll make it," Jim said. "You never know."

Renaldo looked at him grimly. "I know. At his age, with 80 percent of his body burned—it's off the board, Jim."

They stood in silence for a long while. Then Jim asked, "Shall we go?"

"I guess," Renaldo said. "I hate it in that hospital. I get so angry I scare myself. I swear, if I run into Santos or one of his punks, I don't think

I could stop myself. I'd kill him, I swear I'd kill him."

"I understand how you feel," Jim said. "This, on top of Granny's death—it can't be right that the thugs who did that could still be walking around. But violence isn't the answer. I found that out in Vietnam."

"What is the answer?" Renaldo asked with intensity. "What in the hell do we do about them? I know that if I went out and bashed Santos' brains in, that would be a crime. But to do nothing, to let them get away scot-free, that would be an even worse crime. If I don't do something, I'm not going to be able to live with myself."

It was one of those rare times in life when someone else expressed in words exactly what was going on in one's own mind. Renaldo's impassioned statement triggered a decision by Jim. He suddenly knew exactly what he wanted to do.

"I think we have a way to go," Jim said to Renaldo. "Let me tell you what's been happening at the clinic today."

Jim explained the flood of phone calls, and his conversation with Vinnie Civitello. He finished by saying, "I know you've got the big fight coming up. I don't know how this fits into those plans."

"I can fight two battles at once," Renaldo said. "I've always been a worker. This is just a second fight I want to win for Slapsy. When do we start?"

"Right away. We've got a lot of planning to

do. We've got to have a way to screen people. Training procedures. Operating plans. And I think we have to have something to identify us."

"A name?" Renaldo asked.

"More than that. The public has to have a way to recognize us. To distinguish us from the hoodlums and punks we're trying to discourage. Maybe a uniform."

"Wouldn't that be too expensive? A lot of the kids who come with us don't have much money."

"You're right. Maybe a jacket, or ..." His voice trailed off as his eye caught an object on the desk.

"I've got it. It's perfect."

"What do you mean?"

"In Slapsy's honor. We'll all wear red berets."

Renaldo smiled. "That's perfect. The Red Berets we'll be."

sixteen

"Eric, what's that?" Jim asked.

Eric set down the three-foot-square cardboard box, then said, "Wow, that's heavy."

"What is it?" Jim asked again.

Eric smiled. "Contribution from dad. Two gross of whistles."

"That's nearly three hundred. We don't need that many."

"Dad suggested we hand them out. When we hand out those flyers telling people who we are and what we're trying to do. The idea is that even if the Red Berets aren't around, somebody might be in earshot who can help somebody in trouble. We don't want New Yorkers carrying knives or guns, so maybe we can have a couple million people with whistles looking out for themselves and each other."

"Terrific idea," Jim said. "I really like it."

"Dad suggested we might contact some whistle manufacturers. They might donate some, or help us promote the idea."

"We'll try that later. Right now we've got enough to do organizing our first patrols."

Juanita stuck her head in the door. "Jim. Another person to see you."

Jim groaned. "I've been interviewing for two days straight."

"How's it going?"

"Well, I hope. Considering I'm not a psychologist or anything. I'm trying to weed out the kids who are looking for a thrill, for a chance to bust some heads. I may be a hard ass, but I'm only taking people who are in school or who have a job."

"Why's that?"

"The last thing we need is for somebody wearing a Red Beret to get busted carrying dope or a gun or something like that. I can't ask people to take a lie detector test, and I can't hire a detective to investigate each one. I figure if a person is going to school full time or working on a regular job, that's an indication they understand responsibility. The rest I have to leave up to my gut reaction."

"Sounds good," Eric said.

"We'll find out starting tomorrow night," Jim said.

Juanita poked her head in again. "Jim."

"Okay, boss," he said, "send him in."

The man who came in the door and shook hands with Jim looked like a bright-colored beach ball with legs and arms. He wore a peach-colored long-sleeve shirt, baggy orange and blue tartan slacks, a misshapen blue cloth hat, and beige Adidas sneakers. As he walked, his sneakers splayed out in a wide angle in a sort of jaunty duck walk.

"Maxey Ritz," he introduced himself with a big smile.

Jim studied him for a moment. The man's face was jowly, with a prominent nose that descended into flaring nostrils. His lips were thick, as were eyebrows that seemed to be in constant motion as he talked. What was left of his hair was salt-and-pepper gray, and was plastered down in a futile attempt to cover his bald spot. Jim thought the man was in his sixties.

Jim offered him a seat, then sat behind his own desk.

"You're probably wondering," the man began, "what's Maxey Ritz, an old codger, doing taking up my valuable time. Well, I'll tell you. I read that article in the *News* a couple days ago, and since then I've been telling myself, Maxey, you get yourself down there. Shoulda been here the first day."

The enthusiasm in the man's voice brought a smile to Jim's face. "I appreciate that, Mr. Ritz. But—"

"Call me Maxey," he interrupted. "Everybody calls me Maxey. Ziegfeld, Minsky, all the big names. Fifty-six years on the boards, played every burlesque house in the country. Making people laugh—that was a career, I tell you."

This guy was a real character, Jim thought. An amusing character, though. "Pleased to meet you, Maxey. I can't say I know much about burlesque, though."

Maxey shook his head. "Nobody does anymore. Finished up at the Trocadero in Philly about 1962. Porno finally killed us off."

"Well," Jim said. "I appreciate your coming in. But the patrols we're setting up are pretty strenuous."

"I ride the subways every day," Maxey said. "Been riding them for years. All the years I spent on the hoof, I'm a railroad buff. Have to stick pretty close to home nowadays, so the subway's my hobby, you might say. Not much I can't tell you about every mile of the system."

Jim was growing a little impatient. "That's interesting. But I don't—"

Maxey leaned forward, placing his hands on the edge of the desk. "I can see it in your eyes, young fella. Time to get to the meat, as we used to say in burlesque. Well, I'll tell you the meat. I was riding the Dyer Avenue line, coming home from visiting a friend. The night before Thanksgiving. On the train on which your friend was killed."

Jim was jolted. "You what?"

"I'm ashamed of myself. Riding the subway as much as I do, you tend to keep to yourself. I saw them moving through the car and I knew trouble was coming. But I got off at the next stop and hurried right home to Audrey. Didn't know until yesterday the poor lady had been stabbed."

"You saw them?"

"Must have been them. I was in the car ahead, the third from the last. They were moving toward the rear of the train. I saw what looked like a knife handle in one of their pockets." He shook his head. "I'm ashamed of myself. I should have told the token-booth clerk or something."

"You couldn't have done anything then. I'm glad you came forward now. Do you think you'd recognize them?"

"Maxey Ritz? Fifty-six years in show business— never forgot a joke, never forgot a routine, never forgot a step—and I never forgot a face. When things got rough, I'd work the door at one of the Shubert houses on Broadway. They knew me from way back when. You let the wrong guy in the stage door, you hear about it. I didn't make many mistakes, I'll tell you."

"Will you talk to the police?"

"I'll do better than that, young fella," Maxey said. "I'll ride along and point them out, if they try again, which they will. And I can do more. You know, since my missus died three years ago, it's been me and Audrey in that apartment—Audrey is my parakeet. All my friends are dead or in Florida, or they just sit around all day watching television. To me that's the same as dying. I gotta keep on the move, that's why I ride the trains. Anything you want to know about the trains, I'll tell you. I'll set up schedules, tell you how to cover the most territory, tell you what and where the problems are likely to be. I talk to people, too, people who know things. The news vendors and the conductors and the shopping-bag ladies, at least some of them. They all know Maxey."

Jim pondered for a moment. His first reaction had been to dismiss the guy as a harmless old kook. But beneath the bluster was a genuine concern and a genuine intelligence. The same kind of savvy based on experience that Granny and Slapsy Huggins had.

He made a decision. Maxey Ritz, if he wanted to, was going to become the oldest Red Beret.

Their kiss was deep and lingering. When their lips parted, Sara said, "I've been waiting a long time for that."

"I know," Jim said. "I feel guilty about it."

"Good," Sara said with a smile. "That's probably the reason for the flowers."

"Ouch," Jim said.

"But no matter the reason, the flowers are nice. And so are you."

They kissed again, this one lingering on and on.

"Mmmmmm," Jim finally said. "That was nice."

"That's just an appetizer."

"Good," Jim said. "I'm starving."

"If you spent more time here, you wouldn't have such an edge on your appetite."

Jim smiled. "Who says I want to cut down on my appetite."

"Why I do believe you're a dirty old man, behind that serious facade."

"I used to be a dirty old man," Jim said. "Now I feel ninety years old, sometimes."

"You do look tired," she said as they moved toward the kitchen of her one-bedroom apartment. "I'm worried about you. And what's you're doing."

"I'm doing what I have to do," he said.

"How long is that going to take?" she asked.

"I'm not sure," he said. "I'm not sure where it's going."

"I wish I knew where we were going," Sara said.

"I know I've been distant," he said. "But—"

"Don't apologize," she said. "I'm not blaming you for anything. I want to tell you what I've been thinking about for my own life. Then you can think about how that fits in with yours."

"Fair enough," Jim said.

"Mostly," she said, "I've been thinking about where I want to be. This city seems so cold, so lonely. I'm tired of the steady stream of tragedies I see in the hospital every day. I grew up a country girl. I've been thinking more and more about a small-town practice. Where I could be part of a community. Where I could see children brought into the world, and watch them grow up and have children of their own." She paused, looking into his eyes. "Where I could have children of my own."

Jim stood for a moment, reading the sincerity in her blue eyes. Then he said, "That makes a lot of sense. You deserve that."

"What do you deserve, Jim?" she asked. "What do you want for your life? Now, it seems all you do is give and give and give, and get nothing in return."

"Sometimes," he said, "I think that way too. Sometimes I get resentful. But I also love how I feel when I help somebody. For all its faults, I love this city. I've thought a hundred times about leaving it, but—well, I haven't come up with any answers."

She put her arms around him. "I'm not making any demands, Jim. That was the whole issue of my leaving Bill. I'm not saying you have to drop everything today or this week or this month. But, soon, I have to know what you want and if I fit in. Is that fair?"

He kissed her gently. "Very fair. Too fair. I'll think about it. I promise you."

She rubbed her hand on his chest. "Good. And that's enough talk. What do you say, after our appetizer, we move on to the main course?"

seventeen

Jim ignored the extended hand. The smile vanished from Anthony Brown's face. He sat down in the chair opposite the desk and said, "Well. You got quite a collection of boy scouts out there."

"That has nothing to do with you."

"It concerns me a great deal," Brown said. "After all, we're the ones who are bankrolling you."

"Correction," Jim said. "That's one of the reasons I called you. You *were* bankrolling us. But I'm not taking another cent."

"That's foolish. You need—"

"I don't need blood money," Jim said with feeling.

"Wait a second. That's a hell of an accusation."

"It's not an accusation. It's a fact. I don't exactly know how your slimy racket with the Savage Skulls works. But I sure as hell hope the police find out and you get what you deserve."

Brown's face was red with anger. He rose and stood menacingly by the desk. "Listen, Mr. Boy Scout. You better watch what you call people. That's libel, for openers. I'm really going to enjoy watching you getting your ass kicked out on the street when you find nobody's going to pay you for sticking your nose in other people's business. You'll be selling pencils on the street."

"Maybe," Jim said. "But maybe a few less scum like you and your buddy Salvadore Santos will be on those streets."

Brown stiffened. "I've taken just about enough." He turned.

"Wait," Jim said. "One more thing."

Brown turned back. "Yea?"

Quickly, Jim snapped a picture with a Polaroid camera he had taken from a desk drawer.

Brown blinked at the flash. Then he sprang forward. "Give me that," he shouted.

Jim stepped back from the desk.

"I'm getting that camera," Brown snarled. "Or I'm going to break your ass up so—"

"Whose ass is gonna get broken?"

Brown turned. Renaldo stood in the doorway, arms crossed, glaring at him.

Brown took a step forward. Renaldo's arms dropped to his side. Brown stopped.

"Out," Renaldo commanded. "Now."

Brown stood still for a moment, debating. Then he turned toward Jim and said, "I'm going to remember this."

"If you don't get out, you'll have a lot more to remember," Renaldo said.

Brown shot Jim a last hostile glance, then without looking at Renaldo slipped past him.

Jim exhaled as he disappeared. "Thanks," he said to Renaldo.

"You get the picture?"

"Yes," Jim said.

"I'll take it over to Vinnie. Do I have time?"

"I'm going to give the briefing in a few minutes. You should make it back by the time I'm done."

The waiting room was filled by the nearly forty young people. Jim called for their attention.

"You were all briefed when you were interviewed," Jim began. "I want to go over a few things before you go out."

He picked up a brand-new red beret from a stack on the table. "You all know what this is. What it means, more than anything, is 'friend.' As you've been told, we're not patrolling the subways because we're trying to do the job of the police. We're out there not to arrest criminals, but to discourage crime. We want to educate people. What we're saying is, if good people are good citizens, there is no reason to be afraid. The only reason hoodlums and criminals have taken over is because people look the other way, refuse to get involved. This red beret says that we care. That we're not going to look the other way. That we'll help."

He put the beret down and picked up a whistle. "This is your weapon. We're not bullys, we're not fighters. Our purpose is to discourage trouble by our presence. We'll band together, to watch out for the passengers and each other."

"If something do go down, though," said a lanky teenager in the first row, "we be ready."

"You'll be ready to call the cops," Jim said firmly. "Your patrol leader will designate one of you to head for the phone, or for the conductor or the token booth, the instant the whistle sounds. The rest of you stay together. If somebody draws a knife or a gun, back off until help comes. We don't want anybody getting hurt."

He looked around the room. The faces were serious. They were good kids.

"One final thing. You're going to get harassed out there. People are going to call you names, bump you, maybe even spit on you. Whatever happens, you can't let yourself be provoked. One or two bad incidents and the public will think we're another gang, with some sort of con game behind it. You understand?"

There were nods of agreement.

Jim smiled. "Now, on to the good side. This is the first appearance of the red beret. A lot of people are going to ask you questions. Some might even offer you money, which you'll refuse. The attention will be flattering, but don't get too carried away. You still have to do your job—out the door at every stop, keep your eyes open. So be alert. Be proud. And come back safely."

The teenagers jumped to their feet and cheered. They surged forward, grabbing their berets off the table. Then the patrol leaders formed them into four groups, and they headed out on patrol.

Jim watched them leave. The office suddenly seemed empty.

"Good job, Jim."

Jim turned to see Jill Prentice in the doorway to a treatment room. He smiled. "I didn't know you were here."

"Good reporters know how to be invisible. What are your plans on this big night?"

"I'll be out checking up and supervising."

"Need somebody to ride shotgun?"

"Can't say no. Come on."

10:15 P.M. The Pelham local leaving 110th Street, Manhattan.

"Look here. We done got ourselves a boy scout."

Carlos Ortega pulled himself up to his full five feet six inches and stared straight ahead.

One of the four hecklers put his face right up next to Carlos's face. "You deaf, boy? Or just too dumb? What kind of hat you wearing?"

"It's a red beret," Carlos replied.

"Red beret," another mocked. "That looks like a hat for faggots. You want to suck my dick, boy scout?"

Carlos reddened.

The leader snatched the beret. "I thinks I want me a fag hat."

"Hey," Carlos shouted. "Give me that." He lunged forward. The two teenagers behind him grabbed his arms.

"The fag wants to do some fighting," said the kid who grabbed his beret. "We show him what we do to fags."

The train pulled into 103rd Street, and the doors opened. "Let's bring him along. We'll show him a real good time when—"

He stopped abruptly as he turned toward the door. In the opening stood a grim Renaldo. Behind him were three other Red Berets, all boxers from Huggins's gym.

The leader blanched. His eyes seemed to retreat back into his head. "Uh, we was, uh," he started to mumble, backing up.

"Give it back to him," Renaldo said.

"Okay. I was just—"

"Okay, sir," Renaldo commanded.

"Okay—sir," the punk said, handing the beret to Carlos."

"Now, split."

In an instant, the four were gone.

"Wow," Carlos said with a sigh of relief.

Renaldo smiled. "Don't worry. We'll always be here. They'll get to know soon enough."

11:35 P.M. The uptown express stopped at Fourteenth Street. Willy Carson started to board a car. A moment later, he backed off.

Eric called out, "What's wrong?"

Willy ran over and jumped into the car a second before the door closed. "Man, what a stink. Drunk in the corner. Must have thrown up and taken a dump in his pants. Ain't nobody going in there."

Eric thought for a moment, then said, "You can stay in here. But pop out and check the car at every stop."

Willy went down to the end of the car. As

the train moved, he thought to himself, some excitment. Riding around all night watching drunks sleep it off. What he wanted was some action. As it was, all that was happening was that his feet were getting tired.

The first two stops, he popped out, ran to the door of the next car, and peered in. The drunk was still curled up in the corner. The third time he checked, though, the man had rolled on to the floor. Willy was just about to turn away when he heard a choking noise.

He took a step forward. The man's head was slightly raised, his eyes were open, and he was gagging.

The stench was overwhelming, and for an instant Willy almost turned away. Then he blew his whistle, twice, and ran forward.

When he knelt, he could see the old man was choking on his own vomit. Instinctively, he cleaned the open mouth out with his fingers, then rolled the man over and pounded on his back. The man's face was blue, and his eyes were bulging.

Willy pounded repeatedly. The man coughed and phlegm flew out. Willy winced, suddenly aware of the stink again. But he could hear the rasp of breath being taken in.

Things began to happen quickly when Jim came running up beside him. Twenty minutes later, when the man was removed from the platform by stretcher, Jim said to Willy, "You saved his life. I'm proud of you."

Willy looked away, embarrassed. "Just an old wino."

Jim put his hand on his shoulder. "He's a person. A troubled person, maybe. But he deserves to live just like everyone else. And he will, thanks to you."

Willy felt a strange, wonderful feeling begin to grow within him. He, Willy Carson, had saved a man's life. Damn, his mother was going to be proud.

12:10 A.M. The Woodlawn Express. Northbound.

Baseline Jones leaned against the door as the train rumbled through the Bronx. For one of the few times in his life, he felt totally drained of energy.

To be able to spend his evenings on the subway, he'd started to drive the cab on the graveyard shift—2:00 A.M. to 10:00 A.M. By the time the rush hour came around, he was so tired he was a traffic hazard. When he got off, he went home, caught four and a half hours of sleep, then hiked to the Education Center for his reading lessons.

The exhaustion was only part of the problem with the schedule. The other was that he had no time for basketball. Before the last two weeks, he had trouble remembering two consecutive days when he hadn't been on the court. All the time he was growing up, the hours upon hours on the playground had been the most important part of his life. His reading problem made school a torture; home was a series of run-down, crowded apartments and a constant struggle to keep food on the table and clothes on people's backs.

But on the court, he was a king. While he'd practiced hour after hour, year after year, it seemed to him that he had a natural ability that had been stamped on his genes. With the ball in his hands, he felt a power, a control over his environment that existed nowhere else in his life. Every time he executed that jab fake, took the hard step toward the baseline, then soared up, up through the air to slam the ball through the hoop, it was a mystical experience he seemed to enjoy for the first time.

Basketball, however, was a boy's game. Baseline, despite his jive talk, wasn't a dumb jock. He had always taken seriously his responsibilities at home. Now, his relationship with Juanita was getting serious and they'd talked of marriage. And, finally, there was this involvement with Jim and the Red Berets. He'd survived the hazards of a ghetto childhood with a combination of quick wits and his superb basketball skills. Still, there had been plenty of times when he'd been scared and plenty of times he'd been lucky. He didn't want his kids to have to go through the hassles he did. That's why he was committing his precious time, and basketball would have to suffer.

The train jolted to a halt. Baseline noticed they'd emerged from the ground and were on the elevated portion of the run. He stepped outside, looking both ways. He counted the seven other Red Berets, then he stepped back inside.

The train moved and Baseline started to slip

back into his reflections. Then he heard what sounded like a choking noise.

He hadn't seen them get on at the last stop. A slender, light-skinned black girl, who couldn't have been more than seventeen. Huddled next to her, thumb in his mouth, was a chubby two-year-old boy. The girl carried a baby clutched to her breast. She rocked the baby gently back and forth as she sobbed.

Baseline saw the mother and boy wore light-weight clothing far too light for the bitter early December weather. The mother looked haggard and frightened.

He moved over and squatted down in front of her. "Hey," he said in a warm, soft voice, "what's wrong, momma?"

She turned away, clutching the baby even tighter.

"That's okay," Baseline said. "I'm not gonna hurt you. You need some help?"

The door to the next car had opened. Then Baseline was shoved roughly to the floor.

"There you are, bitch," a man snarled. He was unshaven and beer bellied, and he wore dirty work clothes and an old army field jacket.

"Hey," Baseline said, scrambling to his feet. "What do you think you're doing?"

The man shoved him again, then turned back toward the girl. Her eyes had widened in fright and she was whimpering.

The man grabbed her. "Come on, bitch."

"Leave her alone," Baseline said.

The man turned, glaring. "You want your ass whipped, motherfucker?"

"Leave the girl alone."

"This is my woman. You stay the fuck out of the way." He looked at the girl. "Get up," he commanded.

"No," she stammered.

The man slapped her. The girl shrieked and fell back on the seat. The man cocked his arm again and shouted, "Get up, cunt."

Baseline grabbed his arm. The man staggered a step backwards. When he got his balance, he shoved his shoulder into Baseline's stomach. Baseline fell, his back hitting the edge of a seat.

The man came toward him, muttering, "I'll show you."

Baseline fumbled inside his shirt, then pulled out his metal whistle and blew.

The man stopped, confused by the sound. The train slid to a stop. When the man got his balance, he aimed a kick at Baseline's ribs. The basketball player rolled out of the way.

Baseline saw Chang in the door about the same time the man did. The man turned and threw a roundhouse right. Chang calmly dodged the punch, stepped inside, and hit the guy once in the stomach. The man's eyes bulged out, then he crumpled.

When the man got his breath, he tried to get up. Then he saw that eight people wearing red berets were standing around him.

"You like these odds?" Baseline said.

"Wait. I ain't done nothing," the man protested.

Chang and another dark-haired kid grabbed his arms and hoisted him to his feet.

"You're waiting for the transit cops," Baseline said. He looked at Marguerite, who had just come into the car. "You see to the lady."

Marguerite went to the girl's side. She put her arm around her shoulder. "It's all right, honey. You tell me what's wrong."

The girl sobbed and embraced her.

eighteen

The Daily News
December 3, 1982

This urban melodrama was no less tragic for being a variation of stories played out every day in New York City.

The slender, shy girl was a widow at seventeen. With a two-year-old toddler and a six-month-old infant, she struggled unsuccessfully to make ends meet in a dingy, tiny South Bronx apartment. When she fell behind on her rent, the landlord threatened eviction. In days, she'd be out on the cold winter streets, she was told, unless—unless she gave her body to meet the landlord's demands.

When she refused, his words became more threatening. Then one nightmarish evening, he took what he wanted by force. Bruised and battered, she fled in the middle of the night, leaving behind all she owned. He caught up with her on a lonely subway train hurtling through the darkness.

On any other night, she may have been forced

back to debasement and humiliation. But last night, there was another man on that subway car. This man wore a red beret....

The mayor of New York answered four questions about the budget currently being debated in the state legislature. He pointed to a reporter from the *Soho News* next.

"Mayor, what's your reaction to the Red Berets?"

"The who?"

"The young people who've begun patrolling the subways to fight crime."

"Patrolling the subways is the job of the Transit Police," the mayor stated. "Commissioner Shelton and his men do a fine job."

"But subway crime has jumped 36 percent in the last year. Don't you think they need some help?"

"We're providing that help," the mayor snapped. "We've authorized the hiring of an additional 200 officers, and we've changed the assignment procedures to get more men out at high-crime periods on high-crime trains."

"Jill Prentice of the *News* rode with these Red Berets and she said she didn't see a single Transit cop on patrol. She didn't see a cop until these kids had caught two criminals and called 911."

The mayor shrugged. "Maybe Miss Prentice needs her eyes examined. Commissioner Shelton assures me his men are out there. And the last thing this city needs is vigilantes. Not while I'm the mayor. Next question."

*   .   *   *

Transit Police Captain Bill Devlin slammed his fist down hard on the copy of the *Daily News* sitting on his desk. "Dammit," he swore. "A bunch of niggers and spics running around making us look like fools."

He unleashed a string of expletives.

Lieutenant Blair said, "That guy Knight. Didn't he come in to see you? Can you talk to him?"

"Fuck him. He's like those peaceniks back in the Vietnam War. Creating a fucking mess just to get his name and picture in the paper."

"It'll blow over soon, captain. After all, what harm are they doing?"

Devlin's face got even redder. "What harm are they doing? We're the laughing stock of the city. Every city cop is snickering up his sleeve today. And wait until it comes to budget time. They'll be telling us to deputize grandmothers, for chrissake."

"So what do we do?"

Devlin leaned forward. "I'll tell you what we do. We watch these, these Red Berets like a hawk. I want the word to go out. I want to see summonses on my desk. They drop a cigarette butt, I want action. Crime fighters, my ass."

"I can't believe the mayor said that about you," Jim said.

Jill Prentice smiled. "He's said a lot worse in private. He's not my audience."

"You certainly have a hell of an audience. You're responsible for this whole concept taking off."

"No," she said. "All I did was write about it.

It's you and Renaldo and Baseline and the others who made it work. You can't manufacture a story where there isn't one. I was fortunate enough to run into real heroes. And the public wants to know about them."

"I guess they do. I've been besieged. Everybody wants an interview, wants to ride along with us. But I've turned them down."

"Why?"

"Because it's your story," Jim said.

"That's nonsense, Jim. I appreciate the sentiment. But it makes me feel like a press agent. I didn't discover you or artificially promote you. I'm glad I wrote the first article, but that's it. I think you should get as much publicity as you can. Every column of print, every foot of film, will help you toward your goal."

"I suppose you're right. Still—I don't want to feel like a press hound."

"You? Never."

"Thanks," he said.

Jill looked at him for a moment. "Is there something else? You sound like something else is wrong."

Jim looked down for a moment. Then he sid, "Yes, there is something else. Along with the good phone calls, we've been getting some of the other kind."

"What other kind?"

"The kooks. The ones who make threats. I'm afraid the same thing is happening that happens to cops. We've been portrayed as bigger-than-life heroes. Any nut who wants some press attention himself may find us an easy target.

Hell, unlike the cops, we're not even armed."

Jill thought for a moment. "I can see that could be a problem. I can't pretend those people aren't walking around out there. But that's the risk anybody takes when they try to effect social change."

Jim grimaced. "Big words. I know the risk. If it was myself, that would be one thing. But those kids. There's enough danger as it is—Baseline could have been really hurt by that guy last night."

"Jim," Jill said firmly. "That's the way it is."

Jim looked at her. Then he broke into a wry smile. "You sound like my old army instructors. And you're right. We can't pull back now. But I still can't help wondering how I'm going to feel the first time somebody is really hurt badly."

Santos held the receiver until he heard the click at the other end. Then he slammed the phone down. He paced for a few minutes, muttering. Then he grabbed a bottle of Southern Comfort from the bar and took a slug.

The others sat, watching him, not saying a word.

Finally, he slumped into the chair by the desk, then swiveled to face them. When he spoke, his voice was heavy with sarcasm.

"The man wants us to be good. The man wants us to lay back and let these jerks run around."

"Why?" Garcia asked. "We got ten times as many guys."

"I know," Santos said. "The man says let them

have their fun for a few days. The papers come, take pictures of them helping old ladies. Then, when the reporters go home, these guys will get tired and go home too."

"He could be right," said Stern.

"What?" Santos said.

Stern looked at him calmly. He was a fat kid with thick glasses, a big nose, and a face so blotchy from acne that his Savage Skull scar could barely be seen. He was the last person in the world anybody would have suspected to be in the inner clique of a gang. But he was a genius with money, and he knew where to get his hands on everything from cars to explosives. He was the only person who could talk back to Santos.

"Who wants to run around on the subway all night?" Stern asked rhetorically. "They won't last two weeks. Why should we worry?"

"Because everybody's gonna see that," Santos reported. "We spend months running all the punks, all the other gangs out of the area. Now they see these boy scouts with their little hats running around, see them talking about it on TV and in the papers, see them on the subway—everybody's gonna think the Skulls have turned pussy. People are gonna stop paying protection. And those assholes will be coming back in peddling dope again."

"Doesn't your man know that?" Stern asked. "He's no dummy."

"He doesn't have to go out to clean up the mess afterwards. And what are all the squads gonna do the next couple weeks? They'll get itchy. We'll have all kinds of problems."

Santos got to his feet again.

"I'll tell you what they're gonna do," he said. "They're gonna say, I need the money, screw the Skulls. Our guys will get on the train to Brooklyn or Queens and they'll start pulling jobs. By the time we get going again, a third of those dummies will have got themselves nabbed. Then we gotta recruit all over again. I say, fuck that."

"So what do we do?" Torres asked.

"I'll tell you what we do," Santos said. "We go after them. I went to school with Knight. He's a chicken, he even chickened out in Vietnam. A couple of his guys get messed up bad, they'll all run home."

"Yea," Torres said. "They ain't got no balls."

"And all those hotshot reporters," Santos added, "They'll have a story then. All over the papers and the TV, everybody will be reading about how the Skulls don't take no shit. Instead of a mess, we got things easier than ever."

Stern grimaced. "I don't know, Sal. What's the man gonna say?"

"You let me worry about the man," Santos snapped. He turned to Torres. "Listen up. Here's what you're gonna do . . ."

nineteen

"I think you ought to stay home tonight, Maxey," Jim said.

"I don't think you ought to think," the small roundish man said as he bounced along beside Jim. Tonight he was decked out in green and yellow plaid pants with a bright red sweater under his gray, fur-lined jacket. "Beside," he added, "I can't stay home. Audrey is entertaining."

"A parakeet is entertaining?"

"Twin pigeons," Maxey replied, shaking his head. "I told her, if you're gonna fool around, why not a high-class bird like a cardinal? She told me I'm lucky she doesn't have a taste for crows."

Jim laughed.

"I don't think it's funny," Maxey said. "But then again, Audrey hasn't seen me with any high-class birds recently either."

They reached the top of the escalator. Maxey

veered off toward the newsstand. "Speaking of birds," he said to Jim in a low voice. Then he called out, "Mrs. Kowalski, you doll. How are you?"

The heavyset old woman behind the counter broke into a big smile. "Just fine, Mr. Ritz."

"What's this Mr. Ritz? Come on darling. All my girl friends call me Maxey."

"What would my husband say?" she asked with a blush.

"He doesn't have to know," Maxey replied, giving her an exaggerated wink. Then he asked, "You see in the paper the other day about the Polish terrorist who tried to blow up a bus?"

The old woman looked puzzled. "No."

"The guy was so dumb, he burned his lips on the exhaust pipe."

Jim roared. A minute later, the news vendor got the joke and joined in.

"See you later, doll," Maxey said.

As they walked away, Jim said, "You seem to know everybody."

"As I told you, what else do I have to do? Maybe I don't get paid for it anymore. But I still like to make people laugh. And who needs it more than the people who have to make their living in the subway?"

"You're right."

"And I'm right about going with you tonight. Believe me, any trouble starts, you'll find me under the seat. After all, what do I have left except my good looks?"

The tension was so great that it hurt Tony to

breathe. His jaw ached, and he was unable to stop a tic that made his right eye blink.

Torres asked, "You nervous, kid?"

Tony's mouth was too dry to talk. He nodded.

Torres smiled. "That's okay. Everybody, they get a little tight. Even your brother, and he's one cool dude. I was with him the first time."

Tony moistened his lips, then asked, "The first time?"

"Yea," Torres said with a thin smile. "In the Mafia, they call it making your bones. That's when you really become a Skull, man. When the shit gets heavy and somebody goes down."

A knot had formed in Tony's stomach. He'd been able to call Jim to tell him that the Skulls were going out on the subway tonight. But he had no idea it was going to be this serious. If there was any way he could have gotten out of that room, he would have. But all he could do was sit and worry.

"And somebody is going down tonight, huh, Gomez?" Torres said.

"All the way," Gomez said. "Low as they can go." He took a drag on his cigarette, then asked, "When are we moving, man?"

"We wait."

"How long?"

"We're waiting until late. Guys are out on lookout. When the phone rings, we move."

"Tony told you the Skulls were definitely going out tonight?" Renaldo asked.

"Yes," Jim replied.

"And the Transit cops didn't listen?"

"You should have heard what Devlin called me. I'll tell you, I wouldn't trust myself alone in a room with him, he makes me so angry."

Renaldo grimaced. He was swaying back and forth as the train hurtled at high speed in the long run between Fifty-ninth and Eighty-sixth Streets. "I wish we were like the secret agents in those books," he said. "I wish that kid had a small microphone on him. Then we could find out where those guys are working. We've been riding for three hours and we haven't seen anything."

"If we ride all night and nothing happens, that's fine," Jim said.

"Something is going to happen tonight," Renaldo said. "I feel it. It's like before a bout. You train and you train, you watch films—it's like preparing for a chess match. Then you sit in your dressing room the night of the bout and the fear hits. About an hour before, you're in your trunks, it's too early to get up a sweat. You start thinking about the guy, and suddenly it's like he's ten feet tall and made out of steel. If you could get away with it, you'd run the hell out of there. Or fake an injury, or throw up. But then a voice tells you, you got to fight the man sometime. You want to rise up the ladder toward the championship, you got to take him. You did all the work, so it might as well be tonight."

"I see what you mean," Jim said. "But we're not moving up any championship ladder. We're not trying to prove anything."

"Aren't we?"

Jim pursed his lips. "Maybe. Anyway, it's out of our control. The ball is in their court."

Tony's mind had been working furiously all during the long wait. Finally, he stood up.

"Where are you going? We're moving."

"I got to go to the bathroom."

"Forget it," Torres snapped.

Gomez grabbed his arm. "Hey, the kid's nervous. We don't want him pissing on himself."

Torres considered it for a moment. "Okay. Make it quick."

"Where we hitting them?" Gomez asked as Tony left.

"Ace saw Knight on a northbound train leaving Eighty-sixth. They gotta come back south to go home. We'll wait for them there."

"Fourteenth Street?"

"Yea."

Tony came back into the room. Torres looked at him. "You got the weapons?"

Solemnly, Tony patted the pockets of the overcoat. He nodded.

"Let's go," Torres said.

The near empty train rattled through the darkness. When it stopped at Fifty-ninth Street, Renaldo peered out onto the deserted platform, saw ten heads at the doors of all the cars, then looked at the clock. It was nearly 2:00 A.M.

When the doors closed, he said to Jim, "What do you think?"

Jim shrugged. "I don't know. I'm too tired to think."

"Maybe their plans changed."

"Who knows?"

The train stopped at Grand Central Station, then picked up speed for the long run to Fourteenth Street. Jim slumped into a seat, numb with fatigue. The tension had sapped what little energy he had. He'd been living on four hours' sleep or less for the last two weeks, and it had finally caught up with him. Somehow, he had to get some rest.

Renaldo nudged him. "We're home."

Jim looked up. He hadn't noticed the train had stopped at Fourteenth Street. With a sigh, he hoisted himself to his feet and walked out of the car.

The members of the patrol slowly assembled. Jim was surprised to see Maxey Ritz.

"I thought you'd gotten off at home," Jim said.

"Fell asleep," Maxey said. "I'll get an uptown train."

Jim frowned. "I don't think that's a good idea."

"I'll give him a lift," Baseline said. "Gotta pick up the cab now anyway."

"Great," Jim said. He looked around. He counted nine people. "Guess we got everybody."

They moved up the stairs from the IRT platform. Their footsteps echoed eerily in the catacomblike station. Without the crowds of people that thronged through the station during the day, the gray dinginess seemed forbidding, like a long-undiscovered tomb.

At the top of the stairs, the lights had been smashed. They moved through the darkness, then turned right down a lighted corridor.

For the instant it took his eyes to adjust, Jim didn't see them. Then he stopped.

Torres was standing, arms folded, grinning smugly. Gomez stood to his left, Tony to his right. Behind him were a large group of other Savage Skulls.

"Look," Torres called out in a mocking voice. "The heroes are here. Nice pretty hats, like the girls wear."

Jim sensed Renaldo tense beside him. He touched the boxer's arm in a cautionary gesture. Then he asked in a deliberately matter-of-fact tone, "What do you want?"

"Want? Why should we want something?"

"You ain't here for a social call," Baseline said from behind Jim.

Torres smiled. "We wanted to see what heroes look like. Big shots with all the reporters." He nudged Gomez. "See, amigo, now we know. They all look like pussies."

Jim stood, staring at the provocatively arrogant gang members. Finally, he said, "We haven't got all night. Let's go."

He took a step forward. Torres's face turned menacing. "Now," he snapped to Tony.

His hand shaking, the boy reached into his pocket. An instant later, a gleaming .38 caliber revolver was in Torres's hand.

"Stop," Torres commanded.

Jim halted.

"I'll tell you what we want, motherfucker. This

is our turf you jerks have been walking over. Nobody walks over the Savage Skulls."

Jim's stomach was knotting, and his heart was beating so rapidly he could hear it. It had been a lot of years since he'd faced a gun. As he drew in one long painful breath, the memory swept over him—all the blood, the sea of blood of hundreds of men spilling out in hundreds of hamlets and jungles and rice paddies.

Then, with another breath, the memory was gone. When he spoke, his voice was firm. "The gun is foolish."

Torres's eyes flashed warfare. "Foolish, huh? Listen, you—"

"Jim. That's them."

"What?" Jim said. Maxey Ritz had come up next to him.

"That hoodlum with the gun. And the one next to him. They were the ones on the train that night Granny was killed."

"Tell the old man to shut up," Torres yelled angrily.

"They're the ones that killed her," Maxey said.

"Shut up," Torres shouted again.

A bottled-up surge of fury and venom exploded within Jim. He lunged forward at Torres.

The Savage Skull pulled the trigger. Click. Click. Click. The hammer fell on empty chambers.

"Shit," he grunted in the instant before Jim smashed his fist into his sternum. Torres tumbled backwards.

"The blades," Gomez yelled at Tony.

For an instant, the boy froze. Then he dashed toward the Red Berets.

"Motherfucker," Gomez spat. Then he saw the bulk of Renaldo moving at him. He turned and ran.

The rest of the Skulls took flight. The Red Berets surged forward. Jim, who'd stood breathless for a second staring at Torres, dove for the murderer. Torres scrambled away, then leaped to his feet as he followed his gang.

Baseline caught the first one, a heavyset black kid in a denim jacket. He grabbed his collar and slammed him into the concrete wall. "Forget him," Jim shouted. "I want Granny's killers."

They sped past a shuttered newsstand and a Nedick's hot dog counter. Gomez, ten yards ahead, darted down the stairway toward the BMT platform. Renaldo veered off in that direction, followed by two other Red Berets.

Jim hesitated a second. Then he saw Torres vault the turnstile and sprint past the token booth toward the stairs to the street. Jim took off after him, with Baseline at his shoulder and the twins several steps behind.

Tony came to a stop just before the turnstiles. He watched the Red Berets disappear up the stairs. Suddenly, he was alone and scared. Where could he go?

Then a hand touched his shoulder and he turned. "Don't worry, son," Maxey said. "Maxey Ritz will take care of you."

The boy stared at the kindly face of the old man.

Maxey took his arm and guided him through

the turnstile. He ckecked to see that the token-booth clerk had called the police. Then he came back to Tony.

"You did a brave thing, son," he said. "I'll see that you'll be all right."

Gomez had jumped off the platform onto the tracks. Renaldo jumped down and ran a few steps into the tunnel. He started down the murky depths, listening. All he heard were the inexplicable sounds of the tunnel—rustlings, creakings, the faint rush of wind. Beyond, the signal lights gleamed like blood red jewels in the darkness.

"What are we going to do?" Chang asked.

"Shhh," Renaldo whispered.

Then he heard a clattering of feet. Ahead, he got the fleeting impression of a slender body flashing from behind a pillar down the tracks.

Renaldo took off in pursuit. He ran at less than full speed, concentrating on keeping his footing as he stayed between the rails. "Be careful," he hissed back at his companions.

They rounded a curve. Ahead, several hundred yards away, a naked bulb burned over an emergency exit. Renaldo saw Gomez clearly now, leaping for the ladder. He accelerated.

Then Renaldo tripped. He sprawled onto the slimy tunnel floor, his left knee crashing into the rail. His lower leg went numb.

Chang pulled at his arm. "You okay?"

"Yes," Renaldo panted. "Let's get him."

The ladder was slippery with dampness and grime. Gomez's lungs burned, and he felt like he had a hundred pound weight on his back as he climbed.

At the top, he paused. He heard the sound of someone falling back in the tunnel and a surge of hope gave him strength. He pushed on the emergency-exit grating. It didn't budge. He tried again. Nothing.

The third time, the rusty hinges creaked. He shoved with all his energy and the grate moved upwards as a shower of particles fell on him. He let the weight of the grate help him climb upward. He was free, he thought. Those jerks—

Suddenly, his ankle felt like it had been caught in a vise. A jolt of adrenaline went through him. He tried kicking out, but the ankle turned, sending a shooting pain through the joint.

"One more kick, asshole," Renaldo said sternly, "and I'll tear this leg right off."

The night wind whistled through the canyons of the city. The cold air slapped Jim as he paused at the edge of Union Square. A moment earlier, he'd seen Torres dart across Fourteenth Street and into the park that was the notorious hangout for dope dealers, junkies, and other jetsam of New York street life.

The park was three blocks long and one wide block wide. Jim's mind raced as he developed a plan.

"Eric," he said, "You and John cover the north end. One of you on each corner. If you see him, whistle."

They ran off. He turned to Marguerite and Baseline. "You two take a corner down here. The cops should be along in a few minutes."

"What are you going to do?" Baseline asked.

"Flush him out," Jim replied.

"Be careful, man."

Jim smiled. "I used to do this for a living."

Torres stopped in the middle of the park. He bent over, hands on knees, gasping for breath. His lungs burned and he had a pain in his side like somebody had stabbed him with a knife.

He wished he had a knife right now. He could almost feel it, the handle of the blade in his grasp. With a blade he could take anybody.

The pounding of the blood through his head subsided a little. He stood up and looked around. In the summer the park would be full of dudes all night long, drinking wine, blowing weed. But it was freezing cold now, and besides, the Skulls had driven off all the independent dealers working their turf.

Torres listened. He didn't hear any pounding feet yet amid the hum of traffic from the streets around the park. He started moving north, ready to leave the path at any time. The only shapes he saw were lumps on the benches, winos wrapped in rags and old newspapers.

He slowed as he reached the end of the square. He looked out through the bushes. He saw the dude wearing the red beret standing on the corner of Seventeenth and Broadway.

He could make a dash for it, but there was no cover. He didn't know if he could outrun the guy.

So he turned right, moving east. The northeast part of the park was cut off diagonally by a road lined with cars parked head in. Cautiously, Torres left the bushes, crossed the sidewalk, and used the cars for cover to creep along.

Halfway, moving in a crouch, he saw a gleam. An empty quart bottle was sticking out of the top of a trash can. A warm, excited feeling went through him as he pulled it out and slapped the butt end into his palm. Now he had a little edge.

John Siebert stood on the traffic island, tense and alert. His whistle was in his mouth for use at the first sign of the creep they were chasing.

The problem was that he couldn't hear anybody else's whistle. Most of the time, he didn't think of his deafness as a handicap. But now, stalking for the killer of Granny Moore, he was keenly aware that he could use that extra sense.

He'd been startled twice, once by a drunk stumbling out of the bushes, the second time by a nighttime cyclist coming up behind him. He barely stopped himself from blowing his whistle. A false alarm could create an opening for the killer to escape.

John swiveled his head back and forth, like a beacon. The streetlights and the headlights of moving cars created moving shadows that were deceptive.

His eyes caught movement a few yards away, between the cars parked on the outer side of the road. He tensed, his lips tightening on the whistle as he stared. Seconds passed and he saw nothing.

With an exhale of held breath, he relaxed. He turned back the other way. He had to be careful—

Only because of his especially good peripheral vision did he pick up the movement at all. He started to blow the whistle, then stopped himself. As he pivoted he saw the glint of something raised above his head. He instinctively raised his right arm and the numbing blow deflected off his wrist to his shoulder. He stumbled, but managed to get off one blast on the whistle. Then an explosion went off inside his head and he slumped, unconscious, to the pavement.

Jim had been moving with cautious speed along the path. His eyes had adjusted to the darkness, but still he knew he could easily miss a man in the shadows. He was gambling that Torres's only thought would be escape, so he was concentrating on the perimeters of the park.

Fortunately, he was near the east side of the park when he heard the whistle. He accelerated instantly as he leaped a bench, tore through the brush, and hit the concrete sidewalk.

A jolt of concern hit him when he saw the body on the sidewalk. For an instant, he hesitated between stopping to help his friend and chasing the figure disappearing down Seventeenth Street. Then he saw Eric running toward him and he made his decision. He had to catch the killer.

Just a few moments earlier, he had been exhausted. Now, as he sprinted down the street, he got his second wind. All those miles of jogging every day finally paid off. The stride of the teenager ahead of him was wobbly and the distance between them was narrowing quickly.

Torres crossed Irving Place and headed toward Stuyvesant Square. Jim could see him clearly now, less than half a block away. Then Torres stopped abruptly. He turned to face the onrushing Jim, the bottle raised over his head.

Jim halted a dozen steps away. His quarry was panting heavily, and his face shone with perspiration.

"Put it down," Jim commanded. "There's nowhere to go."

With a quick flick of his wrist, Torres slammed the bottle into the edge of the brick building. Grinning, he jabbed the broken edge toward Jim. "Yea, motherfucker," he snarled.

"You got nowhere to go," Jim said. "The cops will be here any minute."

"Fuck the cops," Torres growled, moving forward.

Jim, on his toes, stayed just out of reach. "You're hurting. Want to run some more?"

Torres glared at him savagely. "Pussy. Faggot," he taunted.

"You're brave with that weapon," Jim said. "Especially with women and children."

Torres grinned demonically. "The old lady," he said. "The knife went in so easy."

"What?"

"She died so nice," Torres mocked. "Just like you're gonna get it. Her blood, on the floor of that train. Lots and lots of blood."

The rage burned white hot in Jim, and his reason was buried under the red-hot lava flow of emotion. He charged.

His momentum carried him past Torres, who stepped aside and slashed. The bottle missed him by a hair. But when Jim turned back, the razorlike glass edged sliced the flesh under his chin, blood erupting over the hand that held the bottle.

Jim lashed out with his foot, catching Torres in the knee cap. Torres spun, and the bottle came out of the darkness again. Jim blocked the thrust with a downward karate chop. Then he grabbed the forearm with both hands, yanking it upward against his blood-soaked neck, wrenching the arm diagonally. The bottle creased the cloth of his jacket. Jim spiraled the arm dwnward, twisting the wrist now in his grasp, crashing his shoulder into Torres's body. He yanked again as the teenager tipped sideways off balance.

Jim heard the clatter of the bottle on the sidewalk. He lurched toward the sound. As he bent, a kick caught him in the side of the head. He rolled, twice, until he smashed into the side of the building. Leaping to his feet, he tried desperately to focus amid the shadows. In the thin light of the streetlamp, he caught the flash of a hand. He lunged at it, gripping it in both of his hands. He snapped back, as hard as he could.

The wrist broke. A scream of terrible pain echoed through the night air, mixing with the sounds of sirens in the distance.

twenty

Heinrich Siebert looked stricken, paralyzed by grief. His normally florid skin had turned gray, and his fleshy face sagged. He partially leaned on Eric as he shuffled down the corridor away from the hospital room that held his son.

"My boy," he said. "He doesn't even know me."

"Dad," Eric said. "Let's go. We'll get coffee."

They were approaching the waiting room. Mr. Siebert saw Jim sitting in a plastic chair. His eyes narrowed, and his face started to turn red.

"Why? tell me why?" he shouted, moving toward Jim. "Why did you do this to my son?"

Jim looked up, startled. His own face was pale and he still felt weak and nauseous from his throat wound, which took twenty stitches to close.

"Mr. Siebert. I—"

"My boy. You're crazy, running around with

208

the animals. He was a good son. I should take you and throttle you."

"No, dad," Eric said firmly. He grabbed his father by the upper arms. "You don't know what you're saying."

"My son," Mr. Siebert intoned, his voice now more of a wail.

"I think he could use a sedative."

Eric saw Sara, dressed in a white doctor's coat, next to him. "Can you give him one?"

"Bring him this way."

As Jim watched them move off, his heart felt like it was being squeezed by an iron fist. In the moment in which he'd stood over the whining, writhing killer of Granny Moore, he'd been as high as a kite. The intense animal sense of triumph flushed through his veins. He'd felt revenged, the pagan ferocity of the warrior.

Long ago, however, he'd foresworn that ferocity. During the ride to the hospital for his own treatment, then during the long wait in the dingy, pea green room littered with cigarette butts and soda cans, the weariness had washed away the triumph. With the exhaustion came the despair of knowing that his revenge may have cost the life of John Siebert, his friend.

He was so lost in thought he didn't realize Sara had sat next to him.

"Jim, it's time for you to go home."

"How is John?"

"It's too early to tell. You can't help him by sitting here. That cut came within a half inch of your jugular vein and you lost a lot of blood."

He looked at her with determined eyes. "Tell

me how John is. I want to know exactly what's happening."

"Okay," she said. "I'll tell you. The bottle hit him about here." Sara pointed to a spot on the right front side of her head, just above the hairline. "The skull at that point was really crushed. He must have lost consciousness instantly. He's in a coma now."

"That sounds awful."

"That doesn't mean he can't recover," Sara said. "A coma is the body's way of resting, in a way. I've seen people, a lot of people, come out of a coma after a few days and be perfectly normal."

"What about John? Are you saying he's going to be all right?"

Sara frowned. "I don't know. I'm not an expert in neurosurgery. I don't even think the specialists can predict right now."

"Why not? Are they hiding something?" Jim asked.

"No. You see, there's so much we don't know about the brain. The response of the brain to injury is swelling, just like an ankle swells when you sprain it. The problem is that inside the skull there is very little room for expansion. Unless the swelling is stopped, the brain stem is literally squeezed to death."

"But John's alive."

"They got him here quickly," Sara said. "Bellevue has a lot of experience with traumatic head wounds. They injected some drugs to help control the swelling, then rushed him into surgery. The neurosurgeon cut away part of the skull, cleaned out the fragments of bone and damaged brain cells, and vacuumed out dangerous blood clots. During the operation, John's blood pressure stabilized and the swelling seemed under control."

"There was brain damage then. Is he going to be—be different if he survives?" Jim asked.

"It's hard to tell. I think the chances—the chances are he'll be able to function normally. The brain is very resilient in a way, and he didn't lose that many cells. On the other hand, a blow that hard reverberates like a shock wave through the brain. Sometimes there is damage that doesn't even show on a CAT scan. Damage that won't be apparent when he wakes up—or for months afterwards."

Jim took her hand. "When will that be? When will he wake up?"

"With luck, three or four days. That's why it's no use, your sitting here. You need your rest."

"You're right," Jim admitted. "I'm so tired I can't think."

Sara stood. "I've got an idea. I'll take you to Connecticut. Right now. Nobody will know you're there. Mom and dad are in Florida for two weeks. You can rest all you want."

"What about your schedule?"

"It doesn't matter. This is more important."

Jim got to his feet. He fought a brief wave of dizziness, and Sara steadied him. "Thanks."

"We'll go down the freight elevator and out the back," Sara said.

"Why?"

"A herd of reporters has been waiting downstairs for hours."

"I hate to duck them."

"You don't have the strength," Sara said. "Doctor's orders, you're going with me."

"Of course, I'm in favor of apprehending murderers," the mayor said emphatically. "No one has spoken up more often than I have about a firmer stance on crime in this city. But I can not, I will not approve vigilantism."

"Don't citizens have a right to defend themselves?" a reporter asked.

"Of course they do," the mayor said. "Did I say they didn't? But we can't have gangs of people prowling the streets or subways, taking the law into their own hands. After all, we have a constitution and criminal-justice procedures the police must follow."

Jill Prentice rose. "Are you saying that the Red Berets are hoodlums?"

"Don't put words in my mouth, young lady. They may be fine young men, for all I know. But one of them is lying in a hospital unconscious. According to Commissioner Shelton of the Transit Police, we almost had a riot in Union Square Station last night. I want every citizen to do his duty as a citizen—obey the law, cooperate with the police. But let the police do police work."

"Even if crime is soaring? Even if murderers go free?" Jill asked.

"You can't have people breaking the law to stop other people breaking the law."

"How are the Red Berets breaking the law? Aren't there such things as citizens' arrests?"

The mayor glared at her. "Commissioner Shelton will hold a press conference this afternoon. I don't want to talk about this anymore."

"I thought—"

"Your job is not to think," Anthony Brown said sarcastically. "I told you, the orders were to leave them alone. But no, you have to go out and play cowboy. Look what happens."

He held up a copy of the *Daily News* with a front-page headline, "Red Berets Nab Slayers." "Every day they become bigger heroes," Brown added, shaking his head. "I thought you were smarter than the average street punk, Santos. I guess I was wrong."

"I had to do something. They were all over my turf."

"Your turf? Listen, kid, you don't own nothing. We're setting up an operation that will make a fortune, and you're playing kids' games. You want to play like an animal, I'll send you up to the Bronx Zoo."

Santos's lips were pressed together so hard they were white. His hands were clenched in his lap. "All right," he finally said in a low tone, "Maybe—maybe I made a mistake."

Brown settled in the chair behind his desk. He took a cigarette from his case, lit it, then leaned back to watch the smoke drift toward the ceiling. Finally, he said, "Okay. Now we have to get rid of these—these crime fighters. The organization is going to have to contribute some of its clout. I want to know everything you know about these guys. Knight. The boxer. All of them."

"All right. I—"

"One thing first, Santos," Brown said sternly. "This time is the last time, if you don't do it our way. You even glance the other way, the ball game is over. You understand?"

twenty-one

Renaldo slowed to a walk, then moved through the midday crowd of shoppers on Fourteenth Street. His gray sweat suit was completely soaked through with perspiration, despite air temperatures in the upper thirties. His breathing was heavy, but not labored. When he glanced at his watch, he smiled in satisfaction. He'd had a good workout today.

A lot of boxers, especially heavyweights, slogged along slowly in their road work, more concerned about the number of miles they covered than the quality of the work. Renaldo trained like a competitive runner, pushing himself as if he were preparing for a marathon.

Today was speed work. Eight miles in slightly over seven minutes a mile. Tomorrow he'd stretch it out, a slower fifteen-mile run for stamina. The running was tedious and often painful. But every time he thought about cutting a run short, he saw in his mind's eye the last rounds of a fight, his opponent breathing through his mouth, his eyes glazing with fatigue. Then Renaldo would reach down to the well for that carefully nurtured reserve of energy that would carry him on to victory.

His breathing had returned to normal after a block walk, when he reached the door of the 14th Street Gym. The place was a definite step down from Slapsy's gym. The stairs were dark and filthy. A sign at the top warned Anyone caught stealing will be barred from the gym. Inside, paint peeled from walls and ceilings, stuffing leaked out of the heavy bags, and the locker room was the size of a prison cell.

Only two things were the same. One was the heady smell of canvas and liniment and sweat. The other was the single dream of a championship shared by the men who waited their turn to pound the hell out of each other in the ring.

In the long hours spent at Slapsy's bedside, Renaldo couldn't see how he could bring himself to fight again. But now his desire to prove himself, to be champion, was stronger than ever. He'd resumed his brutally hard training regimen.

Renaldo walked across the gym to get a drink of water. Then he slumped to a bench to untie his running shoes.

"I've been waiting for you," a voice said.

Renaldo looked up. He recognized Bob Duncan of the *New York Post*, a young, long-haired boxing writer. Renaldo thought that Duncan made an unusual effort to be fair and honest in his reporting. Renaldo had found a lot of other boxing writers to whom neither adjective could be applied.

Renaldo smiled and said, "Slumming today, huh, Bob? You must be hard up for a story."

Duncan's expression was serious. "I came to ask you about Sammy Curran's announcement. I guess you haven't heard."

"Heard what?"

"Curran announced that your fight with Thunder Wilkins was off."

Renaldo's mouth dropped open. He was stunned. "He can't do that. We have a contract."

"He says the contract's been broken."

"By who?"

"By you," Duncan replied. "He called you a thug. He made a bunch of statements about fighters who take to the streets to use their fists ought to be banned from the sport. He mentioned some kid in the Bronx who tried to file assault charges against you a few nights ago."

"That kid was a rapist," Renaldo said. "Besides, the charges were dropped."

Duncan shrugged. "I don't think Curran gives a shit about the facts. He was just interested in laying a real heavy rap on you."

Renaldo pounded his open hand against the wall. "That's ridiculous." He put his hands on his waist, trying to breathe deeply to calm himself. "Am I crazy? I'm out trying to stop punks from sticking knives in people, and I'm a thug? He can't be serious."

"Curran doesn't fool around."

"I don't either," Renaldo said grimly. "He can't get away with this. I'll sue."

"Sure. And maybe you'll win. After a few years in court. After $20,000 or $30,000 in legal bills. And no fights to bring in the money to pay them."

Renaldo sighed. "God, I wish Slapsy wasn't lying in that goddamn oxygen tent. He'd know how to handle this."

"Can I give you some advice?" Duncan asked.

"Of course."

"Curran knows that you're the only guy around except the champ who can give Thunder a big payday. That means somebody had to lean on him real hard to get him to call this off."

"Who's that?"

"Come on, Renaldo. You know this sport's a sewer. The Mob's got influence all over the place. Slapsy was so experienced, so connected, he could tiptoe through without getting dirty. But not many other people can."

"So what are you saying?"

"I think this is a warning. Somebody doesn't like you playing around with these Red Berets. Say you're sorry, promise you'll be a good boy in the future, and you'll find the fight is on again."

"And if I don't?"

"Who knows? Without somebody with clout behind you, you're gonna be really up against it."

"Meyer. You can't do this to me!"

The stocky, bald man turned away.

Baseline grabbed him by the shoulder. "I'm talking to you, man. You listen."

"Jones, you're fired. That's it."

"I'm the best driver you got. Half these other dudes don't last two weeks. The other half are drunks or can't speak English or spend most of the night figuring out how to cheat you."

Meyer tried to get away again.

Baseline, who towered a foot over the man, grabbed him by both shoulders. "Talk to me, Meyer. Talk to me."

Meyer glared at him. Then his face sagged. "You want to know the facts?" he asked in a resigned voice. "I'll tell you the facts. I play the ponies. And the trotters. And basketball and football and baseball."

"Yea," Baseline said. "I know."

"Well, lately, I ain't been doing so hot. I'm in deep. Like the Grand Canyon, that's how deep."

"Then you need your best driver working."

Meyer sighed with exasperation. "Don't you get the message, you're so smart? They can lean all over me anytime they want. I'm no big guy, I run four cabs. They tell me you're fired, the cabs roll. If not, I find four burned-out wrecks in some alley by the docks in Brooklyn. You understand?"

Baseline stared at Meyer. "Who's they?"

"*They?*" Meyer said. "Everybody knows who *they* are. The thing is, Jones, I like you. I'm telling you, you pissed them off. You better keep a close watch on that big black ass of yours."

*　　*　　*

When the doorbell rang, Tony retreated into the back bedroom. He stood, tense, listening while Maxey answered the door.

"You Mr. Ritz?"

"Maxey Ritz. That's me."

The man in the brown topcoat flashed a gold shield. "Detective Reynolds. You got a kid named Tony Melendez here?"

"Why yes. Poor boy, he—"

"Where is he?"

The tone of the detective's voice upset Maxey. "What is this? What's going on?"

"The kid's mother says you kidnapped him."

"Kidnapped? That's ridiculous. The poor boy had nowhere to go. He wanted to come here."

"Show us where he is. Now."

Maxey said, "Okay." He turned and called out, "Tony."

There was no response.

"Tony. Gentlemen to see you."

When there was no response again, Reynolds and his partner brushed by Maxey. The window in the back bedroom was open. Tony wasn't in the room.

Reynolds said to his partner. "Kid must've gone down the fire escape." He turned to Maxey. "Get your coat. You're coming with us."

"I don't understand."

"The kid's a minor. And his mother says he's missing. You've got some talking to do."

Marguerite Washington hung her robe on a hook, then stepped into the shower. She adjusted the water to be as hot as she could stand. Then she closed her eyes, letting the heat sink into her tired muscles.

Practices the last two weeks had been grueling. With the additional pressure of patrolling with the Red Berets, Marguerite found herself struggling to keep up at times. She'd even been forced to stop attending karate classes for the first time in years.

After a few minutes, she picked up the bar of soap and began washing her lithe, firm five-foot-ten-inch body. She was very proud of her physical condition and the skills she'd so laboriously developed. This season, her senior year, was going to be her high point. Her high school was cofavorite to win the city championship. And she had received nearly a hundred letters from colleges interested in offering her a scholarship.

Reluctantly, Marguerite turned off the water and stepped out of the shower. As much as she'd like to linger, she had hours of homework and a term paper to write. Keeping up her grades was another priority, for she was determined to go to a college that combined high academic standards with a good basketball program.

She was drying her hair with a towel as she walked to her locker. Then she stopped, surprised.

The contents of her locker were strewn all over the benches. Standing there, looking at her somberly, were Miss McKeever, her coach, and Mrs. Delancy, the assistant principal.

"You've got some explaining to do, young lady," Mrs. Delancy said sternly.

"What is this?" Marguerite asked.

"You're suspended immediately," Miss Mc-Keever said. "I don't know how you could do this."

"Do what?" Marguerite asked.

Then she stared in disbelief as Miss McKeever held up two marijuana cigarettes. "We found these in your locker."

The shotgun blast hit the center of the plate glass window, shattering it instantly.

They poured through the opening, working quickly and methodically. Every drawer, every file cabinet was dumped. Then they soaked the contents with gasoline.

Two were struggling with a huge iron safe when Cisco inspected the storeroom.

"Leave it," he ordered.

"But there's dope in here, man."

"I said, leave it." He smiled. "We'll leave the man something."

An hour later, Cisco stood on a rooftop with Santos watching the firemen try in vain to douse the blaze that was totally destroying the storefront that had housed the Lower East Side Health Clinic.

"That's it for Knight," Cisco said with a sneer.

"Yea," Santos said. "You've done half your job. You know the other half?"

"My brother."

"I want it long and slow. Nobody but nobody sells out the Savage Skulls."

Jim was sitting by the phone, his head resting in his hands.

Sara came into the room. "Well?" she asked.

He looked at her with pain in his eyes. "It's turned into a nightmare."

"Maybe it's for the best, Jim," Sara said, rubbing her hand over his back. "Now we have time for us. We'll get in the car tomorrow and start driving north. When we find the town that's right, we'll know it."

"And what will I do while you're practicing?"

"Whatever you want to do. You've given enough to everybody else. It's time to take care of yourself. And me."

He took her hand, put it up to his face, then kissed it. "I've got to go back to New York tomorrow."

"Do you have to?" she asked.

"Yes. My friends need help with the mess they're in. And I've got to see the insurance people about the clinic. And a lot of other things."

"No. You shouldn't go."

"I've got to."

Her expression was morose. Finally, she sighed and asked, "How long will you be?"

"A couple days. Maybe three."

"Promise?"

His heart felt like a huge, heavy chunk of ice. "Promise. This is the end of the Red Berets."

twenty-two

"So you want to take on the mayor?" asked Don Schiller, executive editor of the *Daily News.*

Jill Prentice swept her hand over the mound of mail and telegrams on her desk. "Look at this. And the telephone's been ringing off the hook."

"You feel strongly about this?"

Jill nodded.

Schiller smiled. "So do I. Go ahead. You've got the space. Coordinate it with Wayne Coffey in editorial."

"Great. Thanks."

Before he left the office, Schiller added, "One more thing."

"Yes?"

"When you see that guy Jim Knight, tell him for me I think he's come up with a hell of an idea."

Jill had never seen anything like the response

she'd received to the latest front-page story of the Red Berets' dramatic capture of the two suspects in the killing of Granny Moore. While her earlier stories about Jim and his young friends had stimulated interest, they didn't have the emotional impact of the battle with the Savage Skulls.

Part of the response was due to sympathy for the brave John Siebert, now in a coma at Bellevue. But the intensity of the outpouring stemmed, Jill felt, from the negative, sarcastic response of the mayor, the Transit Police commissioner, and other public officials. The average citizen in New York, Jill believed, had a profound feeling of helplessness. To people plagued by crime, filthy streets, substandard schools, decaying highways, and dangerous mass transit systems, the city government responded, "That's the way things are. We're doing the best we can. Don't bother us."

The message of the Red Berets was, however, that "the city belongs to us. The streets belong to us, the subways belong to us, the parks belong to us, the buses belong to us." After all, the Declaration of Independence stated that "Governments are instituted among men, deriving their just powers from the consent of the governed, that whenever any form of government becomes destructive of these ends, it is the right of the people to alter or to abolish it."

With crime striking fear into the heart of every decent, law-abiding New Yorker, it was time for the citizens to do their duty, to exercise their right to control their own destiny. If, despite their best efforts, the police couldn't do the job, then the public would have to drive out the jackals. In his effort to find the vicious murderers of his friend, Jim Knight had sounded a clarion call that reverberated in the hearts of the people of his city.

Beth had convinced the management of her paper to let her publicize that response. In one day, in hundreds of calls and letters, were the human dramas typical of the nation's cities:

Jackson Heights, Queens

Pamela Leonard, a slender, pretty seventeen-year-old girl with rich, black hair and smooth mahogany skin, stood patiently waiting for the number 7 subway train that would take her home for a late dinner. The daughter of Leroy Leonard, a paraplegic due to an injury in Vietnam, and Viola Leonard, who worked as a checkout clerk in a supermarket, Pamela knew her parents had to struggle to make ends meet. So she worked all through high school, three nights a week and Saturdays, at her uncle's shoe-repair shop. The money paid for music lessons.

As usual, she was carrying her flute with her. She took every opportunity to practice—free periods at school, even her breaks at work. Her teacher thought she had a great deal of promise, and Pamela had applied for a scholarship at a music conservatory.

She was thinking of a new piece she was

working on, playing the tune in her mind, when the lights of the train appeared. Without warning, somebody crashed into her, propelling her forward. She desperately fought to regain her balance. Then, with an agonized scream, she tumbled onto the tracks as the engineer of the train frantically applied the brakes.

The next morning, her anguished family waited in the hospital. Finally, the doctor came out to tell them that Pamela would live. But her right arm had been so mangled that there was no hope of reattaching it. She'd never play the flute again.

Pamela's boyfriend, Tim Payne, captain of his high school football team, was particularly outraged by the vicious assault. Pamela was the fourth victim of a psychopath who had terrorized Queens riders for two months. As tears of sorrow and rage filled his eyes, Tim spotted the cover story of the *Daily News* on the waiting-room table.

Fifteen minutes later, he had made up his mind. He'd get the guys on the team together. Then they'd contact the Red Berets.

Tremont Avenue, The Bronx

The brutal war in El Salvador had claimed the lives of two of Eduardo Sanchez's brothers. Every day, when he awoke, he thanked the good Lord who brought him, his wife, and his two sons to America. Although he was still living in a run-down building in a ghetto neighborhood, his life was far better than it had been at home. Eduardo was confident that it would get far better still. He'd driven a taxi until he'd managed to save the money to purchase a small *bodega* in his neighborhood. Working sixteen hours a day, seven days a week, he built the business to the point where he rented the next store as a fruit-and-vegetable stand. The proceeds from both businesses would soon amount to enough money to purchase a small house in a better neighborhood.

One shadow darkened Eduardo's horizon. Following the advice of the other merchants in the neighborhood, he had grudgingly paid the $25 a week protection money to the local street gang. The idea of paying someone not to commit a crime made him angry, but with the cost of replacing broken glass, he could look at it as more insurance.

But as he grew more successful, the demands of the gang grew. Two days before, the gang leader came in to demand that he double the payoff, to $200 a week.

That had been the last straw. Eduardo was a big, strapping man strengthened by long hours of lifting cartons of canned goods and crates of vegetables. He'd lost his temper and bodily thrown the hoodlum out of his store. Afterwards, like a good citizen, he'd gone down to the police station to report the extortion.

The police had done nothing. Last night, his windows had been smashed. Tonight, as the clock moved toward 3:100 A.M., he sat inside the store, armed with a machete. He would protect his property himself, if the police would not.

Three hours later, Eduardo's wife's cousin pulled up in front of the store with a truck laden with produce from the Hunt's Point Market. He found the door to the *bodega* smashed and open. Inside, lying in the middle of his store, was the bullet-ridden body of Eduardo Sanchez.

Word of the brutal slaying passed quickly. Other local merchants, all pushed to the wall by huge protection-money demands, were incensed. Then one, a Jewish stationery store owner named Sol Bernstein, passed around copies of the *Daily News*. The merchants appointed a committee to contact the Red Berets.

Coney Island, Brooklyn

Eighty-four-year-old Irene Storynski had so little—a bed, a worn armchair, a small table and chair, a twelve-inch black and white television set, a chest of drawers, and a few pictures. They were arranged neatly in her tiny, airless one-room apartment in the once grand Coney Island, on the shores of the Atlantic Ocean. After she paid her rent and utilities out of her social security check, Irene had $90 left for a month's food, clothing, and other "luxuries."

Despite the hardship, Irene's life was not without pleasures. She had her cat, Brenton, named after the ship that had brought her to America as a young girl. She had the memories of her happy marriage that had ended with her husband's death twenty years before. And she had her daily walks, to the store, sometimes, to the boardwalk, where she would sit on a bench and drink in the sea air.

That Irene went out so often shocked the other elderly people in her building. They barricaded themselves in their rooms, venturing forth only when absolutely necessary, and then only in the morning hours. Irene, however, had left her homeland because she would have had to live in constant fear. She refused to bow to it in her adopted land.

Irene had been feeling ill, so she hadn't cashed her social security check the day it arrived. Stimulated by the glimpse of blue skys and sunshine through her small window, she went out on Thursday morning. After visiting the bank, she felt so happy at being able to stretch her legs that she treated herself to a small piece of pork to cook with her cabbage, and to a rich pastry from Mother's Bakery for dessert.

Feeling almost wicked at the extravagance, she made her way back to the tenement building. For once, the elevator was working, and she hummed a folk tune to herself as the cage rattled up to the fourth floor. She got off the elevator, took her keys out of her bag, and undid her two locks.

They had been waiting around the corner, near the stairway. As soon as Irene turned the doorknob, they sprinted down the hall and pushed her into the apartment. Irene was stunned for a moment when she slammed into the floor. When she was able to open her eyes, she saw two young teenagers rifling her drawers.

"Please," she begged. "No. I'm poor."

"Shut up," one of them snarled. As he turned toward her, he stepped on the pastry that had flown from her shopping bag when she'd been pushed.

That minor accident, a mere trifle compared to the tragedy of losing her month's income, pushed Irene over the edge.

"Help me," she screamed. "Help me."

"Damn," the taller one spat. He crossed the room and lashed out with his foot. The first kick caught her in the neck, then a second and a third followed to the ribs. She slumped, unconscious. But her attacker, maddened by the violence, kept kicking and kicking and kicking.

Irene's death was typical of the push-in robberies and beatings that had plagued Coney Island and other decaying areas. But the elderly people who knew Irene were finally galvanized by her death, because Irene's undiminished zest for life had touched them. Twenty-four men and women came to a morning meeting at the synagogue. They wrote irate letters for the umpteenth time to the mayor and police commissioner. Then they addressed a special plea for help to the Red Berets.

Washington Heights, Manhattan

The good kids in the neighborhood tried to watch out for Billy Reilly. Although he was twenty years old, he had the mind of a four-year-old. He was big for his size, fat really, and clumsy. But he always had a smile on his face, and in the housing project where he lived he took great pleasure in doing little "chores"—opening doors for ladies, carrying packages, picking up litter in the courtyard. A pat on the back or a cookie would make his whole day.

The problem was that Billy was a perfect target for another kind of teenager. The gangs who hung around the street corners and in the lobbies of the project liked to goof on him and taunt him. When Billy had been younger, he'd once been seriously injured. He'd learned to stay away from the worst troublemakers, but at any overture of friendship, he couldn't help responding.

A fourteen-year-old named Odell Dunk was showing off for his thirteen-year-old girl friend. Dunk, a member of the Terrible Turks, a particularly vicious gang, was going through a routine on how dumb Billy was. The girl didn't believe him. So Odell found Billy helping a woman carrying her laundry downstairs. He smiled and told Billy he wanted to introduce him to his girl friend.

While Billy chattered with the girl, Odell split for a few minutes. He returned with a soda bottle filled with a strange colored liquid. He offered Billy a drink.

At the first touch of the lye to his lips, Billy howled. But Dunk moved quickly, jamming the mouth of the bottle into Billy's mouth. Billy choked and sputtered, his face turning red. He was so weak he couldn't fight Dunk off, despite his larger size.

The agony of Billy's death was unspeakable. Even in the violence-ridden project, numbed residents began to buzz. A group of good teen-agers, who were forced to stay together going to and from school to avoid getting mugged, decided they had to do something more. They called the *Daily News* to find out how they could get in touch with the Red Berets.

Hundreds of letters and phone calls. Jill was thrilled as she prepared her stories for print. She couldn't wait to talk to Jim Knight.

twenty-three

The acrid stench of smoke and ash was over-whelming. Fallen bricks, charred timbers, and mounds of sodden ash clogged the once busy storefront. As Jim picked his way through, the dampness produced a bone-deep chill. His mood was as black as the charcoaled remnants of the clinic that had been his life for eight years.

The area that had been his office was recognizable only when he spotted the file cabinet shrunken and welded shut by the heat. He moved to the spot, kicking at the rubble with the toe of his boot. His desk, the chairs, the table, were black splinters, the largest no bigger than his little finger. Gone were the pictures, the postcards, the thank-you letters from the people he'd helped over the years. The loss was so depressing he felt tears forming.

He stood there, aimlessly spreading the sodden ashes. Then he heard a clink. He bent, running his hand lightly over the spot. His fingers closed on a piece of metal.

He moved back toward the front of the store, into the direct sunlight. He scraped the metal with his fingernail. Holding it up, he recognized the eagle in the middle of the misshapen piece.

He was staring at what was left of his army Commendation Medal. As military awards go, this one ranked far below his combat awards— the Distinguished Service Cross and the Bronze Star. But the Commendation Medal had been awarded for his service as a medic.

The words of Macbeth suddenly popped into his head: "As flies to wanton boys we are to the gods/ They kill us for their sport."

He turned the medal over in his hand. Then he flipped it back into the rubble. It was over, his long futile jesting with the "gods" or whoever controlled destiny. Sara was right. The rest of his life belonged to him.

He climbed over a pile of bricks and out into the street. Without looking back, he walked toward the car.

He stopped in the deli for coffee and a bagel before going to the insurance agent's office. When the plump young girl behind the counter handed him the paper bag, he asked, "How much?"

"Your money's no good here, Jimmy," came a voice from the back room. Jim saw Abe Goldberg, the owner, standing in the doorway.

"When you're the mayor, a big shot," Goldberg added with a huge smile, "you remember Abe's deli, huh?"

"I don't understand."

"We're so proud," Abe gushed. "This neighborhood has got so bad. Now, we're gonna clean out the scum, the animals. Even I'm going to help. Not like before. When I see something, I'll call the police."

"You mean the Red Berets," Jim said. "Well, that's finished. We—"

"Finished?" Goldberg cried in disbelief. "Look at the paper."

Jim looked down. The entire front page was one headline: "New York's Vow: We've Had Enough."

The sky was the dirty yellow of dusk when Jim trudged up the steps of his apartment building. He opened the door, then checked his mail. The slot was jammed full. He dropped the contents into the paper bag that contained the six-pack of beer he'd bought. When he got up to his third-floor apartment, he dumped the contents of the bag out without sifting through them. He'd have plenty of time to do that later.

He opened a can of beer, walked into the living room, turned the radio on to a classical station, then collapsed into his favorite armchair.

His mind was reeling from the day's events. After he'd left the deli, he must have run into a dozen people who'd responded the same way Abe had. Inside him, as he was being clapped on the back and praised, intense emotions flashed, changing as quickly as the images on a kaleidoscope.

There was the sense of pride, of course. But there was also anger and guilt. Anger because the praise implied that these people expected him to continue to selflessly devote his time and energy to protecting them. Guilt because the articles opened up the closet in his mind where he'd tried to lock away the feeling of responsibility that had motivated him nearly all his life.

He took another sip of beer, leaned back, and closed his eyes. The future was hidden behind a swirling cloud. If he married Sara and left the city, he'd be leaving his roots and the people whose hopes had been awakened by what he and the other Red Berets had done. If he stayed, he'd lose Sara. And he'd face the awesome task of building and running a more complicated organization than he'd envisioned. He'd also have to find some way to support himself.

His mind balked at following the endless complications. He tried to focus on the intricate music of Mozart coming over the radio. When the phone rang, he ignored it.

Twenty minutes later came a knock at the door. "No," he groaned to himself.

"Jimmy. I know you're in there."

Jim recognized Renaldo's voice. Reluctantly, he got to his feet and opened the door.

The big boxer smiled. "You're a tough man to find, James."

"Not tough enough, I guess."

"You gonna let me in?"

"Sure," Jim said. "Sorry. I don't mean to take it out on you. You've suffered enough from this whole business."

"That's one of the reasons I wanted to find you," Renaldo said. "Canceling the Thunder Wilkins fight may have been one of the best things that's happened to me."

"Come on," Jim scoffed.

"I'm serious, Jim. After Jill's articles and a piece by Bob Duncan in the *Post*, I must have gotten fifty calls. One was from the lawyer who manages Sugar Ray. He's kept Sugar Ray away from the creeps and hoodlums in the sport. He not only asked if he could manage me, he said he'd bankroll my lawsuit against Thunder and Curran. He said we'd nail their asses to the wall."

"That's great. But how is that going to help your career?"

"That's one of the best parts. I also got a call from the champ, who's a real decent dude. He promised me that if I got a tune-up with any legitimate contender, I get a title shot."

Jim smiled for the first time. "Congratulations."

"One more bit of good news. My new manager is going to bankroll a brand new gym in this area, to replace Slapsy's. I'm going to run the gym. Because I have to train, I'll need a comanager. I thought of you."

"Me? But—"

"You need the bread. And you know how it is, you just have to be there. That'll give you time to run the Red Berets."

Jim grew sober. He looked away. "I don't think so, Renaldo. I have other plans. I don't see how I can stay."

Renaldo stood. "Do me one favor?"

"Of course."

"Come talk to Jill with me. Before you make up your mind for good."

They walked down the front steps of Jim's apartment building and turned left, toward Avenue C.

"Jim. Jim."

The voice came from an alley two buildings down.

"Who is it?"

"It's me. Tony."

They moved out of the range of the streetlight, into the shadows.

The boy looked cold and scared. He told them he'd been hiding out in abandoned buildings since he'd fled down the fire escape outside of Maxey Ritz's apartment.

"Where can I go?" the boy asked plaintively.

"We'll take care of you," Jim said. "Don't worry."

Jim reached into his back pocket, took out his wallet, and extracted three keys from a compartment. "This one is to my front door," he showed Tony. "This one is the top lock, this one the bottom lock of the apartment. You go upstairs, fix yourself something to eat, and crawl into bed."

"I can sleep on the couch."

"Use the bed. I won't be back until late. Don't

answer the phone or the buzzer. And don't open the door."

The boy looked down, his lower lip trembling. Jim's heart went out to him, and he put his hand reassuringly around his shoulder.

"I know you'd like me to be with you," Jim said. "But I can't. You're a real hero. I know you'll be fine."

Tony looked up at him. "I understand. Okay."

Jim and Renaldo watched him walk up the steps of Jim's building.

"Brave kid," Renaldo remarked.

Jim smiled. "Hell of a kid. Reminds me of another kid his age who slept in that apartment a few years ago. A kid who turned out to be a hell of a guy."

"You mean me?"

"No. King Tut. Of course, I mean you," Jim said. "I don't know how, but I'm going to find a way to see that Tony comes out of this all right. Heck, I owe him a lot. If he hadn't had the guts and the smarts to unload Torres's gun, I wouldn't be here now."

Jill topped off the cups of coffee. Then she asked Jim, "You're still not convinced? After reading all this?"

Jim once again glanced over the mound of papers on the coffee table. "I think it's tremendous. But there are people who are trained to run large organizations."

"There aren't people like you, Jim," Jill replied. "Belive me, I've covered politics in New York for ten years. The quality of leadership is too dismal to discuss."

"What makes you think I'd be any better?"

"Renaldo. Baseline. And the others. The way you treat them and the way they treat you. You have several rare qualities. I believe you're honest, and I believe that you deeply, genuinely care about people. Those you deal with instinctively pick that up."

"But—"

"But, nothing," Jill said firmly. "When an organization like this starts, all kinds of suspicions are going to be raised. People will charge that the Red Berets is a paramilitary group, or some kind of cult. Or that the leaders are in it for the money or for a publicity boost that will propel them toward political office. Most people in leadership positions have selfish motives and are vulnerable to suspicion and innuendo. I don't think you have selfish motives and I think that is the best and only antidote to rumor and gossip."

Jim rose and moved over to the window of Jill's apartment. He looked out the twenty-fourth-floor window, over the expanse of the Hudson river shimmering in the moonlight. The water seemed so peaceful, so calm. Into his mind came the image of the serene rural life Sara wanted for both of them.

Finally, Jim turned. "I appreciate the compliments. I really do. But I know myself. It's not for me."

"I think you're making a mistake," Jill said. "Renaldo, you told me Jim—"

Renaldo raised his huge right hand. "Hold it, Jill. We're talking volunteers, right? The man doesn't want to volunteer, that's it. It isn't as if he hasn't made enough sacrifices over the years."

Jill pursed her lips, looking down at the mound of papers. Then she looked at Jim with a thin smile. "I guess that's it."

Jim answered, "I guess so." He was moved by the disappointment he read in her eyes. He added, "The best part of this for me has been working with you, Jill. You're an extraordinary person. I'll miss you."

Jill rose and extended her hand. "Good luck."

Jim took her hand. When he met her gaze, he felt a strong, strange urge to change his mind. Then it passed. "Good luck," he said.

An odd smell hit Jim's nostrils as he trudged up the stairs past the second floor of his apartment building. His body tensed, reacting before his mind to the sensation from the past. Then, as his heart beat louder, he knew what the odor was. He raced up the remaining stairs two at a time.

The door to his apartment was ajar. When he pushed it open, the acrid, sulfurous smell was stronger. He flicked on the bedroom light.

The sight was so gut-wrenching he almost doubled over. Tony lay splayed out on the bed, half under the sheet, half exposed. His head lolled backward over the edge, his open eyes staring unseeingly toward the junction of ceiling and wall. Blood dripped from the corner of his mouth to the floor. Blood also dripped from what must have been a dozen wounds in his bullet-ridden body.

Jim was in the living room, staring at the wall, as the detectives and police technicians swirled around him. As he gazed at the plain white surface, it was as if the wall had turned into a movie screen projecting images from his past and his future.

He felt a growing conviction, the longer he sat, that for the last year he had been living in the fog. Suddenly, that fog lifted. Gone was his confusion. Gone was his doubt.

Vinnie Civitello sat down next to him.

"They must have come down from the roof," Vinnie said. "The front window was unlatched. They must have used silencers—the neighbors didn't hear anything."

"They were after me," Jim said without emotion.

"Maybe. They were out after the kid too. After all, he changed sides, and the Skulls don't put up with that shit."

Jim didn't say anything.

Vinnie got to his feet. "I've got to get my report typed up. Maybe, just to be safe, you ought to lay low for a while. Go back out to Connecticut."

Jim looked up. There was fire in his eyes. "I'm not going anywhere. Not for a long time."

twenty-four

The next three weeks were a blur of frenzied activity. Some nights Jim managed as little as three hours' sleep. Finally, as Christmas approached, the organization began to take shape.

On Friday, Christmas Eve, Jim was totally exhausted. The only remaining appointment on his calendar was lunch with a writer from *New York* magazine. As he sat in his office, he recoiled for a moment from the thought of answering the same questions one more time. But he knew that was his job. His reward would be an entire weekend with nothing to do.

He took a cab to Raoul's, a dark, trendy Soho bar and restaurant. He sat at the bar, sipping a Scotch and water. As he started to feel the warmth of the liquor inside him, some of the tension began leaking out. He could have sat there all afternoon, just sipping and staring at the television set.

Carl Waldman arrived fifteen minutes later. They shook hands and went to a table in the back room. After some small talk and a round of drinks, they began to talk about the Red Berets.

"That's interesting," Waldman commented after a while, "but tell me, what about money? Who's paying for all this?"

"Nobody's paying," Jim replied. "The only donations we're accepting are time. There are enough deserving nonprofit organizations who desperately need financial contributions. Besides, once we accept the first dime, someobdy's going to say, I knew it all along—this is a get-rich scam for the leaders."

"You're not accepting a cent?"

Jim smiled. "Every once in a while somebody hands one of us a subway token. I think that's a way of saying thank you, and of course the Red Beret is free to take it. But no money."

"What about subway fares. Do you think the Transit Authority should let you ride for free?"

"We've approached the TA about that. But so far, if you listen to the chairman and Commissioner Shelton, we're a bigger menace than the robbers and muggers."

"Are you a gang?" Waldman asked. "You've been involved in some heavy violence."

Jim pulled a red beret from his pocket. He held it up for Carl to see. "What this says is, we care. We don't need guns or knives or clubs to get rid of fear in this city. All we need is for people to stand together. Our aim is to prevent crimes from taking place, not to act as a posse to corral criminals after a felony has been comitted."

"Isn't looking for murderers the way your campaign began?"

"Yes," Jim admitted. "But we've begun a new approach. We want our organization to be a neighborhood organization, people helping themselves. For example, we've changed our manner of operation on the subway. In fact, we're going to follow the TA's own suggestions for avoiding being a victim."

"How's that?"

"The TA recommends waiting in the center of the platform, in sight of the token booth, if possible. Then riding in the center car of the train, with the conductor, who has a radio. That got us to thinking that everybody has to enter and leave trains through stations. Instead of riding the trains, the Red Berets will stay in the stations in their own neighborhoods. We can watch people waiting on the platforms and on the stairways and corridors. We can escort people to the street and wait with them for a cab or a bus. And we can watch for suspicious people getting on or off the train."

"By suspicious, do you mean gangs of youth who do so much of the damage?"

"Partly."

"But how are you going to stop the gangs without a battle?"

"For one thing, it will be harder for them to operate if everyone rides the middle cars in off hours. They're going to think twice about mugging somebody on a platform with eight or ten of us around watching."

"So you want to be a deterrent?"

"Exactly."

Waldman punched the "stop" button on his tape recorder, turned the cassette over, then pressed the "play" and "record" buttons. "Okay," he said as the tape began to turn again. "Back to the violence issue again. What if a crime does take place? What do your people do?"

"There's supposed to be a Transit cop in most stations. We'll alert him or her."

"And if he's not there?"

"We're training our people to avoid confrontation with criminals carrying weapons. We'll follow the criminal, get a description, alert the police." Jim paused to drain the last of his drink. He motioned to the waitress to bring another. Then he continued, "I can't emphasize deterrence too much. For example, in Brooklyn, we've gotten together a group of senior citizens and high school kids. Each apartment building is going to have several designated shopping days per week. The elderly people will go shopping together, then return together. The high school kids will accompany them and escort every single senior citizen inside his or her own apartment. That eliminates the push-in type robberies that are so common now."

The new drink arrived, and Jim took a sip. The liquor was really affecting him, unsheathing his tongue. After all the tension of the last weeks, it felt good to talk, to get everything off his chest the way he wanted to.

"Another example," Jim continued. "A housing project in Washington Heights, a neighborhood that's started to fight its way back. A group of residents, high school students and some adults, have formed a Red Beret group. Two or three of them will ride every elevator, up and down, all night. Others will be in the lobbies and walking through the parking lots. Again, their aim is to deter crime."

"I understand what you're saying," Waldman commented. "But what if a crime is in progress? What if you interrupt a rape?"

The muscles of Jim's face tightened at the mention of the word *rape*. He grimaced. Then he said, "If it's a matter of someone being brutalized, we'd have to try to stop it. But we're trying to avoid violence. To avoid being vigilantes."

Carl studied him for a moment. Then he said, "That question seemed to bother you a lot. This discussion of violence animated you. I was wondering, especially since you'd been in the war, what brought that about. You were in combat, weren't you?"

Jim debated. He hadn't talked about the army with anyone for years. But today he felt like getting everything off his chest.

"I'll tell you," Jim said. "We were in Laos, patrolling, when it happened ..."

He told the entire story without interruption. By the time he finished, their meals had arrived. They ate in silence.

After he'd finished his fish, Carl said, "That's quite a story. And quite a decision you made."

"It has nothing to do with the Red Berets. Or, only a little bit. I was reminded of if when I caught that animal who killed Granny Moore. For a moment, the revenge was intensely satisfying. But it would have been infinately better if the murder had never happened. I suppose on one level that's obvious. But it led me to the conclusion that deterring crime had to be our objective."

"So your message is to band together and stand up against crime?"

"Exactly," Jim replied.

After Tony's tragic murder, Jim was unable to face living in that apartment, the one he'd occupied since he'd been a child. He'd moved into a smaller apartment on the second floor of the building in which Renaldo was constructing the new gym. Normally, the construction crews worked until the early evening hours. Since today was Christmas Eve, they'd quit at noon, and the building was quiet when Jim returned.

The three drinks and the big lunch had made Jim sleepy. He spread out on the couch, picked up a book, and almost immediately nodded off.

It was dark outside when the phone awakened him. For a moment he lay listening to the piercing ring, not quite sure where he was. Then he shook off the grogginess, stumbled across the room, and picked up the receiver.

"Jim. It's me."

He inhaled sharply at the sound of Sara's voice. This was the first time he'd heard it since that awful scene three weeks before when he'd told her of his decision to remain in New York City.

"Hi," he said tentatively.

There was silence on the other end of the line for a moment. Then Sara said, "I'm in Connecticut. At mom and dad's."

"That's good. How are they?"

"Fine, as usual." A long pause. "Jim, I miss you. I miss you a lot."

His stomach was tight. "I've missed you too."

"Jim, please come out here. Mother and dad would love to have you. We can take long walks and talk."

"I don't know," Jim said. "I—"

"I've got a job," Sara said. "In Concord, New Hampshire. Not exactly a small town, but far from a big city. A wonderful old doctor who's looking to retire soon. I've even bought a house. Four bedrooms, a huge living room with a fireplace, eight acres of land, and my own creek running by. I'm embarrassed to tell you how little I paid for it. The mortgage payments, insurance, and taxes will be less than I paid for a one-bedroom apartment in Manhattan."

"That's wonderful," Jim said. He paused, moistening his suddenly dry lips with his tongue. "Sara," he continued, "it's no use. I'm committed to staying here. Not forever, maybe. But for a long time, until this organization is firmly established. I'm needed here."

"I need you too," Sara said, a hint of anger

in her voice. "I'm not the kind of person who falls in and out of love with people all the time. We were going to start a new life. Together."

"You were going to start a new life. My life has been here. I've just discovered that it's going to remain here."

"Are you saying it was my fault then? Are you saying I led you on and tried to drag you away? That's not the way I remember it. You were just as—"

"Sara," Jim cut in, "there's no point in this. We went over this three weeks ago. I take all the responsibility. It's my fault for letting things go as far as they did. I hurt you. I can't tell you how sorry I am about that."

He could hear her crying. He held the receiver, waiting until she regained her composure.

When she spoke, her voice was barely a whisper. "I guess—I guess you're not coming."

"There will be a time when we can be friends. I—I don't think it's now."

He could hear her crying again. "Merry Christmas," she said.

"Merry Christmas. I ..." His voice trailed off when he heard the click at the other end.

He hung up and sat in the armchair. The room was a jumble of half-unpacked boxes and haphazardly arranged furniture. For the first time in almost thirty years, with the exception of his military service, he wasn't spending Christmas in his old apartment. A suffocating loneliness came over him.

His loneliness, he had realized in the last three weeks, was part of the reason behind his attraction to Sara. He needed somebody to love. He was so physically attracted to Sara and his need had been so great that he'd assumed they were emotionally compatible too.

Jim realized now that wasn't the case, just as he had realized that his place was in New York City. Though he felt very badly, though he would love to have her with him now, he now knew it never would have worked.

He got up, got a beer, and settled down to read. The phone rang several times, but he didn't want to deal with anybody, so he ignored it. At seven o'clock, their was a knock at the door.

"Jimmy. Open up. It's an emergency."

The word shook him out of his lethargy. He unlocked the door.

"Get your coat," Baseline said.

Jim noted the somber expression on his face. He grabbed his coat, which had been laying on a pile of boxes. Then he followed Baseline down the stairs to the street.

Baseline's cab was double-parked at the curb. When the publicity about him being fired for joining the Red Berets was in the papers, he'd been able to choose from a dozen offers. Now he drove a brand-new Checker.

Jim jumped in the front seat. Baseline headed north on First Avenue. "What's the problem?" Jim asked.

"Hey, you yell at Michelangelo when he's painting? Let this artist drive."

Jim, puzzled, sat back. Baseline turned left when they got to Fourteenth Street. A few blocks later, he made a sharp U-turn and pulled to the curb.

"Get out," he said to Jim.

Jim opened the door and stood on the sidewalk. They were in front of Lüchöw's, the famous old German restaurant.

"I don't understand," Jim said.

Baseline took his elbow. "You just come with me. Here, my good man," he added, tossing the keys to the doorman. "See that my vehicle is properly parked."

The interior of the restaurant was resplendent with Christmas decorations. The maître d' led Jim and Baseline to a private room.

"Merry Christmas!" came the cry when they walked in the door.

Jim was stunned. Milling around a table, holding drinks and nibbling hors d' oeuvres, were all his friends—Renaldo and Maria, Chang, Rafael, Marguerite, Juanita, even Maxey Ritz.

"Jim," boomed a voice behind him. "What a wonderful Christmas."

He turned. Heinrich Siebert stood there, beaming. "Mr. Siebert. Merry Christmas."

The hardware-store owner stepped back. "See who comes home for the holidays."

Jim broke into a huge smile when he spotted John Siebert sitting in a chair. His head was bandaged, but he looked terrific. John got to his feet as Jim approached, and they hugged.

"How do you feel?" Jim asked.

"Fine. Well, I get tired. But it's good to be out of the hospital."

A drink was placed in Jim's hand. "This is a wonderful idea," Jim exclaimed.

"Lois Lane did it," Baseline said. "Got the *Daily Planet* to spring for it and everything."

"Lois Lane?"

"I guess I'm Lois."

Jim saw Jill Prentice step next to Baseline. She kissed Jim on the cheek.

He couldn't believe how terrific she looked. And how happy he was to see her. "Merry Christmas," he said.

"Merry Christmas. Now, come on. Have some food."

They stood on the sidewalk afterwards.

"Looks like we closed up the place," Jim said to Jill. "It was a wonderful Christmas Eve. I can't remember when I've enjoyed myself more."

"It was nice. Even the man upstairs is doing his job."

Jim watched the gentle, soft snow drift downward through the city night. "It's so perfect I can almost see the horse-drawn sleighs now."

"Hey," Jill said. "That gives me an idea. Are you in a hurry?"

"I've got no place to go."

"Then let's grab a taxi."

A half hour later, they were nestled under a heavy blanket in a horse-drawn carriage slowly clopping through Central Park.

"This is terrific," Jim said. "I've never done this before."

"I do it all the time. Just like I find the time to

ride up to the top of the Empire State Building, ride out to the Statue of Liberty, and catch a show at Radio City Music Hall. I've never stopped being a tourist. I love New York in a way only a small-town girl from Indiana can."

"I didn't know you came from Indiana."

"Born and raised," Jill said. "It's probably why I love the diversity, the energy, the excitement of the city. It's also why I'm an idealist. I can't stop thinking about what a wonderful place this would be and could be and should be. If I didn't have my column, I'd be one of those people who march around day and night wearing signboards."

"You have a lot of fans."

"Because I write about interesting people. Like Mr. James Knight."

"Posh on that," he said with a smile. "I'm as dull as they come."

"You have a way of putting yourself down, Jim. I can't understand it. You want to know what I think, I think you ought to enjoy your success a little more. You deserve it."

Jim turned to look at her. "You're embarrassing me."

"I'm going to embarrass you even more." Her right hand reached out and pulled Jim's head toward her. Their lips met softly, once, then twice, then pressed into a longer, deeper kiss.

When they parted, Jim gazed into her soft brown eyes. Then he said, "For once, you're dead flat wrong."

"About what?"

"I'm not embarrassed."

He put his arms around her and held her close as the carriage moved through the fairy-tale night.

twenty-five

Anthony Brown rubbed the snifter back and forth in his palms, warming the amber liquid. Then he took a sip of the brandy. "They had to change their approach," he said. "Just when we were ready to start."

Mike Latella looked over at him. "Maybe it won't cause a problem."

"Sure," Brown scoffed. "Eight, ten guys around a token booth." He shook his head. "The perfect way to merchandise. The drugs and the cash are perfectly secure, locked up behind bulletproof glass. Easy access. Nobody gets suspicious about people going in and out, like in a building. Customer slips a couple bills in the change slot in the token booth, gets back a token from the clerk—and a glassine envelope or two."

"Absolutely perfect," Mike commented.

"Perfect. Until those assholes started this boy-scout shit."

"Maybe it's time for some heavy force. Break a few heads."

Brown grimaced. "We tried that. They're like goddamn roaches, you step on a few, there's twice as many when you look around. Naw, discouraging them didn't work."

"I guess you're right. They became martyrs. The public loves reading about them."

"That's it," Brown said excitedly.

"What?"

"The public. That's how we have to go after them. We've got to see that they get some real bad publicity."

"How we going to do that?"

Brown smiled. "You just wait and see. In the meantime, let Santos know I want to see him."

The second free throw whistled through the net. When the ball hit the floor, the team captain signaled for a time-out. The substitutes sitting on the bench got up so that the exhausted five on the floor could get a minute's rest.

The coach, a lean, intense man, knelt in front of them. "One point down. Twenty-two seconds left. We need defensive pressure and we need it now."

"No problem," Baseline said, wiping his face with a towel.

"Time for you to start playing instead of talking, Jones," the coach snapped. "Listen up. I want the 1-2-1-1 press. Hawk, you're on the guy inbounding the ball. The guards have to deny. When they do get the ball in play, clamp on the trap. Hard. Understand?"

Five heads nodded.

The coach looked at Baseline. "If the guards get in trouble, they'll go long to Big Sky. That's your job, Jones."

"The Sky is high, but Baseline can fly," he said.

The horn sounded and the referee whistled the teams back onto the court.

"Hands in," the coach said. The team gathered in a tight circle and piled their hands on top of each other. "Defense!" they shouted.

The players moved out onto the hardwood. An immense seven-foot-tall player trotted the length of the court and set up under his own basket. Baseline, the last man back on the press, stood fifteen feet ahead of him, watching the play develop.

The referee handed the ball to a stocky white guard in a red jersey under the far basket. The guard, momentarily flustered by Hawk wildly waving his hands, took a few steps to his left and bounced the ball to the other guard, who dribbled toward the sideline.

A white jersey appeared in his path, blocking his lane. As he stopped dribbling, a second white jersey completed the trap. The referee counted off one, two, three, as the red jersey looked in vain to pass. In desperation, he lofted the ball the length of the court.

The seven-footer took two giant steps to his right, then coiled for a leap. As the ball approached, the giant jumped, his hands nearly eleven feet in the air. But just as he was about to grab the ball another set of hands came out of nowhere to tip the leather sphere.

The giant landed with a frustrated grunt. A white jersey picked up the ball and fired a pass up the sidelines to a teammate, who glanced at the clock. Eight seconds left. The player with the ball took a dribble to his left, then launched a twenty-foot jump shot. The players stood, watching the flight of the ball.

"Damn," the coach muttered as the shot hit the back rim. The ball bounded high in the air. But once again Baseline came flying, up, up. He grabbed the ball above the rim and rammed it home. An instant later, the final buzzer sounded.

The white team whooped in celebration. Baseline walked slowly up to the bench and picked up his warm-up jacket and gym bag. Eric and Marguerite came up to him.

"Man," Eric said, "that big guy has over half a foot on you. I don't know how you got that pass."

Baseline grinned. "Aviation is my specialty."

"Forty-six-inch vertical jump," Marguerite said. "That's only two inches less than David Thompson of the N.B.A. The man can fly."

"The lady knows what she's talking about," Baseline said. "And let me warn you," he added. "You play one on one with this lady, she'll tie up your ass and hand it back to you like a Christmas present."

Eric shook his head. "I'm a wrestler, not a basketball player."

"Come on," Marguerite said. "We got to get on patrol."

"I'll be a minute," Baseline said. "No reason to shower. Don't have to smell nice for the subway."

As Baseline walked off toward the locker room, Eric said to Marguerite, "Boy, he's good."

"He's great. And he's a real hero to a lot of people around here. Him sticking up for me a few weeks ago when somebody planted that marijuana in my locker made all the difference in the world. If I get that college scholarship, he'll be a big reason."

It was Monday, the first shopping day after Christmas. Until nearly eleven o'clock, the corridors of the Union Square subway station were filled with people toting shopping bags full of presents they'd stood in long lines to exchange. By midnight, though, the cavernous underground terminal seemed quiet and empty.

Baseline was restless. He liked riding the trains better. At least there was the routine of getting on and off at every stop. Plus new people to look at and talk to. He knew Jim was probably right about this being the right way to do it. But he hadn't figured out a good way to avoid becoming bored.

A dozen Red Berets patrolled the station. Baseline answered a question from a couple of cheerful Chinese kids who'd just joined up. Then he meandered away to check the BMT platform.

He was near the bottom of the stairs when he heard a loud groan. Then he saw a figure doubled over, leaning against a wall at the far end.

He ran the length of the patform and leaned down. "What's wrong, man?"

The instant he spoke, the guy started shouting, "Help. Help."

Baseline straightened, puzzled. "Hey, what's the matter?"

"Hands up, nigger," came the command from behind him.

Baseline spun. A beefy Transit cop glared at him.

"I wasn't doing anything," Baseline protested.

"Sure," the cop said sarcastically. "I said hands up."

"I told you—"

"He tried to rob me, man," the guy behind Baseline said.

Baseline turned. "Hey, I didn't—"

The cop brought his nightstick down in a vicious blow to the back of his skull. Baseline's tall, thin body collapsed to the concrete. As the cop knelt, the guy who'd moments before cried for help slipped a bulging envelope into Baseline's jacket pocket. Then he slipped off through a small knot of people who had gathered to watch.

"There must be a mistake," Jim said.

The desk sergeant shrugged. "Resisting arrest. Possession of heroin. Those are the charges."

"That's impossible."

"Bail hearing will be in the morning. You better get your buddy a lawyer."

Jim stood, both hands on the high counter, leaning forward. Jill touched his arm. "Come on, Jim," she said. "We can't do anything here."

"I can't believe this," Jim said. "Baseline's the last person in the world who would have heroin on him."

"We've got work to do. I know a terrific criminal lawyer. This is obviously a frame, but that doesn't mean it won't be hard to fight."

"I guess you're right," Jim said. He put his arm around her shoulder and they started for the door.

They stopped when blinded by a flash bulb.

"What a sweet picture," exclaimed a high-pitched voice. "A reporter ever so close to her source."

Jim saw in front of him a thin, pale man with very closely cropped blond hair. The man was dressed in a three-piece suit and was carrying an open stenographer's notebook. To his left was a photographer.

"I understand one of your good little sheep has strayed," the man said.

"I'm sure there's been a mistake," Jim began. "He never—"

"Don't waste your breath," Jill said. "Mr. Philip Clark of the *Post* won't be interested in a denial. That doesn't rate a lurid headline."

"Venom," Clark commented. "My dear, I'm surprised. I admit I was suspicious when I saw all those pages devoted to the Red Berets. I'm truly shocked to find out you've been playing beddy-bye."

Jim stiffened. "That's not fair."

"It's okay," Jill said, touching his arm. "Darling Philip prefers bikers. He's probably sizing you up for a black leather jacket right now."

"Touché, darling," Clark said. "But enough chatter. I've got to do a big story on another bad boy. It doesn't surprise me at all that these angels have tarnished halos. I'm sure it will interest our readers immensely."

"Wait a minute," Jim protested. "Even if this absurd charge were true, that doesn't cast a shadow on what we're doing."

"Doesn't it? I think it does. I think there must be a reason for the amazing spread of altruism through this wicked city. I would suggest a financial reason."

Jim's jaw tightened. "I've dealt with that question. We haven't taken a cent, and we're not looking for a cent."

"My word!" Clark exclaimed. "I think I'll stand back, so I'm not in the way when the Lord reaches down and takes you bodily into heaven. Unless, of course, there's some tarnishes on your little halo too."

"I don't like the tone of this conversation, Clark."

"Well, as we say in the business darling, fuck you."

Jim was furious. "You goddamn—"

"Let's get out of here," Jill said. "There's no point in this, Jim."

"Ta ta," Clark said. "Look for the *Post* tomorrow."

twenty-six

The meeting with Mike Seitzinger, Jill's criminal-lawyer friend, lasted over an hour. Absorbed by his friend Baseline's problems, Jim was dismayed to see a dozen reporters and cameramen waiting for him amid the construction debris of the soon-to-be-opened boxing club. Tight lipped, he was pushing his way through the crowd to his office when a copy of the afternoon *Post* was thrust in front of him.

The headline read: "Red Beret Chief Former Mental Patient."

Jim grabbed the paper and opened it. The first thing his eyes saw was the by-line on the headline story. Philip Clark. That son of a bitch, he thought.

A barrage of questions was flying at him. Jim announced he wanted to read the story carefully. Then he'd come out to answer questions.

Twenty minutes later, Jim was explaining what had happened during that crucial period in his military career. "The examination by an army psychologist was a routine part of my application for noncombat status," Jim said. "My hospital stay was solely related to treatment for a tropical disease I picked up in Laos."

"The article said you saw the psychiatrist more than once," a reporter commented.

"The psychiatrist was instrumental in getting my application approved. He hardly would have done that if he thought I was crazy."

"How can we check that?"

"Ask Clark," Jim snapped. "He must have had access to my records somehow. Actually, anybody has my permission to check anything. I've got nothing to hide."

"What about you and Jill Prentice?" another reporter asked.

Jim grimaced. "That's nobody's business."

"Nobody's business?" scoffed a television reporter, a cynical, gray-haired man from one of the city's independent stations. "I know what my boss would say if I filmed nothing but stories with my girl friend."

"The Red Berets haven't gotten an inch of print we haven't deserved," Jim said sharply. "Community service deserves attention."

"Is selling drugs community service?" the gray-haired reporter asked.

Jim's blood was boiling. "I'll give you a story, if you want. Jones was set up. There's a lot of people who are very unhappy with what the Red Berets are doing. They'll do anything to see us hurt."

"What do you mean?"

Jim, in high gear, rattled off what he knew about Anthony Brown, the Savage Skulls, and their possible involvement in arson, robbery, and other crimes.

After a number of questions, one reporter asked, "Are you saying the Mob bribed a cop to take part in framing this Red Beret?"

"I can't prove anything," Jim said. "But you can draw your own conclusions."

"That's pretty harsh," another reporter commented. "What do you have against the Transit Police?"

"I've got nothing against them. They seem to have something against us. They don't seem to realize we're there to help them fight crime."

"Commissioner Shelton says the Transit Police can handle the problem."

"Commissioner Shelton is wrong," Jim replied.

That evening, Jim and Jill were sharing a bottle of wine in a small bar in Greenwich Village.

"You really shot from the hip today," Jill said.

"I'm not a politician," Jim said. "I don't have to get up and mouth a lot of platitudes. I really can't understand what's wrong with telling the truth."

"Are you sure it is the truth? Some of what you said is speculation."

"So let people investigate and prove me wrong. It's time somebody shook things up."

Jill looked at him. "People who shake things

up better be prepared for somebody trying to shake them down."

"What do you mean?"

Jill reached out for his hand. "I mean, you have to be careful. You've got some powerful enemies."

"That's not a reason to back away from what I believe in," Jim said.

"No," Jill said. "It's not. But it's a reason to be cautious. And to tell the others to be cautious. I've got a feeling a storm is about to hit."

"Then we'll weather it," Jim said. "There's no turning back now."

Renaldo stood on the platform, underneath the clock. While his eyes automatically registered the arrival and departure of trains and the passengers, his mind worked over the turmoil of the last weeks.

Granny Moore dead. Slapsy near death. That poor kid murdered in Jim's apartment. Now Baseline arrested for the ludicrous charge of possessing drugs.

It was like one of those old silent movies, Renaldo decided. A guy, maybe Buster Keaton, slips on a banana peel. He trips another guy, then a few more guys fall, then all of a sudden cars are running into each other and a full-scale riot is going on.

Only what was happening to the Red Berets wasn't funny. Not in the least. They had to stop the chain reaction before further damage was done.

"Hey, you."

A Transit patrolman, a tall, thin young guy with shaggy hair sticking out from under his hat, was approaching Renaldo.

"Hello, officer," Renaldo said.

"What the fuck you think you're doing?" the cop asked. "Pick that up."

"What?"

"Don't give me no lip, wise guy. The cup."

Renaldo looked down. A crushed Styrofoam coffee cup was a few inches from his left foot.

"I didn't drop that," Renaldo said.

"I said pick it up. Don't you spics understand English?"

Involuntarily, Renaldo's hands started to tighten into fists. "What did you call me?"

"That's it, jerk," the cop said. He pulled a ticket book out of his back pocket. "A summons for littering. Bad enough trash like you Red Berets hanging around, you have to treat the place like a garbage dump."

Renaldo was literally shaking with anger. The muscles of his face were so tight he could feel sweat breaking out on his upper lip.

The cop saw the look on his face and smiled. "You gonna try something, big guy? Huh? You want to add assaulting an officer? You shitheads think we're all crooked anyway. Why don't you try me?"

For an instant, Renaldo almost gave in to the urge to break the skinny cop in half. But with a great exercise of self-discipline, he just stared.

The cop met his gaze for an instant. Then he looked down, finishing the ticket.

*   *   *

Billy Dunn had just reached the top of the stairs to the platform for the Eighth Avenue line at the West Fourth Street Station. Tonight was his third as a Red Beret. He stopped at the top of the stairs, looking back over his shoulder for Bear Barker, his friend.

Then he heard the scream and whirled. He saw it so clearly, like a show on TV. The kid in a blue parka and white sneakers snatched the purse of the lady he'd pushed to the ground, then sprinted up the ramp toward the exit.

Billy was after him like a shot. He had never been good at basketball or baseball or anything where you had to throw or catch. But he could run like the wind. Even though he had been ohly a freshmen last year, he'd won half his races on the varsity track team.

At the top of the ramp, Billy darted right. He pushed through the gate, where he saw a flash of white sneaker disappear up the stairs to his right. He took the stairs two at a time.

The thief was slowed by the crowd exiting from the Waverly Theater next to the subway stop. Billy dashed into the street, dodging cars to circle the throng. As the thief veered left onto West Fourth Street, Bill got close enough to touch him. The kid swung the purse and Billy grabbed it.

For a brief moment, they were locked in a tug of war. Then the thief let go. Billy tumbled backward. For a moment he was stunned. By the time he got to his feet, the thief was gone.

But Billy had the satisfaction of recovering the purse. He headed back underground. As he pulled open the gate leading to the platform, a hand grabbed him. "Where do you think you're going?"

Billy looked up at the transit cop. "I got the purse back. For the lady."

The cop eyed him suspiciously. "What lady. What in the hell are you pulling?"

Just then a well-dressed woman in her forties approached the turnstile, accompanied by three other Red Berets. "Oh, my purse!" she exclaimed. "Thank you."

Billy handed her the bag. "I didn't catch the kid. I'm sorry."

"You're so wonderful," the woman said. "All of you. I feel so much safer."

The cop was glaring. "All right, kid," he said, grabbing Billy's arm again. "You're coming with me."

"Why?"

"You didn't pay. That's a crime."

"But officer," the woman said, "this boy was returning my purse."

"I don't care what he's doing," the cop said.

"That's outrageous," the lady protested. She touched the officer's sleeve.

The cop pulled his arm away. "You touch me again, lady," he snarled. "I'm taking you in too."

The elevated platform in Queens was windswept and frigid. Tim Payne stood, his hands tucked up under his armpits to keep warm. The rest of his friends had gone home a half hour ago, and he was at the limit of his endurance. One more train and he'd call it a night.

Unfortunately, it was another night without capturing the psycho who pushed Tim's girl friend Pam under a train on this very platform. Tim took some satisfaction in the fact that the attacks had not been repeated since the Red Berets had begun their patrols. But he still didn't waver from his vow to put behind bars the creep who ruined the career of the girl he loved.

At this time of night, the trains ran twenty minutes apart. An eastbound train rumbled into the station, discharging several passengers on the opposite side. Then it pulled off. Tim watched the red rear lights disappear into the dark night.

When he looked back at the turnstile, he froze. A short, stocky figure in a long overcoat was limping toward the opposite end.

Tim pulled himself back into the shadows of the post that supported the roof covering the elevated tracks. He breathed deeply, trying to quiet his pounding heart. He couldn't see the man's face, the face that Pam swore was forever etched into her memory, the face she saw in that frightening instant she tottered on the edge of the platform. Pam had not seen any other detail except the face. But a woman who had witnessed the vicious assault had thought the attacker had limped before he began the lunge that nearly sent Pam to her death.

Tim didn't know what to do now. The token

booth wasn't open this time of night. The pay
phone was on the other end of the platform,
near where the man was standing. Tim could
go downstairs to make a call to the cops, but
a train was due any minute. He was afraid the
man would be gone.

His thought was interrupted when he saw Mr.
and Mrs. Poulos walk onto the platform. They
owned a deli on Roosevelt Avenue. Every night,
they closed up at midnight and took the train
to their home in Astoria. Behind him, Tim could
hear the rumble of that approaching train.

The man in the overcoat started moving toward the Poulos. Tim was moving forward too.
The noise from the train grew louder. The man
broke into a run. Tim dashed forward, tackling
him a few strides before he would have crashed
into Mrs. Poulos.

Tim hit him hard, just like he did as a linebacker on the football team. The man grunted
as he hit the platform, but he was strong and
full of fight. They grappled, rolling over. Tim's
back hit a post and he involuntarily loosened
his grip. The psycho's hands moved up toward
his throat, and Tim barely got one hand in the
way.

His opponent put all his weight on his two
hands. Tim's shoulder and wrist were alive with
an intense pain, like a dentist drilling into a
nerve. His teeth clenched, Tim started upward
at the malevolent eyes, the unshaven face, the
stained, uneven teeth. The man's breath was so
heavy with liquor that it made Tim choke.

The hands moved closer to his throat. Tim

concentrated on pushing with all his might. Fight, he told himself. His arm was beginning to numb. He braced for one last effort. Then he pushed as hard as he could, using every reserve of strength he'd built up in three years of lifting weights for football.

The suddenness of the thrust caught the psycho off balance. Tim freed his other hand and pushed again. The man fell back. Quick as a cat, Tim leaped to his feet.

They circled, like two wrestlers. The man charged, but Tim dodged. It seemed to Tim that the man was dragging his bad leg more. He decided to go for that leg. But the man was surprisingly quick. He dropped, upending Tim, who somersaulted over him.

Tim landed on his back at the edge of the platform. Below him were the tracks, including the third rail with its 600 volts of electricity. Tim's head and shoulders were over the edge. His attacker jumped, hoping to force Tim's fall. Tim caught the weight in his powerful arms. Then he twisted with all his might and slammed the man into the concrete. He heard the crack of the man's head hitting. Then the man lay still.

Instantly, exhaustion flooded over him. He lay, eyes closed, taking in huge gulps of air. Slowly he sat up, then got to his feet. He didn't think he could have fought another minute. Never in his football career had his arms been this tired.

"Hands up."

Tim's heart leapt with joy as he heard the

command. He turned to the cop. "Thank God," he said. "I couldn't—"

The cop's gun was pointed at him. The cop's face was a harsh mask. "You. Hands up. Against the wall."

twenty-seven

"It looks like the cops have declared war," Jim commented. "I can't believe that poor kid Tim had to spend the night in jail."

Renaldo shrugged. "Can't say that was all due to the Red Berets. He was black and young, the other guy was older and white. The cop made the usual assumption."

"He shouldn't have," Jim said. "At least his girl friend's identification of her attacker cleared that one up. But if things keep going, we'll need an army of lawyers."

"You're going to have them," Jill said as she emerged from the office.

"How's that?"

"Mike Seitzinger's been on the phone all morning. To other lawyers. And he's met with a group of law students from NYU."

"So?"

"They're going to patrol with us. Mike's got at least twenty signed up for next week. Any problems come up, with a cop or a criminal or anyone, we'll have an attorney as eyewitness. Plus, most of them are going to carry tape recorders, just so there's proof of what was said."

"Will it work?" Renaldo asked. "The cop that gave me a ticket, it was my word against his."

"It's not infallible," Jill said. "But I doubt whether the commissioner is going to want half his force tied up in lawsuits. And he's the one who's causing our problems."

"That's true," Jim said. "I've talked to a number of Transit cops who privately support what we're doing."

"They're being pressured. And the way to ease that pressure is to go to the top."

"How?"

"A meeting with the mayor," Jill said.

"What will that accomplish?"

"Think about what we could do if we worked in cooperation with the Transit Police. If we coordinated patrols, kept in touch by radio. We can put ten people out for every cop. Instead of handling routine chores, they could be concentrating on real police work—making arrests."

"Why would the mayor agree to that?"

"Because his constituency is going to force him. The mayor's a shrewd politician. The working people who are most concerned about crime are the base of his support. When we show him they believe in the Red Berets, he's going to have to jump on board."

"How do we do that?"

"Petitions," Jill replied. "I've already typed up

a form to take to the printer. We'll have someone in every subway station, every housing project, every local business district. Then we'll take the petitions to city hall."

"That's very shrewd," Jim said.

Renaldo looked at Jill. "You keep saying 'we.' You sound like our PR agent."

Jill smiled. "As of now, I am. I've been thinking over what Phil Clark said. As obnoxious as he was, he's right. I'm not objective as far as the Red Berets are concerned. I've taken an indefinite leave of absence from the *News*."

"Are you sure?" Jim asked. "You love reporting. And how are you going to live?"

"I've been working so hard the last few years I haven't had a chance to spend a lot of money. Besides," she added, looking at Jim, "I'm gambling I have prospects."

"Prospects?"

Jill kissed Jim on the lips. "They say that two can live as cheaply as one."

Jill leaned back in the chair, rubbing her closed eyes. It was 12:30 in the morning, and the pages in front of her were beginning to blur. But she wanted to stay up until Jim returned. He'd insisted on picking up the petitions from the Manhattan subway stations.

They were both anxious to see how the petition campaign was going. When the story had hit the eleven o'clock television news, there had been the expected howl from the mayor about people telling him how to do his job. But there had also been an exploratory private phone call from one of the mayor's aides. When the petition drive gathered strength, the winds at City Hall would blow in a different direction.

The phone rang. Jill picked it up and recognized Renaldo's deep voice.

"Where are you?" Jill asked.

"I'm still at Fourteenth Street. I've been waiting for Jim for an hour."

She felt a chill. "He should have been there a long time ago. He left here at a little after 11:30."

"Are you sure he was coming to meet me?"

"That's what he said. Maybe he changed his mind. Maybe he—"

"Jill, I'm worried," Renaldo interrupted. "I'll leave somebody here and head back. You call the police."

"The poice," she said quickly. "I don't think—"

"Have you ever known Jim to change his plans without calling?"

She swallowed against the lump of fear in her throat. "No," she replied.

"Then call the police."

The car hit a pothole and bucked. Jim slammed into the lid of the trunk. The blow jolted him toward consciousness.

His first sensation was the pain, like a bad toothache, ricocheting back and forth inside his skull like a handball bouncing on a court. Then he gagged as he took in the thick air. It was like breathing through a greasy rag. Then nausea slammed him like a whitecap hitting the beach, and he vomited noisily. Each spasm sent a sharper pain through his head.

When it was over, he rolled as far as he could from the stench. His head was slowly clearing. He started to raise his hand toward his head, but it wouldn't move.

Then he knew his hands were tied. From the vibration of the darkness in which he lay, he knew he was in the trunk of a car.

He concentrated, trying to make some sense of the jigsaw puzzle that was his memory. He'd kissed Jill good-bye, then walked down the flight of stairs to the street. His mind had been preoccupied as he covered the three blocks to the subway. He passed an alley between a dry cleaner's and a boarded-up tenement without a glance. Then came a blinding pain. He couldn't remember anything else.

Now, he became aware of the fear building in him. He could feel his heart beating rapidly. For a moment, the emotion ran wild, out of control. In his mind's eye he saw a parakeet he had as a kid. One day a cat got in the apartment through an open window. Even though it was safe in its cage, the bird had leaped off the perch, its wings fluttering impossibly fast. Then it gave a short cry and fell, its heart burst from terror.

The memory helped him regain control. He held his breath, trying to stop the hyperventilating that had added to his anxiety. He kept the air in until his lungs ached. Then he exhaled, very slowly. When he took in air again, he tried to fill his lungs completely.

In a few minutes, he was able to turn his mind away from his body to his predicament. The sound of the tires spinning on the rough pavement was the only sound he heard. As he listened, the car started to brake and he braced his feet against the side of the trunk to avoid rolling into his own vomit. They turned left, came to a complete stop (must be a light), then started up again. He soon had the sensation of going downhill, then up a rise, then down again.

He heard gravel beneath the car. Then the car came to a halt. Suddenly, he heard voices. Doors slammed and a key rattled in the trunk lock.

When the trunk opened, Jim was blinded by a strong flashlight. Hands grabbed him and dragged him roughly out of the trunk to the ground.

Jim lay, face in the gravel, trying to catch his breath. Then, pushing with his bound hands, he tried to get to his knees. A vicious kick hit him in the rib cage and he collapsed.

Jim heard laughter.

"Look at Mr. Big Shot."

"He's gonna arrest us," came a second mocking voice. "Watch out."

More laughter. Jim blinked, trying to focus. There was a full moon, and as his blurred vision cleared, he saw he was lying in what looked like a small parking lot surrounded by trees. A fence separated the parking lot from the woods, except for a narrow opening off to his left.

"Hey, hero," a voice called. Then Jim was kicked again. A sharp, stabbing pain nearly caused him to black out. He coughed, and he tasted blood in the back of his throat. A hand grabbed his hair and pulled his head back. "Why didn't you listen, smart ass? You got enough warnings to mind your own business."

Jim felt a surge of anger. He tried to spit, but his mouth was bone dry.

"Why don't you talk, hero? You talk good on TV. You talk good to the newspaper reporters. I hear you fuck them too."

"F—ff—."

"What are you trying to say?"

"F—fuck you," Jim managed to murmur.

An open-handed blow hit him in the side of the head.

"Pick him up," came the command.

Jim was hoisted by the armpits.

A punch hit him in the stomach. He sagged.

"You're still a smart ass."

Jim tried to focus on the dark form in front of him.

He was hit again, and again. In the stomach, the side, the face. His mind longed for unconsciousness, but he couldn't get over the edge.

Finally, it was over. Jim was flung to the ground. He tumbled, coming to rest on his back. Every breath was like a knife stuck in his side, and his head felt like someone had stuck the needle of a bicycle pump in his ear and started to inflate.

"Get the bottle, Cisco."

Jim heard a match being struck, and the sweet smell of marijuana wafted through the cold, still December air.

The whiff triggered another memory in Jim's mind. Out on patrol, in Vietnam, after he had become a medic. He'd watch the soldiers plunk themselves down after a typical day's nightmarish slog through rice paddies or jungle, fighting the heat and the thirst and the insects and the fear, heavy as a lead blanket. Then would come the night, and they'd light up the joints to lift their heads out of the war and float it back to some place of peace, so that they could get a little sleep. The relief was so sweet that it became a habit, and Jim watched many of them stay high all day, those poor kids flung into a living hell they didn't understand.

That was the hardest part of the war for Jim to take. After being part of the crackerjack Special Forces units that operated with minimum casualties in the heart of enemy territory, watching the ill-trained, shoddily led kids was like watching Christians thrown to the lions. He understood why they used drugs, but it dulled their reflexes and just made it worse.

In the beginning, he'd tried to tell them. Tried to teach the NCOs some of what he'd learned in Special Forces. But soon he gave up. Then he'd just watch them get hit. Then he'd bind their wounds and inject the morphine as so many of them met their ends.

The memory seemed to energize him as he lay in that parking lot. His captors were ignoring him for the moment. He took a look at the gate. The woods were about twenty feet away.

Very slowly, he started to roll to the left, to get his arms under him. Every inch he moved brought pain from what he was sure were broken ribs. He fought against nausea, closing his eyes and swallowing against the bile rising in his throat.

Finally, he completed the roll. Gravel cut into his cheek as he waited to see if his captors had noticed. But all he heard was the drone of conversation.

He forced himself to take several deep breaths. Remember your training, he told himself. Remember those awful sixteen-hour marches in 120-degree heat with a sixty-pound pack on your back. You made it because you were tough, because you were a Green Beret.

Now he wore a Red Beret. He was needed more than ever, so he had to escape.

He spread his hands as far as the rope would let him. He tensed, then shoved, pulling his feet under him. He stumbled the first step, almost falling. Then he took a second, and a third, reeling like a Bowery drunk.

Incredibly, he nearly got to the fence before they noticed.

"Hey, stop."

The weird thought hit Jim as he barely cleared a log in front of the gate. Stupid, yelling at him to stop, like he was a runaway dog. He wasn't going to let anybody that stupid catch him.

The path in the woods went to the right, sloping downward. Jim moved along, ineptly, feeling like he was running in three feet of water. With the jolt of every step, his head was pounding in pain. But he didn't give in to it, and he began to get a rhythm. He picked up the pace.

He could hear them running behind him. The light was fainter than in the parking lot, and the path, eroded by rainstorms, was rutted and treacherous. He nearly turned an ankle on a root as he reached a fork.

Hurriedly, he looked around. To the right, the path seemed to double back to the parking lot. To the left, through the leafless trees, he saw shimmering water down below. If he could reach the water, he might get away. So he veered left.

The path was steeper now, and he had to slow. They were gaining on him. His shoes were no good for this. If it hadn't been winter, he would have been wearing his running shoes. Damn, the absurd thought echoed in his head.

Ahead, a huge fallen tree blocked the path. He couldn't go left or right, as far as he could see. So he started to climb over it, awkward with his hands bound. When he hoisted himself on top, he was silhouetted against the sky. He heard the sharp crack of a pistol, and a bullet whizzed by. A second bullet embedded in the trunk beneath him.

He jumped, then felt his ankle give. He hobbled, a circle of fire eating into his ankle joint. He got into the rhythm again and the pain started to dull.

The path was running along the edge of a thirty- or forty-foot drop-off. Below were railroad tracks, four sets, side by side. Then there was the water, which he recognized as the Hudson. To his right, the woods rose steeply, and he instantly knew he'd never be able to climb.

The next shot was the closest of all. The path was straight, and in the bright moonlight he had no cover. He only had one option and he took it.

He dove to the left, tucking his body up into a ball as much as he could. He tumbled over and over, his body banging rocks and limbs. The last five feet were a straight drop-off. His hands lost their grip on his head and his body opened up as it slammed onto the tracks.

Miraculously, he was only momentarily unconscious. He lay, panting heavily. His arms responded to commands from his brain, the muscles tensing. So did his legs, although his bad ankle throbbed.

He could also hear the clatter, a few yards to the left, where his pursuers were sliding down the slope. He grabbed the rail closest to him, then, using his good leg, got to his feet.

A wave of dizziness felled him. When he reached out, he saw that his hand had missed the electrified third rail by inches. Somehow, with superhuman strength, he got to his feet again. He stumbled toward the water. A thin ray of hope drove him. A few more yards to the water and—

The bullet hit him in the right shoulder, sending a shock wave through his entire body. He spun, then dropped. His head cracked against a rail, then blackness descended.

A moment later, the three were around him.

"He's dead," Cisco said.

"We got to make sure," Santos said. "We don't—"

He stopped when he heard the sound. Looking north, the dual headlights of a train were rounding the bend, bearing down on them.

"Let's dump him in the river," Homicide Healy said.

"Leave him here," Cisco said.

"No," Santos said. "Cide's right. The train hits him, they radio the cops right away. In the river."

They bent and picked up the limp form, grunting with the effort. Hurriedly, they stepped over the rails. A mound of rocks lined the bank. They climbed on top.

"Now," Santos commanded. They heaved. The body flew outward a few feet, then hit the water with a giant splash.

"I found this near the corner," Renaldo said. He held out a dirty Red Beret.

Jill stared at it, open mouthed. Then the spasm of grief shook her. She collapsed, sobbing, into the boxer's arms.

twenty-eight

The slap of the ice-cold water snapped Jim back to consciousness. He turned his head, coughing up swallowed water. He gasped for breath, trying to kick over on his back.

His limbs were numb. His right arm wouldn't move at all. The current was strong, and he felt it carrying him farther from shore.

For an instant he closed his eyes. A wave of exhaustion passed over him. Letting the water take him would be so easy.

But something inside him wouldn't let that happen. With a burst of energy, he completed the roll to his back. Trying to swim normally was useless. All he could do was frog kick furiously with his legs. Knowing it would be useless to fight the current directly, he aimed his body at an angle, toward the shore a hundred yards ahead in the direction the current was carrying him.

He was winded almost immediately. With his

ribs, breathing was excruciating. But he ignored it all. To take his mind off the suffering he counted the motions of each kick, as if he was doing exercises. One, two, three, four. One, two, three, four.

His concentration was so intense he didn't realize he was at the shore until his head rammed a rock. He spun, grabbing the rock with his good hand. He was too weak to pull himself up at that point. He propelled himself along until he came to a gap in the rocks. He crawled out of the water, then vomited out what must have been a gallon of river water.

He lay back, gathering his strength. As he stared upward at the stars, he began to shiver violently. A white layer of frost covered the ground. If he didn't move, he'd freeze to death.

He got to his knees. He knew he had to move along the tracks. In the distance, he spotted a bridge spanning the river. Unmistakably the George Washington Bridge. That meant he was north of the bridge along the river.

He decided to go south. When he got to his feet, he staggered along like a baby walking for the first time. He didn't know how many times he fell. Every time he fought a battle with himself, fighting the urge to take a rest.

After what seemed like hours, he saw up ahead a building with light in the windows. He started to move faster. He fell once again, bruising his already battered body. Finally, he reached a flight of stairs that led to the lighted second floor. Two thirds of the way up, his legs

buckled beneath him. He fell, tumbling backwards down the stairs.

"I'm through playing with these shitheads,"
Vinnie Civitello said.

Renaldo was staring at the tenement that
contained the headquarters of the Savage Skulls.
"It's illegal, isn't it?" he asked.

"You don't have to come if you don't want
to."

"I want to," Renaldo said firmly.

"Stay close to the building. I don't think they'll
have anybody downstairs, but if they do, we'll
have to wait." Vinnie reached over the back
seat and grabbed a black bag. "Ready?"

Renaldo nodded. They got out of the un-
marked sedan, then moved through the shadows toward their target. The hallway was empty.
They walked through the unlocked front door,
past the stairs, then through the door to the
basement steps.

Vinnie flicked on a powerful flashlight as
Renaldo closed the door behind him. As they
descended, they could hear the scurrying of
rats, and they saw tiny eyes reflected in the
beam of the torch.

At the bottom of the stairs, Vinnie paused.
"This way," he finally said.

They made their way down a narrow corridor
through rooms clogged with junk discarded
over decades. The acrid smell of the dust they
kicked up made Renaldo choke. The place
gave him the creeps, and it was all he could
do to avoid turning back.

Finally, they found a square box attached to the wall of the furnace room. "Here it is," Vinnie said. "Hold the light."

Vinne jerked off the cover, and the telephone wires were revealed. The pairs were in vertical rows.

"How do you know which one Santos uses?" Renaldo asked.

"I don't," Vinnie said. "But I'll find out."

He took a hand telephone from the black bag. He attached the alligator clips to a pair of terminals at random. It took him three tries to find a live line. Then he dialed the Savage Skulls' number.

When the phone rang, Vinnie ran his fingers along the pairs of terminals. His hand jumped from a mild shock when he touched the second pair from the top on the left side. "That's it," he said.

He pulled off the alligator clips, disconnecting whoever answered upstairs. He took a length of telephone wire from the bag, then stripped off the insulation from one end. Loosening the terminals with a screwdriver, he wrapped the bare end of the wire around the base, then tightened them. He ran the wire up along the other telephone wires, wrapping it around several times so it looked like part of the normal connection. He ran the wire to the ceiling and across the room to the other wall. Branching off here, he dropped his wire to the floor.

He let it hang while he pulled a small tape recorder from the bag. He attached the telephone wire to the jacks on the recorder. Finally, he put the recorder into the drawer of an abandoned bureau.

With the flashlight, he inspected his work. "Not a chance anybody will notice," he said. "Let's check it out."

"How?"

"Watch."

Vinnie attached the hand telephone to a pair of terminals again and dialed the Skulls' number. He waited one ring, then pulled off the clips. When he crossed the room to inspect the recorder, the tape had moved forward.

"All set. Let's get out of here."

"Aren't we going to wait?"

"It could be hours before anything interesting happens. We've got a lot of other things to check. Besides, you like it here?"

Renaldo grimaced at the thought of sitting in the dark, damp, cold, foul-smelling basement. "Not really."

A few blocks down Avenue C, Vinnie pulled the cab over to the curb. Renaldo jumped out to call Jill. When he came back to the car, there was excitement in his voice. "Jim's alive," he announced.

"Where?"

"Montefiore Hospital in the Bronx."

"What happened to him?"

"Jill doesn't know. She had just called a cab to go up there."

"We're on our way," Vinnie said.

"Where did you pick him up?"

THE RED BERETS 293

"Spuyten Dyvil Switching yard," replied the uniformed cop from the 50th Precinct. "The railroad guy found him."

"How was he?" Renaldo asked, stepping up next to Vinnie.

The cop shrugged. "Unconscious. But breathing. Looked like he'd been worked over pretty good, then tossed in the river. He had a gunshot wound in the right shoulder, but not too much bleeding. You'll have to ask the docs anything else."

"Thanks," Vinnie said. He turned to Renaldo. "I'll go in and see what I can find out."

He was back shortly. "They kicked me out. They're still working on him."

"They didn't tell you anything?"

"Not much," Vinnie said. Then he smiled. "But a nurse told me not to worry. They think he's going to make it."

The phone rang in Santos's office. When he picked it up, a voice snarled, "You stupid bastard."

"What?"

"Knight's alive."

Santos sat forward. "That's impossible. We threw him in the river."

"Well, he's in the hospital. Alive."

"We'll go after him."

"No," Anthony Brown said. "Fat chance you'll get near him. Knight's out of commission, at least. We can deal with him later. Right now, I'm concerned about business."

"The protection is all set. Every station's gonna be covered."

"They better be," Brown warned. "The merchandise is going into the token booths tomorrow night. Another fuck-up and you're in the river. And I guarantee you won't come up for air."

"But—"

"But, nothing. We start tomorrow." Brown slammed down the receiver.

In the basement, the tape recorder clicked off.

twenty-nine

"Turn to Channel 2."

"Jim, you shouldn't get yourself upset."

"I want to see it again."

"Jim, please."

He squeezed Jill's arm gently with his unbandaged hand. "I want to see it. I'm not going to jump up out of bed." He smiled. "Even if I could."

Jill looked at him. Half his body was covered with bandages—his right shoulder and upper arm, his chest, the top of his head, his right hand and forearm. In addition, his right eye was blackened and swollen, and he had a huge lump on his left cheek.

"You look like a candidate for mummy of the year," she said.

"Then turn the channel or I'll invoke the mummy's curse."

Jill flicked the dial on the small hospital television set. The logo for the local CBS news vanished and the anchormen began reading the news. The first story after the first commercial was the one Jim was waiting for.

"Turn it up," Jim requested.

As Jill adjusted the volume, Jim heard the strident voice of the mayor saying, "Of course, I deplore this young man being shot. But I believe this is what happens when people take the law into their own hands. Look at the facts. Since these Red Berets have been out in the streets and in the subways, one of them has been killed, two or three hospitalized, one arrested for assault, another on drug charges—I can go on. Isn't that enough proof that law enforcement should be left to law-enforcement officers."

"Subway riders say they feel safer," a reporter commented.

"Why?" the mayor asked. "I'll tell you why. Because they haven't been mugged or robbed since the Red Berets started. But there is no proof that crime has decreased. In fact, it may have increased, because they've provoked incidents."

"What incidents?"

The mayor ignored the question. He jabbed his finger toward the cameras. "I want to say one more thing. You parents of the Red Berets. Keep your kids home. They should be doing their homework at night, not riding the subway. If you want them safe, if you want them to be good citizens, take away their Red Berets and give them schoolbooks."

Jim said, "Damn." He turned his head away.

Jill switched the set off. "You promised me you wouldn't get upset again."

"I'm not upset." Then he paused and added, "Yes, I am upset. He makes me sound like Rasputin, leading innocent lambs to slaughter."

"Jim, politicians can make anything sound reasonable. Watergate, Kent State, the Bay of Pigs. The reason politicians get elected is because they're experts at manipulating the facts to seize center stage. In any crowd, the guy who shouts the longest and loudest eventually takes over."

"So what do we do?"

Jill smiled. "We start shouting."

"How? I mean, I'm lying here, wrapped up."

"Precisely," Jill said. "We have our ways of manipulation too."

"Eric—"

"I can't, Renaldo."

"Nobody is coming in."

There was a pause on the other end of the line. Then Eric said, "My father's really put his foot down. He's been good about it, even after John got hurt. But this thing with Jim, then what the mayor said, it was the last straw. I mean, I understand. I've been studying in the afternoon, so I haven't been able to help in the store."

Renaldo sighed. Then he said, "I guess I see the man's point. So this is it?"

"Until it blows over."

"See you," Renaldo said. He depressed the button to disconnect the call. Then he lifted his finger without replacing the receiver. The phone had been ringing all night with Red Berets telling him they couldn't make it tonight. Renaldo couldn't listen to another call, so he'd decided to leave the phone off the hook for a while.

He got up, his mind churning as he undressed. How could things change so quickly? A couple of days ago, they had an army mobilized.

He found himself shaking with frustration. He donned an athletic supporter, gym shorts, and a T-shirt. Then he walked into the still uncompleted gym. He switched on a single bare bulb over the heavy bag, and in the semidarkness began banging away with a ferocity that seemed to shake the entire room.

Vinnie inspected the .38 to make sure it was loaded. Then he put it in the holster at the small of his back and picked up the overcoat.

Of all parts of his outfit, he was proudest of the overcoat. It was huge, at least three sizes too big, and it was marked with every imaginable kind of stain that could come from years of sleeping in gutters. The smell, the deep stench that permeated every fiber, matched the stains.

When Vinnie put it on, the outfit was almost complete. He picked up a filthy knit ski cap, pulled it down over his eyebrows, then took the pint of cheap rotgut whiskey. He swished a few mouthfuls around, spit it out, then poured the rest down his front.

He threw the bottle into the pile of trash at the end of the alley. Slamming down the trunk of his car, he buttoned the key in an inside pocket of the baggy green work trousers and staggered out into the street.

Vinnie had always had a talent for undercover work. He'd only pounded a beat a few years before he'd managed to get into anticrime. As a decoy, he'd been a legend. He'd made so many arrests that he was the youngest officer transferred to the detectives in five years. Only his refusal to play departmental politics had prevented him from rising high in the department.

He didn't use his acting ability much these days. As he moved down Avenue A, then left on Fourteenth Street, he felt himself getting into the role. He'd have to be convincing enough to pass the scrutiny of a Transit cop, if one saw him.

He'd figured what Brown and the Savage Skulls were up to from the wire tap. Since the tap was illegal, he had to see for himself.

Near the corner of Fourteenth Street and First Avenue, he lurched down the steps to the subway. He looked around as if confused, then slumped to the floor, his back against the wall.

There were two teenagers standing next to the token booth. "Get him out of here," the token clerk said. The two looked at each other and grimaced. They started toward Civitello. When they got close, he added the final touch of his role.

"Ugh," one kid howled. "He's pissing on himself."

"Get him out of here."

"You get him out of here. I ain't touching no piss."

Vinnie, his head lolling as if he was nodding off, felt an inner satisfaction. It worked every time.

He sprawled, eyes half closed, for a few minutes. Then the LL train pulled into the station. A handful of passengers clicked through the turnstiles. One, a pencil-thin white kid about sixteen, pushed a wad of bills through the change slot with a shaking hand.

The clerk took a long look at the kid. Then he picked up the bills, counted them twice, and pushed two glassine envelopes back through the slot.

"Hey," the kid said in a high-pitched voice, "you owe me one."

"Take it and get out of here," the clerk said.

"I gave you $60. That's three bags."

"That's two. Get."

The kid's face turned red. "I want the other bag. It's a rip-off."

The token clerk nodded to the two Savage Skulls. They jumped forward, pinning the white kid's arms. The kid started to struggle, and one of the gang members pulled a knife.

"Drop it!" Vinnie Civitello commanded. He was on his feet, gun drawn and pointed. He hadn't wanted to step in, but he couldn't let the kid get hurt.

"I said drop it," he repeated.

The knife clattered to the floor.

"Against the wall. You know the routine."

The teenagers backed up. Vinnie turned to

the token clerk, who stared at him with wide eyes. "You. Out of there."

"I can't."

"You can't my ass. You're already in deep enough. You—"

It seemed the pain came before Vinnie's brain registered the sound of the shot. The bullet tore through his jaw, and he could feel the blood pouring through his mouth. He started to turn. He grunted as a second shot hit him in the chest.

He started to raise his hand to fire. His finger squeezed the trigger, but by that time he was falling and the shot ricocheted off the concrete floor.

Their was a moment of agony as the detective struggled to take a breath. Then he was dead.

Homicide Healy stepped forward. He nudged the body with his toe. Then he said to the two Skulls, "You're lucky I was checking."

"What do we do?"

"Relax," Healy said. He pointed at the swarthy, stocky Puerto Rican. "You call Santos. Tell him to get a car here."

The white kid who'd bought the drugs was slowly edging toward the stairway. Homicide pointed the gun at him. "Stop."

The kid froze. His face was a mask of fear. "Please. Please don't shoot."

"Stay cool. Nothing's gonna happen."

A half hour later, a dark '73 Oldsmobile pulled up to the abandoned docks on the West Side. Soon two bodies, weighted with bricks, were sinking through the murky water to the depths of the Hudson River.

thirty

Jill wheeled Jim into a waiting room. A nest of microphones was set up on a low table facing thirty-odd reporters assembled for the press conference. Jim took two folded sheets of notes from the pocket of his hospital robe and studied them while the TV cameramen adjusted their lights.

He was nervous. He took a sip of water to moisten his mouth, then began:

"I've asked for the opportunity to speak to you, and through you to the people of New York, because I'm angry, outraged, and terribly hurt. The reason I'm so upset is not the personal attacks on me by certain members of the media—most of you have probably read the article on me in this week's *New York,* and I believe that explains my war record in sufficient detail for people to make up their own minds. Nor is the reason for my anger the attempt on my life—I survived and I am confident my attackers will be brought to justice. And, finally, I can even understand the criticism of the way in which the Red Berets have operated under my direction."

He paused for a moment, then continued. "But as a concerned citizen of this city, what I find totally unacceptable in any elected official is the mayor's total disregard of the truth of living conditions in New York. He tells New Yorkers, 'Crime is under control; the police can handle the job.' I want to ask everyone listening: Do you feel safe? Do you think the police are stopping crime? Can you walk the streets and ride the subways without fear?"

Jim looked into the television cameras, his jaw set sternly. "The answer, of course, is no. New York is paralyzed by crime. That's why the Red Berets, young people with the courage to make this city a better place to live, have been riding the subway. But what does the mayor tell their parents? Lock the kids up at night so they'll be safe.

"I ask you," Jim said vehemently, "doesn't this mean we're supposed to lock ourselves up? The mayor tell us to stop crime, we should put more locks on our doors, bars on our windows, and not venture outside until dawn. New York is a world turned upside down. The criminals roam the streets free while decent, honest people have to turn their homes into a prison and lock themselves in.

"Obviously, there are powerful forces who don't want to see the situation change. Evidently, one is the mayor and other politicians, who prefer to have the people weak and passive. A second seems to be the leaders of police forces, who find it inconvenient and embarrassing that people want to help them do the job they're supposed to be doing. The third is the vicious criminals who have prospered preying on decent people."

Jim took a deep breath, trying to keep his voice calm as he moved toward his conclusion. "I didn't realize how effective the average citizen could be in fighting back until two nights ago. Evidently, the threat posed to the criminal elements of this city by the Red Berets was so strong they decided they had to kill me. Evidently, the idea of citizens taking control of their own city is so threatening to the mayor and Transit Police commissioner that they have to call press conferences and deploy their forces to make us outlaws instead of the criminals. Well, these efforts almost worked. But I'm alive and the Red Berets are not dead. Today, I call on every citizen—every parent, every voter, every young person, to declare war on the forces that oppress us. Write letters, talk with your friends, and, if you're able, join with the Red Berets. Only by working together can we truly free ourselves from fear. Thank you."

For a moment, their was silence in the room. Then, in the back, a female reporter stood up and began to clap. Soon the applause began to spread, until it echoed off the walls.

Jill had never seen anything like it. She squeezed Jim's hand, tears coming to her eyes.

Then the applause died down, and questions started to fly.

Jim was too drained after his emotional appeal to field the questions. He left Jill to deal with the press, while Renaldo rolled him back to his room.

Ed Schwartz had never seen the mayor angrier. He was pacing back and forth in his first-floor office at City Hall.

"That jerk. That wacko. That's inciting to riot. We'll throw the book at him."

Schwartz listened as the mayor poured out invective. But when the mayor ordered him to call the district attorney, Schwartz gave a firm no.

The mayor froze, glaring. "What do you mean?"

Schwartz rose. For the first time, his legendary calm was ruffled. "I've watched you make an idiot of yourself long enough. Against my better judgment, I sat back while you made the asinine remarks that got us to this point. Now you're about to go off the deep end completely."

The mayor was stunned into silence.

"I'll tell you what is going on," Schwartz continued. "The reason you're mayor is that the middle class loves your ass. What's the biggest fear of the middle class? Crime. So what do you do? Try to tell them they've got nothing to worry about. And you launch an attack on the one genuine hero that's come along in years. So where does that leave you, if you lose their votes? Since the blacks and the Hispanics hate your guts, you'll end up with the votes of a few thousand cops. Enough to maybe run seventh in a six-man field."

"But—" the mayor sputtered.

"But nothing. The only thing to do is sit back and watch. This guy might take a fall, then you can come forward and say I told you so. But if he gets something going, you'd better be prepared to eat a little crow and jump on board."

The mayor stared. Then he said sourly, "I don't like this."

Schwartz shrugged.

"But," the mayor continued, "it won't be the first time."

"How come I haven't heard from you?" Jim asked.

"The switchboard wouldn't let the call through," Renaldo said.

"Sorry. I forgot. You should see this place— stacks of telegrams. And I couldn't have the telephone keep ringing, not with the other patients trying to rest."

"This place has been a madhouse too," Renaldo said. "With the names we took over the phone, and the line outside waiting to sign up, we must have added a couple hundred people."

Jim smiled. "Them mail tomorrow should be interesting."

"Yea."

Jim picked up something in his voice. "Something go wrong?"

"No. Well, maybe. A detective was here. Looking for Vinnie."

"What about Vinnie?"

"Nobody knows where he is. He hasn't checked in the office since last night. He hasn't been home either."

Jim thought for a moment. He'd expected some reaction from Vinnie on the speech. On the other hand, the detective operated on his own a lot. "Got any ideas?" he asked Renaldo.

"Well. I didn't tell the detective. But I'll tell you."

Jim listened to Renaldo tell about the illegal wiretap. When Renaldo finished, Jim asked, "Do you think he's tracing something he heard on the tape?"

"It crossed my mind. I was thinking of going over there to check."

"No," Jim said. "That's risky. We'll wait until tomorrow."

"Then?"

"Then we may have to check."

Anthony Brown was steaming when he hung up. He sat, staring, forefingers pressed to his lips. Finally, he looked at Mike. "That was not a pleasant phone call."

"The boss was pissed, huh?"

"The situation has to be solved."

"We hit Knight ourselves?"

"That would be risky. And it might make him more of a martyr. No, he's the one who has to call off the dogs."

"How are you going to make him do that?"

Brown picked up a copy of that week's *New York* magazine, which was lying on the desk. "I've got an idea. "Call Santos and tell him I want him here."

thirty-one

For a moment, Jill thought it was a nightmare. Then, as she struggled to breathe, she realized a hand was over her mouth. She tried to squirm away, but other hands held her tightly.

The light flicked on. She saw four of them in her bedroom. The two that held her were teenagers. A slightly older olive-skinned man with frighteningly wicked eyes was at the end of the bed.

The fourth man, whose face she couldn't see, said, "Set it up, Santos."

Santos pulled the covers off her bed. As he moved toward Jill, the horrible idea of rape slapped her mind. She twisted and pulled, but to no avail.

Santos grabbed the top of her beige nightgown and ripped it away. A wave of panic washed over Jill, so strong she almost passed out. If she could only scream, could release the huge reservoir of terror inside her, it would be better.

The hand came off her mouth. She exhaled, but her cry was quickly cut off by a piece of adhesive tape that replaced the hand. A second and third piece followed.

Then Jill felt rope tied around her ankles and wrists. The other end of the ropes were tied to the four bed posts, leaving her naked and spread-eagled.

Jill had never felt so vulnerable. In her churning mind came the thought that this was worse than rape. Tears streamed down her face.

Then the fourth man stepped into view. He was older, well dressed, and rugged looking. He smiled, then aimed a camera at her. The flash went off. He waited as the Polaroid print emerged from the camera. When it had developed, he showed it to her.

That was the worst humiliation of all. She closed her eyes and kept them closed as he took two more pictures.

A few minutes later, when she felt the needle in her arm, she was almost grateful, anticipating the blackness that soon followed.

Renaldo was stunned to see Jim in the doorway. Jim was leaning on a cane, and he was winded from the effort of climbing the stairs.

"I didn't know they were going to let you out today."

"They didn't. I left."

"Why. That doesn't sound like a good idea."

Jim, grim faced, tossed a nine- by twelve-inch manila envelope into Renaldo's lap. "Read that."

He watched while Renaldo read the envelope's contents.

"I can't believe this," the boxer said when he finished.

"Of course you can. They're capable of anything. They're murderers. Granny dead. Tony dead. Slapsy dead."

"You heard?"

"Eric came by last night and told me," Jim said. "I'm sorry."

"I'm glad," Renaldo said. "He was in so much pain. That wasn't fair." He looked down for a moment, then added, "I might as well tell you the rest of the bad news."

"Vinnie?" Jim asked.

"He hasn't turned up. But they found his car in an alley off Fourteenth Street. Stripped and burned."

"What do they think?"

"They canvased the neighborhood. Nobody saw him. Or, rather, nobody admits to having seen him." He paused, then added, "It doesn't look good."

"Damn!" Jim exclaimed through gritted teeth, slamming his unbandaged hand on the desk.

"Take it easy," Renalso cautioned. "Are you sure it's okay that you're out?"

"They were only keeping me for observation, because of the concussion. Otherwise, it just feels like I've been run over by a truck. But that doesn't matter. How could I be in the hospital now?"

"What are we going to do?"

"Do?" Jim repeated. "All I know is that I

shouldn't have talked to that writer from *New York* about what happened to those girls raped in Laos. The image of that happening to Jill ..." his voice trailed off, tears of frustration and rage in his eyes.

"We should call the police," Renaldo said. "The FBI too. Kidnapping's a federal rap."

Jim winced. "Lot of good that will do. And I believe them when they warn us about contacting the authorities. I'm sure they have more than one cop on their payroll."

"Jim, take it easy. Losing your temper won't solve the problem."

Jim turned in his chair to face him directly. "Renaldo, we're at one of those points. Those rare turning points in life where we've got to make a giant decision. I've only been there once, in the army. When I suddenly knew that, no matter what the consequences, I couldn't kill anymore."

"And now?"

"Now, there's a different choice. One, I can do what they want. Tuck my tail between my legs, look like an asshole after all I've said in public by disbanding the Red Berets. I do that, I save Jill's life. They take this neighborhood over again, sure. But I'm white, I'm bright, I'm upwardly mobile. I can find a safe place to run to."

"Yes, you could," Renaldo said. "That's probably the smart thing to do."

"Yea. But you wouldn't do it. You're a fighter."

"I'm a boxer. That's a sport, not life."

"We're in a game too," Jim said. "The other

option is, we could play to win. We could go
for a knockout."

"How do you mean?"

"I don't believe in violence. But we've been
sitting back and taking it and taking it. There
comes a time to take off the gloves. To say to
hell with caution and hit them with everything
we have. That would change things in a way
no one would ever forget. Now is the time to
really fight back."

Renaldo studied him. Then he said, "I'm with
you, man. Let's do it."

Renaldo was the last one to take his place
at the table.

"Any trouble?" Jim asked.

"No. I got it." Renaldo held up the cassette
tape.

"Let's hear it."

The tape contained a dozen conversations.
Forty-five minutes later, after listening to the last
one, Jim commented, "Selling the drugs in the
subway must have been what Vinnie heard."

"Do you think he tried to stop it?"

"Vinnie wasn't afraid of anything," Jim said.
He paused, then added, "The only good thing
is that a lot of the Savage Skulls will be in the
subway. It'll make them easier to find."

"We're going after them?" Eric asked.

"We're going to take them all. Tonight, it's
war. Now, for the planning. Step one, we need
a command post set up here."

John Siebert looked at him. "I can't be with
you on the streets. But I can handle the phones."

"Thanks," Jim said. He turned to his left. "Maxey, it's time to make use of all those people you know. News vendors, shoe shiners, the people who hang out in the streets and subways. I'll give you rolls of dimes and cards with this number. If they see any Savage Skulls, they should call John. John in turn will call one of the squad leaders stationed at a pay phone."

"We'll need a lot of people," Renaldo commented.

"We'll be on the phone all day. To all our groups in the other boroughs. Tim Payne in Queens, Cindy Robinson in Brooklyn, all of them."

"I got another idea," Renaldo said. "Things could get rough. Slapsy's death was in the papers today. He had a lot of friends in the business. I think I can round up an army of boxers. Good kids, street-smart kids."

"Will they take orders?"

"If they didn't have discipline, they couldn't fight."

"Great."

"I can help too," Baseline said. "You wouldn't believe the cabbies I've run into who've talked to me about the Red Berets. Nobody gets robbed more than taxi drivers. I'll put out the word and we'll have a fleet at our disposal."

"They've got radios in those cabs, too, don't they?" Marguerite asked.

"Good point," Jim said. "Now, the last matter. Supplies. That's your job, Eric."

"What do you mean?"

"We're going to face people who will be armed. At least with knives."

"We're going to carry weapons?"

"Absolutely not. Or, rather, not the kind of weapons you're thinking of. I've got a different idea."

Jim explained in detail what he wanted. When he finished, Eric smiled. "It's a big job getting that stuff in one day. But my father's got all the connections, I think it can be done."

For the next half hour, they discussed coordination and timing. When he was finished, he asked if there were any questions.

"What about Jill?" Renaldo asked.

Jim looked somber. "That's my job. I've already made contact with Anthony Brown."

"What did you say?"

"I'm meeting him at seven o'clock tonight. At Santos's headquarters."

Renaldo looked surprised. "That's dangerous."

"It may be. But I have two reasons. One is that I'm certain we could find evidence there that would put Santos and all his leaders behind bars for a long time. The second reason is that I want to ask Brown face to face where Jill is being held."

"Why would he tell you that?"

"He'll tell me," Jim said. "If things go according to plan, I guarantee he'll tell me."

thirty-two

"It still looks like an old, cheap wooden cane," Renaldo said.

"I hope so," Jim replied. He put the cane aside. "Now, for the last preparation."

He unscrewed the lid of a jar, then poured some dark purple crystals into a white number 10 envelope.

"What's that?" Renaldo asked.

"They use it to clean swimming pools," Jim said, jiggling the envelope to spread out the crystals evenly. Then he put two rolls of caps inside. Finally, he unscrewed the top of a tube of Brylcream and squeezed out a thick line of the white goo along the inside of the flap. He sealed the envelope.

"That's weird," Baseline said.

Jim smiled. "An old trick I learned in Special Forces. Let's hope it works."

Renaldo said seriously, "I hope the whole plan works."

Jim shrugged. "We have to do what we have to do. You don't want to back off now?"

"No."

"Good," Jim replied. He turned to Baseline. "How about a lift?"

"You got it."

Jim rang the bell. Mike, Brown's henchman, opened the door. Jim, leaning heavily on the cane, moved inside. Mike looked around in the hallway behind Jim before he closed the door.

"I'm alone," Jim said. He put the cane down on an upholstered armchair, then removed his old army field jacket. He felt for a second to insure that the carefully prepared envelope was in the pocket, then he tossed the jacket over the back of the chair.

"I've got to pat you down," Mike said.

Jim, balancing his weight primarily on one foot, raised his arms. "Go ahead."

Mike was quick and efficient. "Okay. The boss is in the office."

Jim picked up the cane and started after him. Mike took a look at the cane. Before he spoke, Jim picked it up and held it out, crook forward. "Go on," he said. "Check it."

Mike stared at the plain wooden handle for a second, then said, "Looks okay."

Anthony Brown was sitting at the desk. He swiveled when Jim entered.

For a moment, they inspected each other in silence. Then Jim asked, "Where's Santos?"

"Doing his job," Brown said. "Besides, I didn't

think it would be productive to have Santos here."

Jim didn't comment. "Can I sit?" he asked.

"Go ahead." Brown nodded at Jim's leg. "Nothing too serious, I hope?"

"Nothing a few months won't heal. No thanks to you."

Brown shrugged. "A man has to do business. If you'd been willing to do business before, we could have saved ourselves a lot of trouble."

"Like fire bombing Huggins's gym?"

For an instant, Brown's jaw muscles tensed. Then he said, "We better stick to the point."

Jim moved slowly toward the couch, then sat. Brown came over and sat in the armchair facing him.

Jim said, "I'm here because I want to discuss exactly how I'm going to proceed. I can't just call another press conference to say, 'Sorry, guys, I didn't mean it. All of you go home.' I'm going to have to do this more slowly and more subtly. I hope you realize that."

"I'm an understanding man," Brown said. "Your lady friend will remain with us, of course. Safe and sound. As long as you do what you're supposed to do."

"Then let's talk."

As they negotiated, Jim kept glancing at the clock. When he'd thrown the jacket over the chair, the crystals had come in contact with the Brylcream and the chemical reaction had begun. The pocket would help retain the heat, so combustion should take about ten minutes.

"I'll give you a list of stations to avoid," Brown

said. "I don't give a shit what you do in the rest, at least for a while."

"Okay. But I'm not totally sure—"

The caps started to explode in machine-gun succession. Both Brown and Mike leaped to their feet. Brown dashed toward the door. Mike reached inside his pocket for his gun.

Jim hooked his arm with the crook of the cane, spinning the gunman toward him. Mike stumbled forward a step. Jim reversed his hold on the cane, grabbing the handle. He swung the cane over his head as Mike went for his gun again. The cane descended. The butt end, which had been drilled out and filled with lead, cracked into his skull.

Brown, in the doorway, spun. A 9mm pistol was in his hand. "Drop the cane," he ordered.

Then came the sound of a siren, incredibly loud. Brown looked away from Jim, who dropped to the floor. He reached inside the jacket of the unconscious Mike and grabbed his weapon. Jim rolled behind the couch for cover as a shot whistled over his head.

A second shot hit the couch. "You won't get away with this," Brown said.

Jim checked to make sure the gun he was holding was loaded and the safety was off. He heard the sound of the apartment door being broken down. Brown had turned to fire a shot at the intruder.

Jim hadn't fired a pistol in nearly nine years. But he'd been a crack marksman, and the gun felt natural in his hand. In one smooth motion, he raised the weapon, aimed, and fired.

The shot hit Brown in the wrist. The gun fell to the floor. He bolted toward the living room, away from Jim.

Renaldo was waiting for him. Brown, a big man, lowered his shoulder and aimed to blast the boxer out of his way. What he met was Renaldo's fist, a vicious right hook to the midsection. He doubled over and crumpled to the floor.

Jim came out of the office. He smiled. "Good work."

"Good timing. I heard the shot and set off the portable siren in the hall."

"Old military technique," Jim said. "Nothing can be as distracting as a sudden loud noise. I saw that in combat time after time."

"Now what do we do?"

"Call downstairs and get the guys to clean this place out. I want every scrap of paper, and anything else that might possibly be evidence. Load it into the van that Eric rented."

"What about our friend?"

"He's coming with us. For a little chat."

Brown was lying on his back, tied to a massage table in the gym. Jim approached him.

"You'll never get away with this," Brown spat angrily. "That bitch is dead, that's for sure."

"I don't think so," Jim said. His voice was almost unnaturally calm. "I think you're going to tell me where she is."

"Forget it. Never."

"Let me tell you something, Mr. Brown. *Never* is a bad word to use. For example, I never would have believed that anyone could order the murder of Slapsy Huggins. The pain and suffering that eighty-two-year-old man went through was awful."

"I didn't—"

"Bullshit!" Jim roared. "I know what the hell you did. You had Santos and his gang torch the place." Jim opened a jar, spilled some liquid into his hand, then rubbed it on Brown's face. Brown coughed and sputtered.

"Yes. That's gasoline," Jim said. "That's what they used. You want to know what it feels like when that gets lit? If you don't, you better tell me where Jill is."

Beads of sweat covered Brown's forehead. He struggled against his bonds.

"I guess you're gonna need to be shown," Jim said. He took a piece of twine and dunked it into the jar of gasoline. Then he took the dampened piece, pushed up Brown's pant leg, and tied it around the hoodlum's calf.

"Where's Jill?" Jim asked.

"Fuck you."

Jim lit a match and touched it to the string. A circle of fire surrounded Brown's leg.

Brown screamed in pain, writhing as much as the ropes would allow.

The flames died quickly. Brown lay, panting heavily. "Goddamn you," he muttered.

"That's what Slapsy felt," Jim said. "Only it wasn't an eighth-of-an-inch strip around his ankle, but 80 percent of his body." He moved closer to Brown. "Now, are you going to tell me where Jill is?"

"No," Brown hissed. "You've done it. You'll never see her alive, if you don't let me go."

"I'm not letting you go," Jim said. "If I'm not going to see her alive, I might as well take my revenge."

Brown saw Jim bend. Then a cold liquid saturated his groin area, dripping down his legs.

"You're gonna like this," Jim said. "You know how sensitive your balls are."

Brown was trembling violently. Entirely gone was the arrogance and bravado. When he spoke, his throat was so tight the voice was a whisper. "You can't. You can't."

"Tell me where Jill is."

"I can't. I—" His eyes widened like a frightened thoroughbred's when he saw Jim light a match.

"Okay," he shouted. "Okay. A warehouse in Chelsea."

Jim held the still burning match. "Where in Chelsea?"

"Nineteenth Street. Between Ninth and Tenth avenues. Gerard Storage. Santos and his buddy are there, in the office on the second floor." Brown stopped to catch his breath. "Please. Put that out."

"You slime," Jim spat. He dropped the match. Brown fainted.

The match hit Brown's pants. The water with which the material had been saturated immediately put out the flame.

thirty-three

Jim thought, this is a night New York will never forget.

He stood, in the semidarkness of a chilly urban winter night, on the steps of City Hall. In front of him, spread forth in City Hall Park, was a waving sea of Red Berets. Double-parked for blocks around the park were their transport, a flotilla of nearly a hundred taxicabs.

Jim had chosen City Hall as the gathering spot for more than practical reasons. Waiting for the signal to begin their mission was an army four hundred strong. It seemed symbolic to Jim that they start from the seat of government. Jim saw tonight as the beginning not of a revolution, but an evolution. Tonight, the citizens of New York would begin to control their own destiny.

As important as what the Red Berets would do tonight was who they were. The members of the Red Berets were not the upper-middle-class intellectuals of other protest movements. Rather, most of them were ghetto kids—whites, blacks, Hispanics, Orientals, all fed up with the vicious criminals whose victims were most often their families and friends. The reward they sought for their effort was not fame or financial gain, but the sense of pride and achievement that would come from making their neighborhood a better place to live.

Jim glanced at his watch. It was nearly 10:00 P.M. Time for them to begin their sweep. He had planned to give a short speech. But talking with so many of them assembled, he found that they were so self-motivated that a pep talk was unnecessary. Besides, he was so choked with emotion that he doubted that he could speak.

So he stood and watched for another minute or two. Then he sounded a blast on the portable siren.

A great cheer went up from the Red Berets. Then they streamed out of the park toward the cabs.

Marguerite Washington saw the tall, muscular Savage Skull eyeing her as she slowly sashayed down the steps to the subway entrance. She smiled at him.

"Hey, momma," he called out. "What's happening?"

His voice reeked of arrogance. But Marguerite forced herself to reply. She walked over to him, bantering as she kept her eyes on the token booth.

It didn't take long. A thin, pathetic-looking girl who looked no more than fourteen or fifteen made a drug buy. Now, Marguerite had her proof. The fury that came from the idea that anyone could make a profit off such misery made it easier for her to do what she had to do.

Marguerite turned away from the Savage Skull. She opened her large canvas bag, took out her whistle, and blew two shrill blasts.

"Hey," the tall hoodlum called angrily.

Marguerite glared at him. "Brother, your ball game is over."

"Hector. Jones," the Savage Skull called.

Two other gang members ran to his side. They took a step toward Marguerite, then stopped as they saw a squad of Red Berets flying down the steps from the street. Another squad was coming from the tracks.

The big punk's eyes flashed menace. He pulled a wicked-looking knife from a sheath attached to his belt. "Out of the way, motherfuckers," he snarled.

"Put it away," Marguerite said.

"Make me," he spat.

Marguerite reached into her bag again. Her hand emerged holding an aerosol can. She pushed the button.

The hoodlum screamed as red enamel paint covered his face. His eyes stung, and he coughed, doubling over. Quickly, the Red Berets moved in and seized him and his two cohorts.

"You know what to do?" Marguerite said.

They pulled the three over to a pillar, stationed the Savage Skulls around it, then handcuffed them together.

"You can't do this," one begged.

"The Savage Skulls are dead," Marguerite said. "And everybody is going to know it."

She moved over with the spray can and coated the hair of the other two gang members. "That will mark them for a while," she said to Hank Weston, her second in command.

"Sure will," Hank said. "What about the token clerk?

Marguerite walked over to the token booth, where a frightened clerk was locked in. "Get out of here!" the clerk yelled through the glass. "I'll call the cops."

"We'll call the cops," Marguerite said. "We know you have drugs in there. And we're going to make sure they stay in there. Will," she called, turning.

One of the Red Berets who had come up from the tracks joined her. He was carrying a large satchel. From it he removed a portable oxyacetylene torch, asbestos gloves, protective goggles, and some thin sheets of metal.

Marguerite nodded at him. He donned the goggles and the gloves, then lit the torch. The clerk watched in horror as he began welding the door to the token booth shut.

"One down," Marguerite commented.

Baboon Reilly lolled indolently as the subway train rattled through the darkness. He'd already picked his victim, a frail elderly man who looked like a shopkeeper on his way home. The stop after next, they'd hit the jerk, then be on their way to the street before the guy knew what hit him.

Reilly was almost sorry the guy was such a wimp. He liked it when they tried to resist. Then he could use his 260 pounds and smash them into walls. He liked the sound when they hit, the crunch of breaking bones.

The train pulled to a stop and the doors banged open. Reilly was instantly alert as the three Red Berets walked into the car.

Reilly got to his feet, a smile spreading over his face. Wimps, all of them. None of these three weighed more than a 150 pounds, soaking wet.

"Hey, girls," Reilly called in a mincing voice.

Rafael, his red beret at a rakish angle, approached, "We've been looking for you, scum."

Reilly scowled. "Scum? Why you assholes," he snarled as he charged.

The three Red Berets snapped open big umbrellas. Reilly's punch crashed through the fabric of Chang's umbrella, and his hand caught in the frame. Using their collective weight, the three Red Berets pushed Reilly back, back to the wall of the car.

Reilly continued to flail with his free arm. Chang stepped forward and clocked him once in the jaw with a snapping left hook. Reilly slumped, out cold.

Chang turned. "Not bad for a lightweight, huh?" he asked.

Rafael said, "Glass jaw."

Chang laughed. "Come on, let's do it."

When the train pulled into Fifty-ninth Street, teams of Red Berets stepped from every car. Behind them were eight Savage Skulls, all handcuffed to poles, all subject to the ridicule of the passengers they'd terrorized for months.

Maxey Ritz said into the phone, "How are you, darling?" He listened, making notes on a pad. "I love you, sweetheart. Thanks a million."

He hung up and turned to John. "That was Big Meg, a flower vender."

"What did she say?"

"The word must be true. She saw a group of them buying gasoline at the station on Canal Street."

John grimaced. "I'll call Eric."

He dialed the pay phone where his brother waited. Of all their targets this evening, one of the most important was Cisco, brother of the slain Tony. The word on the street was that he was the arson specialist of the Skulls. They wanted to make him pay for the death of Slapsy and the destruction of Jim's clinic.

Eric answered on the first ring, listened, then hung up. He hopped into the waiting taxicab.

Earlier that day, a *bodega* owner had seen two of the Savage Skulls casing a recently abandoned tenement on his block, a block that had suffered terribly from deliberately set fires. This evening, Eric was sure, the Skulls were going to torch that building.

The cab pulled up in front of the tenement. Eric jumped out and joined his squad inside.

Then minutes later, Cisco and three other gang members came strolling around the corner. One of them carried a five-gallon can of gasoline.

They pulled back the tin covering to the front door and went inside. "Upstairs," Cisco said. "We'll get the top floor first."

They got to the third-floor landing. As they started up the next flight, Eric called from above, "Hold it right there."

"Get out of here," Cisco yelled. The gang turned and sprinted back down the stairs. In the darkness, they couldn't see the taut wire that the Red Berets had stretched eighteen inches above the last step before the second-floor landing. The first three Savage Skulls hit the wire and tumbled to the floor. From a second-floor apartment a group of Red Berets jumped out and seized them.

Somehow, Cisco, in the rear, was able to stop. He leaped over the wire, slugged a Red Beret who tried to grab him, then bolted into the apartment opposite the one from which the Red Berets had come. When he was followed, he pulled a pistol from his jacket pocket and fired. The bullet hit the doorjamb, and the Red Berets retreated.

Cisco ran to the front of the room. The window had been nailed shut. He picked up a broken chair and smashed the glass, which rained down on the street. He ducked through the window to the fire escape.

Two Red Berets were below him on the sidewalk. Cisco fired two shots, hitting one of the

Red Berets in the arm. His friend pulled him into the doorway.

Cisco grinned, seeing his way to escape clear. Then, on the roof above, Eric hoisted a bucket of roofing tar, balanced it on the edge, then tipped it.

The heavy, gooey pitch hit Cisco as he was halfway down the ladder. He screamed as he lost his grip and fell the remaining eight feet to the ground. The pistol flew out of his hand. Blinded by the tar that totally covered his head and upper body, Cisco groped on his hands and knees.

Three Red Berets grabbed the vicious gang member and handcuffed his hands behind him. From the other buildings on the block, a crowd gathered to cheer the Red Berets and hoot and laugh at the Savage Skull. Manuel Torres, the *bodega* owner who tipped the Red Berets to the attempted arson, came out of his store holding a pillow.

"This hoodlum," Mr. Torres said, "This, I always wanted to do."

With a knife, he cut open the end of the pillow covering and poured the contents over Cisco. The feathers stuck to the hoodlum and the crowd roared.

Eric emerged from the building. "Let's get him to the police."

"I'm gonna sue," Cisco cried.

Eric grinned. "You'll have plenty of time to do that. While you're sitting in a cell."

Ed Schwartz hung up the phone, then said to

the mayor, "Another bunch of reports. One was about five cabbies. They chased down and trapped a pair of muggers near Union Square. This is the busiest night the cops and courts have ever had."

"What are we going to do about it? Commissioner Shelton and Commissioner Reynolds of the NYPD are furious."

"Who cares?" Schwartz said. "Do you know what's happening out there? Even I'm excited. Sullivan had another story to tell me in that last call. At least a dozen members of that gang have gone to police stations tonight to ask for protection. Can you imagine? For once it's the criminals who aren't safe on the streets. It's a great day for New York."

The mayor turned toward the window for a few moments. Then he faced Schwartz and asked, "So what do I do?"

"Let's get out of this office and get your picture taken."

"Where?"

"That's the one problem. I can't seem to locate this guy Knight. For now, we'll have to go to police stations and see the hoards of people they've arrested."

The mayor smiled. "You know, you've convinced me. I think I like this. Arrogant hoodlums handcuffed to subway pillars. Terrific."

thirty-four

The place was a four-story building with a grimy brick front and a vertical line of boarded-up windows where the freight elevator ran. The bottom floor was a tire shop. Next to it was the loading dock for the storage company that had the top three floors.

"How are we going to get in?" Renaldo asked.

"Through the building next door."

They went up the steps of a tenement separated from the warehouse by an alley about six feet wide. The lock on the door was busted. When they were in the vestibule, Jim cautioned, "Be quiet. We don't want any ruckus."

He led the way up the stairs, carefully maneuvering the folded-up aluminum ladder so that it didn't scrape the walls when he went around corners. Baseline and Renaldo followed, carrying the rest of the equipment.

When they reached the top, Jim opened the door to the roof. The air was frigid, but still. They tiptoed across the surface to the edge.

Baseline leaned over and looked downward. The brick walls disappeared into blackness. He couldn't see the ground.

"Man," he said, "this is not my idea of entertainment."

"You're always talking about flying," Renaldo said.

"Only self-propelled aviation," Baseline replied. "My knees are banging like bongos."

"Well, this is the way we have to go," Jim said. He opened up the ladder and stretched it across the gap. The roof on the other side was slightly higher.

"I'll go across first with the duffel bag," Jim said. "Then you two come. Push the other stuff in front of you. And hold the ladder. I'm not interested in taking a dive either."

Jim climbed up on a vent, then stepped onto the first rung. The aluminum bent slightly with his weight, but it held. He moved up quickly and confidently, then signaled to Renaldo. The boxer also crossed quickly.

It took an extra minute for Baseline to get up his courage. He took a tentative step, rested, then went up two more. Then he made the mistake of looking down. He stayed, frozen, his heart thumping wildly.

"Baseline," Jim called in a half whisper. "Look up. You have to move one way or the other. It might as well be up."

Baseline took a deep breath, closing his eyes. Then he completed the climb. "Man, I am glad that is over," he said as Jim assisted him climbing down.

"That's the easy part," Jim said. He moved across to a skylight protected by a grillwork made of thin strips of metal. From the duffel bag Jim took a long pair of cutters. They snipped through the metal easily, and he lifted off the grillwork.

Next, Jim attached a suction cup with a handle to the glass pane on the right of the skylight. After motioning to Renaldo to hold the handle, he cut out the pane of glass. He repeated the sequence on the other three sides, then cut away the metal frame.

Baseline moved next to him to look down through the square opening.

"It's just boxes on the floor," Jim said. "They'll be on the second floor."

Jim turned away and got the ladder. He put it through the skylight and they descended into the darkness.

Jim turned on a flashlight. They were in the center of the floor, surrounded by stacks of large floor-to-ceiling boxes. They walked down a narrow path between the boxes until they came to a door leading out into a corridor.

"Let me go over the plan again," Jim whispered. "Baseline, you're going down the stairs and wait outside the second-floor door."

"When do I move?"

"We'll be coming down the elevator. I'm sure we'll get a loud reception. You get in the office, get Jill, and get her downstairs and out of the building."

"How will you guys get out?" Baseline asked.

"I guess," Jim said grimly, "we'll have to play that one by ear."

Santos put the match to the end of the joint, then inhaled deeply. He held it out toward Jill. "Want some, sugar?"

She shook her head no.

"It'll make those ropes feel a little looser."

She glared at him.

Santos shrugged. "You could use it, to be more relaxed. Of course, if Brown don't get back soon—well, my friend Mr. Healy, he's ready to go."

A shudder of revulsion and dread coursed through Jill. For hours, Homicide Healy had been staring directly at her. She could feel his eyes on her, making her feel unclean. She couldn't bear to imagine what hideous fantasies were going through his warped mind.

"I wonder if that faggot of a boyfriend of yours is doing anything," Santos said. "Probably sitting home crying. Somebody takes my woman, you wouldn't see me doing nothing but going after their scalp. That's the difference, between chickenshits and the Savage Skulls."

Jill could feel her face redden at yet another mention of Jim. She'd been told that the condition of her release was the disbanding of the Red Berets. The idea that hoodlums could get their way through blackmail was repulsive. On the other hand, the fate that awaited her if the demand wasn't met was abhorrent. Try as she could to keep her spirits up, she found herself staring down the black hole of despair.

Santos looked at the clock. "Nearly midnight. We don't see Brown coming through that door—"

"Sal," Homicide interrupted.

"What?"

"The elevator."

The stepped out of the office and crossed the floor. The freight elevator was moving.

"It's probably Brown," Santos said as he watched the arrow over the door move slowly from one to two. Then he gaped as the elevator passed their floor. The creaking of the cables continued until the arrow pointed toward four.

Through the shaft, they could hear the doors open and close two floors above. Santos pulled out his gun. He turned to Healy. "We're not asking any questions."

Healy's eyes were like coal. "Right."

They backed off, one to the right, the other to the left. They crouched behind desks, using the top to support their gun arms.

The elevator descended slowly. Jill, tied to a chair in the office, could see the whole scene through the glass window. The wooden door opened and her heart jumped as she saw Jim and Renaldo.

"No," she screamed.

Santos and Healy opened fire. A dozen shots rang out, and Jill closed her eyes in terror.

There was a moment of silence. Despite her fear, Jill couldn't help opening her eyes. To her surprise, Renaldo and Jim still stood.

Santos couldn't believe it. Then he saw the reason they weren't dead. They were crouch-

ing behind shields of clear glass—probably bulletproof glass—to which they'd attached handles.

"Shit," he mumbled. Then he yelled to Healy,
"Get back to the office."

Jim and Renaldo charged, still holding the
shields in front of them. Healy, closer to the
office, held his ground, waiting for Renaldo to
expose some flesh for him to aim at.

At that moment, Baseline was in the office.
He'd waited in the dark stairwell until the shooting was over. Then he sprinted in and began to
untie Jill. When he was finished, he said, "Come
on. Let's go."

"But, Jim—"

"But, shit. Let's go."

They left the office and started for the stairs.
Out of the corner of his eyes, Healy spotted
him. He swiveled, aimed, and fired. Baseline
crumpled as the bullet tore into his thigh.

Healy swung the pistol toward Jill. But an
instant before he pulled the trigger, Renaldo
crashed into him with the full weight of his 220
pounds. Healy went flying five feet, hitting the
floor with a thud. For a moment, he was stunned.
Then he spotted his pistol a few feet away and
dove for it.

Renaldo grabbed him with one massive hand
and yanked him to his feet. When Healy saw
the look in the heavyweight boxer's eyes, his
arrogance was gone. "No. Please."

Renaldo's training had been to use his skill
only in the gym. But in front of him was a savage murderer. He took a deep breath. Then he
cocked his right arm and hit Healy in the face

as hard as he could. Renaldo heard bone breaking and blood spurted out Healy's nose and mouth. Renaldo let him drop to the floor.

While Renaldo was taking care of Healy, Jim had made a charge for Santos. But when he saw Baseline, he tried to move too fast. He tripped over the shield.

Instead of escaping, Jill had knelt next to Baseline. She didn't see Santos until he grabbed her. He pulled her into the office, then held her with one arm around the neck. With his other hand, he held his pistol to her forehead.

"Don't come any closer or I'll kill her," Santos warned Jim and Renaldo.

"You'll never get out of here," Jim said. "Drop the gun."

"No way."

"What should we do?" Renaldo whispered to Jim.

Jim didn't reply. He stared into the office at the terrified woman and the despicable criminal who held her. He'd never been angrier.

"You slimy coward, Santos," he called. "Your whole life, you've been hiding behind other people. Now you're hiding behind a woman. Big fucking gang leader. Too bad we don't have a little baby for you to beat up."

"What?" Santos said, his voice choked with outrage.

"Big bad Santos," Jim called mockingly. "Sends everybody out to do his dirty work. You wear a skirt around the house, Sal?"

Santos was shaking with anger. "What do you want, chickenshit?"

"Me, chickenshit? You're the one hiding behind a woman. What I want is to take you on. No weapons. One on one. If you beat me, you leave. If you don't agree, you're not getting out of here. Even if you shoot her, you're not going. Fighting me is your only chance."

Santos pondered. Then he asked, "What about the big guy?"

Jim pulled a pair of handcuffs from his pocket. "I'll handcuff him to the post over there. No tricks."

"So do it," Santos said.

Renaldo knew that Jim was still hurting badly from the terrible beating he'd taken just a few days before. "You sure you know what you're doing?" he asked.

Jim's face was a rigid mask of determination. "It's the only way."

Renaldo put his arms around a post, then Jim applied the cuffs. He tested them for Santos to see. "You ready?" he asked.

Santos released Jill. He tossed the gun on a desk and came out of the office.

"All right, hero," Santos said. "Time to see if you fight like you talk."

They circled warily. Jim moved a bit closer with every step, feinting. He lunged with his left, but paid for it with a numbing chop to his shoulder. Then he hit Santos with a stiff-fingered jab to the flesh above the arm pit that made the gang leader gasp with pain and stumble backward.

Jim leaped forward. Santos recovered, grabbing his arms around the biceps. They circled like wrestlers.

Jim sensed, however, that he'd weakened Santos's left side with his first blow. He pressured with his right arm, pulling downward. Santos struggled, the buckled. As the gang leader's knees hit the floor, Jim released his grip and grabbed for the throat. For an instant, he applied pressure. Then the forward momentum of his lunge took over and with an assist of the blow from Santos, he somersaulted over his foe.

Like a cat he was on his feet. He spun. Santos stood there. In his right hand gleamed a long, thin stiletto that he had pulled from his boot.

Before Jim could think, Santos lunged. Jim reacted a hair too slowly. He managed to raise his left arm for protection and step to the side. The blade, however, cut through his elbow, severing the tendon. Blood gushed as the arm dropped uselessly to his side.

Now Santos stalked him. Jim moved back, back, then tripped. Santos was on him, barely managed to snag his wrist with his right arm. Both men were grunting with intense effort. But Santos had the advantage of body weight.

For the first time, the thought came to Jim that he might lose his life. He'd lost a lot of blood and he fought dizziness and the blade came closer to his heart. Then some hidden strength took over as he reacted to the look of triumph on the face of the gang leader, which was inches from his own face.

Jim had never felt more loathing. He took a deep breath, then spit.

The gang leader lost his concentration for an instant as he winced at the saliva hitting his face. Jim pushed with all his might. They rolled and Santos's elbow cracked into the concrete floor. He dropped the knife.

The sudden reversal stunned Santos for an instant. That's all Jim needed to get to his feet. As Santos started to rise, Jim hit him in the side of the head with a vicious kick. Santos fell back. Jim kicked him twice more, once in the stomach, the other in the groin. Santos tried to rise, then slumped, unconscious. The battle was over.

The effort and the loss of blood had Jim reeling like a drunk. Jill got to his side as he fainted.

Three days later, Jim was released from the hospital to take part in a ceremony at City Hall. All the Red Berets were going to be there, including Baseline, whose injury turned out to be only a flesh wound.

They were sitting around the gym, waiting to leave for the mayor's office, when the phone rang.

Jill answered it, then handed it to Jim. "I think you're going to be surprised," she said with a smile.

Jim took the receiver. When the man on the other end of the line identified himself, Jim exclaimed, "Major Hudson. It's great to hear from you."

"It's great to hear about you," the former army psychiatrist said. "Somehow, I knew you'd make your mark."

"You helped me a lot, sir."

"Don't say 'sir.' It's Dr. Hudson these days. And although I did want to congratulate you, it's the Red Berets I want to talk with you about. I have a big favor to ask."

"I owe you a big one," Jim said.

"I live and practice in Chicago now. And we've got a terrible problem the police haven't been able to do anything about. I'd like you, and some of your people, to come out here. We need your help."

Jim thought for a moment. Chicago. He and Jill had talked of expanding. It would be selfish not to take the concept to another city in need.

"The Red Berets will be there," Jim said.

The Destroyer
Warren Murphy

CELEBRATING 10 YEARS IN PRINT
AND OVER 22 MILLION COPIES SOLD!

THE AMERICAN HERO WHO BELIEVES IN AMERICA FIRST

RAKER

by Don Scott #1

New, from America's #1 Series Publisher!

A hardened Vietnam vet with brains, guts and killing power, Raker believes in America the beautiful—right or wrong. Whether it's leftists or terrorists, radicals or separatists, blacks or whites, foreigners or freeloaders, libbers or gays—Raker is sworn to annihilate any man, woman or collective force that threatens the American way.

☐ **41-689-X RAKER #1** $2.25